D1577491

How to Build a Boat

ALSO BY ELAINE FEENEY

Poetry
Where's Katie?
The Radio Was Gospel
Rise

Fiction
As You Were

ELAINE FEENEY

How to Build a Boat

Harvill
Secker

1 3 5 7 9 10 8 6 4 2

Harvill Secker, an imprint of Vintage, is part of the Penguin
Random House group of companies whose addresses can be
found at global.penguinrandomhouse.com

Penguin
Random House
UK

First published by Harvill Secker in 2023

Copyright © Elaine Feeney 2023

Elaine Feeney has asserted their right to be identified as the
author of this Work in accordance with the Copyright, Designs
and Patents Act 1988

penguin.co.uk/vintage

Set in 11.4/16.25 pt Palatino LT Pro Typeset by Jouve (UK), Milton
Keynes

Printed and bound in Great Britain by Clays Ltd, Elcograf S.p.A.

The authorised representative in the EEA is
Penguin Random House Ireland, Morrison Chambers,
32 Nassau Street, Dublin D02 YH68

A CIP catalogue record for this book is available
from the British Library

HB ISBN 9781787303454
TPB ISBN 9781787303461

Penguin Random House is committed to a sustainable future
for our business, our readers and our planet. This book is
made from Forest Stewardship Council® certified paper.

There are some times when I'm in a big forest and I don't know where I'm going. But then somehow I come to the top of a hill and I can see everything more clearly. When that happens it is really exciting.

Maryam Mirzakhani

Prologue

Jamie said: When I grow up I will be as tall as these trees and he sprawled fast like a salamander along a trunk. He climbed to the first branch when Eoin said: Whoa, Jamie, careful, and lifted the boy back to the ground.

Eoin, Jamie said, did you know that resin from trees makes arrow tops and they are so hard they can go right through you?

No, I didn't know that, Eoin said.

Jamie nodded furiously then dragged his damp nose along the red sleeve of his anorak, saying: Did you know that trees turn into all the things?

Tall trees were Jamie's current favourite: the Scots pine matured fast, lived for centuries and housed red squirrels. Jamie loved the colour red. He also loved patterns, books with dust jackets, cats, rain that came with wind, the curvature of objects, Edgar Allan Poe and rivers.

Jamie hated sunny days and the red sky that slung about the trees today was a good sign that a shower threatened. He liked rain pelting his face, soaking the layers of his clothes until they were sopping and heavy on his skin. Winter was Jamie's favourite season, November his favourite month, for November was predictable: nothing happened but a heavy darkness covering the town like a weighted blanket, and the sideways rain was ferocious. Winter was bare and unburdened, leaves disappeared from the big oaks and the River Brú, an unspectacular river, grey on a grey day, blue when the sun shone, became so white on a day of blanket fog, you could not see the opposite bank, an infinite and uninhabitable space.

The white fog excited Jamie, like an infinity of ghosts (though he did not believe in ghosts)

infinity excited him (he believed in infinity)

and ferocious things terrified him, setting alerts flashing in the crevasses of his busy brain.

Soon Jamie and Eoin passed the stone-corbelled icehouse. Its earthen domed roof was overgrown with tufts of grass and knotweed. Here, the river bends and carves into the horizon and Jamie liked to walk this far to get close to the estuary. And though he had never been on a boat to feel its energy beneath him, suddenly he was filled with an urge to do so.

They watched a man sail past in a currach and wave at them. Jamie considered whether the boat looked more like a black slug or an upside-down sea monster. He settled on likening it to a pirate hat he had to wear last year at Terry's sixth birthday party, just shortly after Terry arrived in Emory. The party hat's thin elastic pinched Jamie under his chin until it burned his skin. He ran outside screaming and eventually sat in silence at the end of their garden, watching rumbling cement trucks roll past to new estates until Eoin came and rescued him. And in turn, rescued the party. Terry's mam was saying: I am so sorry, and trying desperately to hug Jamie, his face mashed up against her.

He spun on the heels of his wellies and said: Can we come back tomorrow and go swimming in the river, Eoin? I think if we swim out far, he said, busy waving his arms behind his head, we can get to America. I'll wear armbands . . . Then suddenly he grabbed Eoin by the back pocket of his denims: Watch out, Eoin, your laces are open, and he thought about kids in school who called them lacers.

Thanks, Eoin said, now *ssshhh* or you'll wake the river, and he put his finger to his lips and felt a sudden tightness across his chest. He unzipped his jacket and bent down to tie up his runners.

Jamie said: Rivers do not sleep, not the River Brú anyways and he blew his lips out and said *Brú* again. He liked the way it vibrated. It bursts sometimes, did you know that? My teacher said when that happens it makes a mess. And did you know that Brú means crushing? Jamie said, slamming the heels of his hands together. Did you know that? My teacher said that is what it means and that it is good because rivers are important, but also bad, because if it is strong, he dragged the nose again, it might crush fish and rocks and boats and that's not good, way *way* not good if everyone is gobbled up. He looked at the river and said: Or crushed.

Eoin was distracted by the band of pressure across his chest.

And I looked up *Brú* in the irishenglishenglishirish dictionary and it means hostel too, Jamie said, stopping abruptly and pulling at some eyelashes catching his eye. We have never been to a hostel, Eoin.

Jamie spoke to Eoin at length about various scenarios in any given moment, yet for a chatty child, his teacher said he did not like being among other children for sustained periods of time. She also said that when he had something to say, it was important he spoke fast in that very moment. Eoin argued that this is the way of all children, but nevertheless monthly targets were drawn up: Turn-Taking. Wait and Listen Time. Develop and Maintain Peer Relationships. Still, Jamie was often captured by something and blown off-guard and there were numerous events in his life that while often beautiful and spontaneous, were intense.

Eoin said: We've never been to a hostel because there's many people crammed together in dorms. You'd hate it.

How would you know if I have never been? Jamie replied.

Good question. But I've been, Eoin said. And they're very packed.

Like when you were a boy stuffed up with other boys in school?

Yes, Eoin said, like dorms and too much noise for a busy boy like you to sleep. Besides, you love tents. Now how about I bring you to the swimming pool tomorrow?

But unlike rainwater – Jamie hated the public swimming pool.

When Jamie began to speak in his third year, after making hardly a sound at all until then, he spoke in full and elaborate sentences, mostly poetry, and mostly the poetry of Edgar Allan Poe. He had found Poe in the library and was drawn to a bird perched on a blood-red cover. Jamie loved the library, the hum of the lights, the red carpet, the plastic yellow furniture. It was warm and smelled of feet. He gobbled up books and so his grandmother Marie took him every week, and afterwards for tea in the hotel on the Square with biscuits wrapped in tartan plastic. Marie was drawn to books with women on the cover and sometimes they were accompanied by men with loose ties around their shirtless necks and Jamie could never figure out how she read so many pages in one week and managed to clean every house in Emory. Walking home, he'd sing out: *Whether tempter sent, or whether tempest tossed thee here ashore, Desolate yet all undaunted, on this desert land enchanted* – until Marie banned Poe.

On the day of Jamie's birth, Marie rushed to Christ's College to alert her son that his girlfriend had gone into early labour. It was an oddly sunny day for February and Eoin was bored in a final-year Latin class. All spring everyone was saying: *Oh, your exams are just around the corner.*

But for Noelle Doyle and Eoin O'Neill this turned out to be untrue.

Noelle deferred her exams at the request of the girls' school, who insisted pregnant students did not attend class due to the message it gave to others. Her promising swimming career was paused.

When Marie banged at the class door, Eoin legged it, leaving his school bag and a lunch box full of chicken sandwiches behind. He never returned. For in the hectic moments after giving birth, Noelle Doyle's blood pressure rose. Machines beeped and the baby, swaddled like a warm shoulder of pork, was handed to Eoin as Noelle was taken to the Intensive Care Unit, where, fifty-five minutes later, surrounded by her large family, she died. Her family tumbled out through the doors in blind anger, and screamed at Eoin who held the baby tightly in his arms. One of Noelle's older sisters, the one with corkscrew curls, spat at him, then lunged at him in a half-hug, half-punch, common with grief until security guards separated them and he was still holding the baby when the family walked out of the hospital without looking back or noticing that underneath the small hat on his head, Jamie O'Neill had a mass of auburn hair and furrowed brow, just like his mother.

One New Year's Eve, close to the countdown, Eoin was sat by Jamie on the sofa. He muted the telly and watched an old clip of Noelle competing in a swimming gala. There had been hundreds of clips. Noelle laughing after school. Noelle walking in the woods. Noelle soaked to the skin on a picnic. Noelle pulling faces outside the cinema. Noelle painted like a Dalmatian at Halloween with a black-and-white hair wig. But after a rare night out with the soccer club, Eoin, angry and lonely and drunk in his small, dark living room, deleted the phone's contents. After which, he placed his phone on the laminate floor of the two-up-two-down and smashed it hard under the heel of his foot. After which, he vomited. After which, he passed out until morning when he woke frantic and pacing about with a dry mouth and a pounding headache, and in a lather of sweat and overwhelmed with the desire to disappear. But Jamie woke, crept downstairs and began asking so many questions that Eoin had no choice but to recover and get on with the getting on a young boy requires. And for years after, Eoin replayed each deleted clip in his mind before he'd fall into a fretful sleep, until the clips grew so hazy and faint and there came a time when Eoin couldn't visualise Noelle's face at all,

and though he tried to (re)build it:

smile, red hair, eyes, freckled nose, wide shoulders

parts of her vanished until it was finally impossible to recreate her.

The swimming-gala clip had survived as it had been uploaded to her school's website.

So Jamie, watching his father's face change, grabbed the phone to look for himself. And as 2013 arrived, the year when he would turn seven, he met his mother, all two minutes and eight seconds of her, for the very first time.

Noelle warms up by the side of the pool, whirls her arms and stretches her shoulders back, lifts dark bug goggles onto her broad face, fixes her hair under a red swimming hat, plucks her red Speedo costume from her thighs, does it once more, hops three times on the balls of her feet, finally moves her head side to side. The spectators are filled to the roof in the stands, mostly in school uniform, screaming her name, as though their lives depended on this one mad brief moment, and she dives, and moves quick like a red admiral in the summer sky.

Jamie watches it every day and just before the end

where she punches the air, he pauses the clip, then he plays it, and she turns to Jamie and smiles.

Eoin said: Careful running, not too fast, Jamie.

The early life of the boy had perplexed Eoin. His own boyhood experiences revealed a crude blueprint and soon Marie gathered books in the library for him, too,

but nothing felt right. The closest he'd come to a book making sense was *Unconditional Parenting* by Alfie Kohn. The synopsis was agreeable: you're a parent, deal with it, love unconditionally. No star charts. No nonsense rewards. The tall trees closed in and Eoin had a sudden urge to leave the woods, filling with intrusive thoughts about catastrophic moments –

as was his habit,

which meant he went out of his way to protect Jamie from accidents and accidentally from the world.

They walked along the yellowing path

quicker now

the boy bouncing and he ran ahead and hugged a tree tightly and this gave Eoin time to catch his breath.

Jamie said: Eoin, on the law of averages, boys break fewer bones than you think.

Not sure that's a true statistic, Jamie, Eoin replied. And let's not chance it.

I am not sure of the statistics on this per se, Jamie said.

Per se?

Yes, Latin, by or in itself or themselves; intrinsically, *it is not these facts per se that are important.* But it might be nice to climb a tree and look out across Emory, it is a myth what you always say . . .

What? Eoin asked.

The young lose their lives in strange and unimaginable ways.

Eoin said: Another mouthful. But slightly more accurate.

Jamie scanned Eoin's face for clues. This was a finite sentence. He learned this about human beings early in life: sometimes people just stopped talking.

Soon Jamie grew tall and into the triangular shape of his mother, unusually broad for a young teenager. He had no desire to jump into the river or climb a tree. His mind wandered into other spaces. They did not go to the woods so much now as it was hard to get Jamie off screens and away from the large board in his room where he worked out the interconnection between much of what the day had given to him, including delights and problems.

But there remained one developing obsession together – watching films late into the night. And on nights when Eoin falls asleep, Jamie lifts his dad's arm up and escaping from his clutch, he throws an old blanket over him, before creeping upstairs to bed.

1

Jamie's school uniform hung on his bedroom door and the plastic covering was pinned with a small tag that read: For Collection: Jamie O'Neill. No Charge. Best of Luck, Jamie x

All of Jamie's clothes were laundered before first wear. Vest. Jocks. Red. Good. Socks. Red. First sock. Second. Doctor Seuss. Cat. Hat. Elastic tight. Wait. Turn on Maryam Mirzakhani first. Wait. Think . . . Think first, James . . . If you are to ever whip up. Laugh at yourself for saying 'whip up'. Note the sound of the word, ship, cool whip, Family Guy, repeat it. Cool Whip. Rhymes with ship up. Good. Favourite colour? Red. Cats also. The colours of them. Fur. All of them. Marmalade ones. Hairless ones. Trousers. Yes. Yes. Good pleat. Good. Belt. Tight. Tighter. New hole, not great. Eoin insisted on doing with a fork. Level of exasperation with Eoin: Ten. Breathe. Shirt. White. Good. Tie. Red. Horrible. I do not like green eggs and ham . . . ham . . . I do not like. I do not. Make your bed. I do not LIKE . . . Get up. Check the sky. Get up, put your feet on the ground like Eoin says. Circadian rhythm. Ground yourself. Good. Get up. Leg hairs. Count. Do that first, settle yourself. Body in space. Don't sing. Oh, sing. Get up then. Make it all even.

All of it. Must be even or threes, even or threes. Good man. Don't wear the red socks, do not violate College rules on the first day. I wish . . . I wish . . . I wish I could complain to a manager, tell him I don't want to go to school . . . what is the point?

Jamie played the day out in his mind,

and as his bedroom filled with rain sounds from a sensory machine Eoin picked up in Argos, the walls lifted to pink, reddened and reassured him that he was floating inside a lava lamp.

He wished the day

Monday

being an even date

twenty-six

in the year, however, of an odd number

nineteen

and an odd age, perhaps the oddest and most unlucky age of all

thirteen

the day would go according to plan.

Since he was born at three p.m., three was his lucky number, and he whispered *Good Morning* three times, stretched, then ran his hand along his leg and counted new hairs: Five. Six. Seven. Seven.

An odd number was no cause for celebration (unless it was three)

so

he traced along a warm purple vein and pinched a hair between his finger and thumb and plucked it out of his body – a body which was dangerously volcanic like

Kīlauea in Hawaii, a body that was erupting. He climbed out of bed with his arms stretched backwards, gripping the ladder like a gymnast before dismount. Jamie then ran his hand on neat piles of books on his bottom bunk.

When he started primary school, a slew of birthday invites arrived – polite pattern of parents, but soon they trickled to single figures. And by year two all the colourful invites stuffed in his school bag with monkeys or clowns and elastic writing in different-coloured inks, stopped altogether, aside from new boy Terry's outlier – and that had proved another disaster. At which time, the bottom bunk of Jamie's bed, once considered for sleepovers, was relegated / elevated for Jamie's Books of Great Importance. The books were left in piles along the bare mattress like tortoises with meticulous handwritten notes pressed on their immaculate covers: Date and Place of Publication. Date Started. Date Completed, Initial Reaction and most pressing – Jamie O'Neill's Star Ratings.

The Star Ratings were harsh and among the piles, only one book received five hand-drawn Jamie O'Neill Stars: *The Complete Tales and Poems of Edgar Allan Poe.*

From his bedroom window, he scanned the morning's sky over the identical tiled roofs. Marie's car was gone from next door and he stared at the sky ablaze with red;

Shepherd's warning.

Shepherd's warning.

Red sky at night

delight.

Jamie switched on his computer and sat in his pyjamas,

plucking the remaining hairs from his warm leg. Leg hair perplexed him. Eyebrows stopped sweat and Marie explained how pubic hair safeguards against infection, but he could not understand why he had to grow leg hairs. They were a nuisance, much like hairs on his top lip.

Maryam Mirzakhani's lecture on *Dynamics Moduli Spaces of Curves* opened on YouTube. She appeared, smiling. *These chalks are great,* she said, and Jamie smiled back at the woman with the pixie haircut and green jumper who made him feel safe as she scribbled on the board and spoke in an inspired flurry about flows of defined bundles while drawing beautiful shapes. She was the first woman Fields Medallist, a mathematician who wanted to be a writer, and when she worked, her daughter said, it was as though she were painting.

On Jamie's bedroom whiteboard were lists and extensive drawings of trees and bees and mad shapes of wheels crudely shaded in with black labelled 'mercury' . . . and one list in tiny writing which read:

Perpetual Motion Machines – Design Notes (Binder under desk) Construction Notes (to be completed). Perhaps will have to consider downgrade to a motion machine that relies on a tiny amount of outside pressure to start motion

Riemann surfaces

Noelle swimming: Kinetic-energy created by a swimmer??

Billiards' Tables: Never ending ball motion (Avoid the pockets? Stuff the pockets. Create a table without holes?)

Various shades of red – Jamie-red (inspired by Yves Klein Blue and Vantablack)

Shakespearean insults (add to list daily)

Pine Cones as predictors of rain (Put more on window-sill. Give some to Marie)

Cynipid Wasps and Galls on Oak Trees

Puberty and volcanos and hairs

Three-dimensional jigsaws (Eiffel Tower next)

Where the energy of a dead person is stored??? Re-creating energy . . .

Footnote:

Colours and originality of colour invention is including, but not limited to, the intersection between art, design, science, nature and physics

Next door, Eoin was restless having spent the night tossing about the bed's flat sheet which ended up on the floor. The fibre pinheads of the bare mattress scratched and inflamed his skin. He picked up his phone and dropped it so many times throughout the night that he couldn't recall, and he was good at keeping count: his whole life had turned into measurements and timings. And while Sundaynightitis was a fever he was used to, this was different. Jamie was about to begin secondary school and Eoin was filled with whirling moments of the boy at different stages of life. He tried for hours to remember the first day he'd lost a tooth or his first step. He thought of the days that the boy never stopped chatting, and the times he had not listened back, or was short-tempered. And his regrets, coupled with anxiety, had kept him awake until he settled on a memory of Jamie making a daisy chain one June evening out on the green and gifting it to the scrawny neck of a stray cat.

Jamie! Lad . . . you OK? Eoin said, sticking his head around his son's door. Heard you rummaging. What're you up to at this hour?

The uniform's grey material pooled on the carpet. The oversized blazer with its motto belonged to a different era. Eoin wanted to return it to the shop and say there was some mistake. He pulled the pin from the plastic and retrieved the note.

Jamie said: Yes, Eoin, I'm OK.

Big day, eh? Eoin said, folding the pink laundry tag over. He regretted his words. A build-up was the worst thing that could happen, birthday, Christmas, a trip – anything that incurred a countdown.

Eoin? Jamie said.

Yes?

I've been thinking about the route.

Want us to take the van? Eoin said. We can.

No, Jamie said, but the streets raced in my mind, and I notice that Marie is gone out cleaning already.

Did you want to say goodbye?

No, she said *Good Luck Jamie* yesterday . . . Jamie stopped dead.

Eoin rubbed his eyes again. You'll be OK. I promise.

You can't make that promise, Eoin.

Maybe we should just take the van? I can drop you.

No, Jamie said.

Fair enough, Eoin said.

Eoin?

Yes?

I'm glad there's no women in the College.

Eoin laughed and said: You'll regret saying that.

I will not, Jamie said.

What are you watching? Eoin said.

I'm trying to figure out if Mirzakhani can help me apply the laws of surface geodynamics to build my machine and to get—

I thought you decided to let this go, Eoin said.

No, you decided I should let it go. If I can get to the stage in the swimming pool when Noelle was going at such . . . at such speed . . . then I'll figure out how to replicate her energy output. Or just create a machine that moves at the same speed in a continual motion, then maybe . . .

Maybe what?

Jamie stopped again and grabbed a clump of his hair in a tight fist. Eoin lifted his son's hand from his hair and circled the boy's palm with his index finger. She's not coming back, Jamie, maths or machines won't bring her back.

Jamie tugged his hand free and he banged the space bar and Mirzakhani moved and drew a kind of lotus flower. Then she smiled. Jamie paused the screen again, and shouted: Of course she's not coming back, Eoin. I am not a fool. This is not some irrationality.

I know it's not an irrationality, just don't want you to get your hopes up.

My hopes? Jamie said.

Whatever you're trying to do, perpetual motion machines, your mam. Energy. Eoin yawned and squeezed the little ball he had made of the laundry tag.

Jamie hit the space bar a third time and Mirzakhani continued talking.

17

Fine, be like this, but for fuck's sake, Jamie, you can't meet her. The blood rushed from Eoin's head and the room spun. I know you miss her, he said, softer now.

How can I miss someone I have never met? Jamie said.

Grief was profoundly different for both humans. One felt an intense anger he had never recovered from, the other knew something was missing, a vacuum to where a mother should fit, and he had a fixed determination to fill it.

Eoin changed course and said: Jamie, perpetual motion machines violate the first and second laws of thermodynamics.

I agree. *But* it is possible to build a machine that never stops. I know it is possibly impossible to build one that relies on nothing.

Eoin relaxed. It was the first time Jamie had conceded in this argument.

But, maybe atmospheric pressure. Or a natural energy? Jamie scratched a bite on the back of his hand. It bled.

Maybe, but today is about making some friends, and you have enough on your plate.

No and yes, Jamie said, flatly.

Eoin replied: We know energy cannot be created or destroyed, only transformed. A perpetual motion machine would have to produce work without energy input. I just don't want you to get your hopes up.

Yes, Eoin, and an isolated system will move toward a state of disorder. I never get my hopes up.

Jamie got it. He just didn't want to get it. Noelle had never stopped moving from the first minute he had met her on screen. She was in a constant and limited motion.

I'll leave you to it, Eoin said, as he gently closed his son's bedroom door. Love you.

Jamie said: Yes. Yes, you do.

Jamie went back to his computer screen. He was drawn to the loops on the board in white chalk that Mirzakhani was crossing. She had uncovered brilliant universal patterns in things that excited Jamie, and he was comforted by the idea that dynamical systems were as arbitrary as the human heart firing versus the human heart misfiring. But for now, all practical application of theories and how he might use them for his machine eluded the boy.

On this random Monday, just moments before his first day of secondary school,

Jamie O'Neill knows:

his mother's liver enzymes elevated, and that a complex system overheated in her young body in those precious and devastating moments after giving birth to him –

as was first determined in labour by her proteinuria and he knows from his research

that her urinary protein would be high. She might have had a low platelet count. A bad pain.

That in turn she would have been given infusions of Labetalol and Magnesium Sulphate ($MgSo_4$)

which in turn should have decreased her blood pressure but her organs had already begun to fail

starting with her kidneys.

And ending with her brain.

What Jamie doesn't know is what Noelle Doyle's first thoughts were when she saw him, and for how many minutes she held him. Or if she held him at all. And most pressingly, what went through her mind in those very moments.

He intends / wants to prove that the probability of connected cycles between all of his life's events, and the energy that he obsesses with

(and M Theory to Perpetual Motion Machines and Infinity)

means

that there is an above average probability that there exists a complex web of interconnectedness of everyone who had ever loved him, with everyone that would love him,

and he is the link

and even the energy of those whom he hasn't met is circling about the planet, even the energy of those unknown who will find him through his life

and that as earth is a curved surface, some journeys would create original geodesics, and every Jamie Journey could, in probability, connect many random sets of events and compulsions

but also,

somewhere in the boy's mind was a mortal fear that culminated in planning each day at great length, and not leaving things to chance, because losing one parent was a tragedy, losing two would be careless.

It was 6.30 a.m.

Jamie O'Neill would have made it to London on time for morning classes, never mind the two thousand, eight hundred and sixteen steps to Christ's College.

Exactly.

2

Nervous? Paul Mahon asked his wife, hoarsely. Tess stood looking out of their bedroom window, searching the river. Looks like another good one, she said, glancing over the tall trees as mackerel clouds slipped between the green tops.

Paul said: It's to turn.

Right, she said, quietly.

You sure you're OK?

Yes, Tess said.

Don't overthink it, first day back and the beginning of term always makes you nervous, Tessy.

It's just apprehension, Tess said, shivering into herself. She rubbed her hands quickly along her arms. There was a nip to the autumn air. A fat crow perched beside another on the telephone wire beneath their window. The wire stretched down under their weight.

Tess had been feeling panic for months now. Panic when she woke. Panic before sleep. She had blamed brandy for making her heart race, beer for making her groggy, Xanax for spacing her out, panic from adjusting her antidepressants. She had eaten carelessly over the summer months, a see-saw of bingeing sugar, then intermittent fasting with no routine or motivation. Mostly she blamed the injections, the up and down of it all; bursting-out-in-tears in one moment and in another, mad feelings of overwhelming elation flooding her. It was an unsettling see-sawing. *I don't care, it's not for me, what's for you won't pass you*, and then, mostly, *who deserves a child anyway? State the world is in*

until one thought dominated

who'd bring a child into this world?

It's normal, Paul said, sitting up. He rested his head against the velour headboard. The thing with you, Tessy, is . . . and I've read about this . . .

Paul Mahon rarely ever missed an opportunity to tell someone a personal feature he noticed in that moment, an interpolation he backed up from a book he had read, with a title he could never remember.

Thing is, he said, you're always like this on the first day back, worse than the students. Then, he said as he clicked his fingers, you're grand. He folded his freckled arms. By evening you're back in the swing of it. You work yourself up so much, Tessy – they're just kids.

You're right, Tess said in a thin whisper. Yes, you're right.

And then he was silent. And this denoted agreement.

The last time she was at work in Christ's College, Tess was pregnant.

Early. Eight weeks. Six days. Four hours.

Tess watched over the birds.

As long as I've known you, you worry. By October you'll be floored and that'll put paid to your anxiety. You'll be right as rain then.

Right as rain or floored? Tess said.

Floored, Tessy, so floored you won't have time for anxiety. He puffed up two pillows, and fixing them behind his freckled shoulders, he sat up.

A white feather came free and floated onto the floorboards where it lay quivering. The feather steadied itself. Duck or goose, she considered, which reminded her of a greasy roasted bird sat in the bowl Paul's mother served Christmas dinner on. Every year the same faces at her dinner table. Every year the same ugly platter with large sunflowers handed down for dead fowl.

Mind the boys, she'd say, *girls can mind themselves*.

She would kiss Tess twice, awkwardly, like on a French film and not on the Irish west coast where people are never certain how to greet one another. Tess was set to inherit the platter. *This is for you*, Mrs Mahon said as she carried the heavy dish to the table, *to mind my boys when I'm gone*.

Her sons would clap.

The oldest son began every sentence with *now this is just an opinion* and monologued with such gusto you would be forgiven for taking every word as absolute fact. The younger son was a tech head and excused from general manners and often turned up stoned and obnoxious at family meals. *He's tired*, Mrs Mahon would say and after dinner, the older woman, a stout woman with lashings of sweet perfume and a ruddy face, linked Tess to the kitchen where they washed and dried the dishes and where she talked incessantly about soap operas, online grocery stores, or the state of Brooke's Hotel on the Square, how urgently it needed reupholstering.

Tess held her breath until the feather lay still.

Paul leaned out of bed, tapping his hand flat along the parquet floor until it landed on his laptop and he plonked it on his stomach. The bed sheet was pitched up by his knees.

Tess looked in her wardrobe and groaned.

Wear navy, Paul said, powering up the machine. You look good in navy.

In your marriage, and correct me if I'm wrong, but it's been a couple of weeks now, and I'm sitting here listening to you both, and what I'm hearing is a problem shared really seems to be a problem doubled. Would you both agree? So we need to get past this, this needs effort on both your parts, problems need sharing, you need to be there for one another, retreating into yourself is not helping, Tess. I'm interested in your piece. Paul has articulated much these past weeks, and I would like for the next few weeks to hear from you, Tess. I understand your family environment was very different to Paul's, I think we have all agreed to recognise that, but it is difficult for Paul to fully understand it, we need you to explain it. You are withdrawing again, Tess, and Paul, I think you need to let Tess in, you are overcrowding her, she has opinions and I think we might need to hear them. I understand, you like to fix things, offer solutions, but listening is a solution. I know you are here to save, to try to save this relationship. Am I right? Is this ultimately why you are both here? But you must find the right language for Tess. Maybe you need

to, gently and I mean this with great respect, back off a little. If
she is saying she is stifled, we should listen.

Paul disagreed with the counsellor and considered the sessions a challenge: a time to defend himself with rigorous
rebuttal, and so he took to defending their marriage at
every session, reiterating how good they both had it, even
when time was up. Once he demanded a double session
but the counsellor refused and Paul found it difficult to
understand how she could not give up her lunch break for
them, and even as he went down the stairs to the door of
the industrial estate, he continued protesting. Even as he
turned the key in the ignition of their Honda to drive from
Galway to Emory, he stopped, looked at Tess and said:
That woman is not well, Tessy, as he released the hand-
brake. We could teach her a thing or two about marriage.

That was their last session.

Tess had had a far more concerning childhood, so Paul
suggested she avail of the lady-to-talk-with-on-a-one-to-
one, it might be good for her.

Tess stood in front of their mirror now and lifted her
shoulders up and back. She had developed a habit of
hunching over. She twisted the top off a pot of cold cream,
dabbed some on her cheekbones, patting it in under her
eyes. As it melted into her skin, it made her eyes water.

You want coffee? Tess said, pulling on a navy sweater.

Great, Paul said, tapping on his keyboard – no milk.

Milk made him wheezy and occasionally it ignited a
flare-up.

Tess pushed the balls of her feet into a pair of Converse

without opening laces – a childhood habit – and she held the banister going downstairs, unsteady, cursing quietly.

Downstairs, light flooded the kitchen and last night's takeout remnants were strewn across the marble island. Orange-crusted foil boxes, fried onions, yellow rice grains, chicken bones, red-wine rings on the countertop and beer cans folded over like dead birds were just heaped on a deflated plastic bag. Tess gagged as she picked dried tea-bags from around the sink.

Tess had convinced herself that she'd be pregnant again by the return of school. Even if she couldn't visualise herself with a child. Even when the tests had had two lines, even when the tests had read **PREGNANT**. But this morning's preparation and thoughts of school had blindsided her.

Alexa, play 'Creep' by Radiohead, Tess said, rinsing plates under the tap.

Playing 'Creep' by Radiohead . . .

Alexa Volume 8 . . .

I'm sorry I do not understand your command, playing 'Creep' by Radiohead from Spotify . . .

Alexa, Volume 8, Volu . . . Alexa . . . ALEXA. PLAY FUCKEN 'CREEP'.

I'm sorry, Goodbyeeeeeee.

For fuck's sake, Alexa, Tess said, stomping on the foot lever of the bin. She jerked out two sacks, dry recyclables and sweaty landfill. She walked into the back yard, banging the bags off the French doors. The landfill bag left a stain on the glass. Outside, green weeds sprouted through patio cracks. Paul didn't lay weedkiller – he had conscionable objection to it and spent all summer on his hands and knees, loosening weeds with a little scraper and pulling lanky ones out of the ground, only for another to grow by morning.

Tess spent the summer in a lounger reading books and drinking beers. They had been unable to afford a holiday after the final round of IVF, which had resulted in three embryos. This retrieval was low, *very low for a woman who had yet to reach her fortieth birthday*, Dr Green said. After which, two were implanted. Tess miscarried, weeks of bleeding, pain and crying in bed, crying in the shower, crying running from shops when a baby would call out or a woman pushed a buggy in her way.

Paul's sperms were *flyers* Dr Green said when he saw Tess back in Clinic, crying uncontrollably. *Yes yes yes so painful*, Green'd said again, and then, rather unremarkably, he announced *it just was what it was*.

They had one embryo left.

Somewhere in the hospital in a container were fragments of them both. Tess thought about it when she reached into the small freezer for a rubber ice tray, or parents said at the annual parent–teacher meeting, *He's trouble because he's our last, a surprise, I had two already. Two is loads. Three is a handful.*

One last shot.

Next round they said in the Clinic, as though she should order pints in the pub.

Tess had screamed at Paul as she was miscarrying: I'm fucking barren. Paul was horrified and went to his brother's for a few nights to give her space.

27

Oh fuck you, she'd screamed as he left.

Tess liked the space, then, she even liked the word *barren*, though she never used it in front of the other women in the Clinic's waiting room. There they said: *It's not happening*, or, *We're having problems*. Barren was an explosion, an active word that pounded out of her lips. She thought of the summer in the desert with her first boyfriend, the same summer her Granny Liz, who been there for her all her life, died while Tess was padding along in the stifling heat in another country, the same year her father, Jennings, disappeared into himself on the streets, the year she was so madly in love with Luke that she never wanted to return.

Good things can happen in dry places. Barren cacti, barren villages, fertile Vegas was one example. If anything sprouted inside her aridness, it would be cause for much celebration.

Or consideration.

But Vegas is not all winning. People come out broken.

Tess Mahon, you have an inhospitable womb, she had said loudly to herself in the Clinic. Some people had incomplete cervixes, sperm with low mobility, no tails, half tails, some had incomplete reasons and many, like Tess, defied medical science as to why the world did not want them to reproduce. As egotistical as this sounded, it was how Tess considered her infertility – the world's conspiratorial way of proving that she and Paul were not meant to parent. She had once read an article about women who could not carry a baby for psychological reasons and when she admitted this Dr Green stopped talking to her about *mental fatigue*. Tess accepted fatigue as a reasonable explanation for her hostile body. And because she agreed with him, Dr Green said that Tess Mahon was a most unusual patient.

But she was not unusual. She was detached.

Take for example her mother's death:

Tess was a toddler and too young to remember her mother, but she had no hesitation in talking about her death, if asked. Tess knew her mother was dead. She never felt the *presence* people speak of, only something of what it was to miss a mother on nights she watched her father wriggle across the kitchen floor ending in the corner against the stove in a ball, drunk. Tess accepted her mother was dead. Dead like dogs and goldfish and things on windowsills in arid heat, dead like orchids with sunburn crawling up their leaves.

She also accepted that it was prudent not to trust people.

They were almost a decade married now and to avoid misinterpretations in the way they communicated, they had grown polite and consistent with each other. To Tess, it was as though she had capitulated. She stopped giving Paul her point of view. And Paul had stopped worrying about what ailed Tess. He worked hard. She had stuff, stuff that was absent from her childhood, and in that sense, he was a good provider. In the end Tess fell silent. And not in an all-encompassing and awkward way, just in the way of gentle politeness, like how you might meet and greet the postman or a parent in school. However, lately, her body was less inclined to polite hostility. It was increasingly difficult to override the urges she still had to function, to be held, to cry, to fuck and recently, Tess craved sex without any purpose other than to orgasm and cry out.

Paul had similar feelings, though neither of them broached this with one another, and while language came readily to Tess when dealing with herself alone, having one-way conversations over all of her choices on her long walks in the woods, or on her way to school, now she no longer tabled these discussions with her husband. Together Paul and Tess Mahon had grown politely obtuse. A space, the counsellor said, was major red-flag territory. Though both of them disagreed. Sometimes it felt simply harmonious.

After cleaning the kitchen, Tess pulled a pan out from under the sink. She grabbed ingredients from the fridge. She cut a chunk of cold butter from its foil pack on a wooden chopping board and placed the lump into the ceramic pan. Then she cracked in four large eggs and watched the yolks wobbling. Turning up the heat, she whisked, left the eggs to cook. She lifted a silver coffee pot from the windowsill, taking apart the pieces and rinsing each, drying them carefully before she filled the pot's belly with tap water, and scooped in spoons of coffee, tapping them down into the steel funnel, compressing the coarse powder with the back of the scoop. Tess screwed the parts together and placed it on the hob next to the eggs, and whisked. She chopped wiry chives, sprinkled them in and spooned in crème fraîche, before turning off the wheezing coffee. Finally, Tess served the eggs on two elaborate plates with gold edging and warm soda bread. She drenched hers in salt and it felt rebellious. Salt apparently interfered with her cycle: dehydration: ovulation: the plumping of ovaries: the pushing of eggs to the surface: the scraping for a small return and come mid-term: the dilating: the Petri dishes: re-insertion: last chance.

But just before eating, the memories surged in Tess, and she lost her appetite.

I'm off, Tess said, sponging make-up on her nose. Then she opened a box of cereal and shoved her fist inside, retrieving a free toy cat that she stuffed into her bag.

Bye, Paul, she said. Have a good day.

Paul came running and said: Oh, yeah, here . . . wait . . . here, wait up, love, and he planted a kiss on her lips. All best now, d'you hear me? Head up, Tessy. You'll have holidays in no time. Best part of being a teacher, eh? he said, as she walked out of the front door.

Out on the footpath she turned right after the small garden gate that was left swinging in the gentle breeze.

There was a red sky in the distance.

Shepherd's warning.

June, July and August, Paul called out after her.

3

Jamie walked the potholed street out of the Heights and onto the asphalt main road with its large neon markers. He walked on along the narrow path as cars whizzed by and over the small hill where he sped up (dangerous blind spot) towards the Square, and crossed the first pedestrian crossing at the Odeon with its art-deco facade on Cinema Lane. Jamie liked to walk this street on the opposite side as the sun would lift up and shine on the cinema in the mornings. He enjoyed walking in shade. The rain had stayed in the clouds but Jamie wished for them to open, to burst, and to feel rain on his face – though perhaps Marie was right, better not to sit all day in damp clothes for the possibility of inducing early-onset arthritis.

He passed another set of traffic lights at the Square where kids swung around the pole and some didn't bother to check crossing the road, just darted on without looking. Jamie thought them very careless as he walked by Donoghue's shut-down sweet shop.

And on towards the terrace of the looming cathedral.

Nearly there.

There had been weeks of planning the route, etcetcetc,

so now Eoin's words echoed: Mind the road, look left and right at the crossings, what to say, what not to say, how to conduct yourself and most importantly of all – how to self-soothe. And finally, if things got *badbadbad* how to get to safety and raise an SOS. But Jamie was growing more frustrated with Eoin. He had tired of his dad in cafés, or in restaurants with little room between tables, and especially how cautious he was with him on train journeys – just because they once stopped a train in the middle of nowhere-France to allow father and son to alight in the hazy moments after Jamie panicked.

Jamie was learning things, and as far as general life went, there were really very few people could regulate themselves or take proper care of themselves in any case.

Take for example the old couple he just passed on his walk to school laughing hysterically on the footpath, this was unnerving, the unrestrained way of it. She was outside wearing a bed coat with no socks on,

or the people fumbling at the gates of their houses with too much shopping, not having considered it beforehand, planned out the shopping with more care, and how this amount of bags made them the perfect sitting-ducks for a robber,

or how car drivers blew horns aggressively at each other all morning to attempt to make progress in a traffic jam, and it was unlikely to impossible that any progress would be made as they left the house too late and had only themselves to blame,

as for people who crossed roads without looking – they were asking for it.

And as far as intelligence of the kids in his sixth class last year went, it was *a travesty of epic proportions.*

Eoin said: When you're in big trouble, or if you panic, always look for a . . .

Jamie replied: . . . a woman with a buggy.

The streets of Emory were bustling. Bikes, cars, buses and delivery trucks rushed by. The sounds were madly vibrant and they hurt. His earlobes throbbed. There were humans everywhere, crawling like ants out of doorways and shops and alleys. The schools in town had all re-opened at once, something Eoin had failed to predict, and everywhere was a sea of grey blazers, maroon gym-slips, fur gilets, hoodies, rain jackets, some in pyjamas, and an abundance of squeaky shoes.

Jamie watched two boys with long hair sat on the pavement drawing on each other's arms with markers. Then they coloured each other's fingernails, eventually holding hands and grinning. Behind them, the cathedral spire was taller than the trees in the woods, but nothing about it made Jamie want to approach.

Christ's College was nestled out of view behind the cathedral. Jamie took fast shallow breaths and waited watching as the boys that had drawn great loops and patterns on each other moved on. He stalled to let some cars pass into the grounds, men in shirts and ties sipping out of coffee cups with one hand on the steering wheel. Parents coaxed toddlers along. A woman with a buggy slowed. Jamie noted her bouncy hair, a large watch on her wrist. He counted three children though he could not see the child in the buggy.

You all right, love? she said, turning to Jamie. One child, with curls just like her mother, twirled about and the woman left a foot on the buggy. Love, everything OK? the woman said again.

Jamie looked over his shoulder. Pardon me?

Just wondering if you're all right, love, looks as though you've seen a ghost is all.

Yes, Jamie said, considering her large bottom lip and the small scar on her chin. I mean, no. No, I have not seen a ghost, and yes, I am all right. Thank you. Actually, about the ghost, I have a pallor to my skin – I get it from my mother.

Ah, that'll be West of Ireland skin, she said, kindly, goodgoodgood then, she continued while sticking a straw into a juice box and handing it to the buggy.

Jamie considered her boots fallen in at the arches and her anorak all tucked up into one sleeve.

You do know where you're going, right? she said.

Yes. I am going into the College.

Ah, I see. Is it your first day?

Yes.

Congratulations. But get a move on or you'll be late, good lad, she said, adding, good luck before she walked on, pushing the pram while pulling the small twirly child with her, and watching as her older daughter bounded ahead.

All motion begins with force and opposing motions.

And Jamie was now perplexed by a woman who would wish him congratulations before good luck, and worse, before he had set foot inside the College. Still, her smile was kind, and had he been in trouble at that very moment, then her appearance was very much a moment of luck. He skirted on, zigzagging quickly, concerned now that added to the morning's complications he might also be late, despite lying on high alert all night, despite getting up and out of bed before six a.m. He berated himself as swarms of boys flocked ahead of him – which took his mind off everything, except getting inside the front door.

*

Tess Mahon walked along Emory Woods Road, picking up speed as the cathedral spire came into view. Her jumper was tight under her arms. It was not how she wished to be dressed. She was so poor at making choices now. Paul had distracted her, and she wondered sometimes if it were too much on humans to share such close quarters with another. The only time she was truly alone these days was in the loo. And even then, the sound in their house travelled. She had grown up alone, spending long swathes of time at home when Jennings was out for work, or in the pub. She was used to herself, alone, to the things in her head that occupied her. On this morning all her thoughts were coming fast. Her hands inflated like they often did in times of panic. Her body had carved a roadmap for panic, and everything was quick to inflate in great cortisol surges. Even teaching – the place she felt most control – was making her edgy. She knew it was time to move schools, this place was past its sell-by date. Tess specialised in Additional Needs, but increasingly it felt to her that every kid who did not fit the mould of rote learner was being brushed aside in favour of high grades, and religion. The College was everything Tess Mahon despised about education; closest to the church, farthest from god.

She passed by some students and the sight of them huddled in their groups, some couples kissing, some laughing around phone screens, some smoking cigarettes, unnerved her, as did those zooming past on motorbikes with sports bags across their backs. Tess yielded at the traffic lights to cross the road at Donoghue's. The shutters were down and flat thistles sprouted from the pavement, spiders hung off gossamer and faded sweets advertisements that had fallen from the windows and were trapped behind an ice-cream fridge chained up inside the door. The shop was heavily graffitied:

fuck the police

make rich cunts pay for the recession

Laura is a Lezzie

Fuck fear, the world is ours

As Tess stepped onto the pedestrian crossing, she watched a tall boy with ruffled auburn hair zigzagging along. His rhythm was perfect. He stopped to talk to a woman with a buggy and Tess stood by the wall, watching, as she sprayed Rescue Remedy under her tongue. She liked how it tasted of brandy.

Inside the College she passed by the Oratory and considered the same thing every year she returned to school: what church order builds such a substantial school with an elaborate church, golds and mahoganies, polished parquet floors, and right next to it, an extravagant cathedral with the tallest steeple of any church in the West of Ireland during the years of the Famine? A town which, it is rumoured, during these years had only four beds – two in the Palace of the Bishop. One for the Bishop of Emory, one for his housekeeper. Two smaller beds were in the Army Barracks on Barrack Street off the Square for the top-ranking British officers. Tess thought about the ice-house in Emory Woods, also shared in the nineteenth century by the Big House and the Bishop. Ice came in twice a year, great sheets of it on liners that sailed in along the North Atlantic, and the ice sheets were broken up and taken then to the ice-house along the River Brú on currach boats by the locals, many starving and frozen with the cold and hunger and wondering who needed to add ice to the already cold world they lived in.

*

The cathedral bell rang out fast.
Bell | bang | bell | bang
Half past the hour.
It knocked a start out of Jamie who was stood in line behind other boys in blazers and school bags clasped to them. A few leaves whipped up in the rusty gulley at the entrance and a bird perched on the head of a marble statue.

A full-size laminated picture of Jesus was nailed to the main door, his heart plucked out of his chest and rainbow shards of light shooting from him. This was new and it threw Jamie. He memorised it for tomorrow. Eoin warned him that there could be new things. He said not to panic if this happens. But Jamie preferred when Eoin said nothing. Saying *not to panic* was like telling him not to think of an elephant in a tutu, or a sink hole suddenly opening up. Jamie catastrophised on sink holes for days, but it was better than the sensation of holes on his face that once lasted for months.

To take his mind off the queue, Jamie considered food. Eoin promised to make his favourite dinner after his first day, which Eoin believed to be moules-frites. Last eaten 2017. France. Tent. First and last holiday. But Jamie's favourite dinner was actually Marie's macaroni and cheese. Moules-frites was a dish that only worked in France. It is an experience meal, and tastes best in the sun. Sat at the counter in the tiny kitchen down the Heights with his dad scrolling on his phone and slurping fish juice with raw onions just wasn't the same. But Jamie was learning that sometimes the feelings of other people are more important than sensations in your stomach.

He hummed 'Paint It, Black' by the Rolling Stones as the line shortened to single file, then he started humming louder, until he was mouthing the lyrics to the song with his head thrown backwards and staring at the sky. By the time there was nothing or no one between him and the large door, he stopped dead. He started to sing again as he pushed the heavy door, wishing that he could go back and live in the tent in France. But Eoin said that every-one needs to meet others, and though he trusted Eoin, to what end he needed to socialise with these boys that pushed around him now was anyone's guess and Jamie never placed much faith in guesses – which were very dif-ferent to educated estimates, based on probability.

He went along with swarms of boys making their way to the Hall with the lockers. He was fixed on the Hall. Get-ting there, being there, sitting there. Hopefully he'd spot Terry there.

Eoin had told him to sit in the Locker Hall and wait for the year head to collect him, and look out for someone from his old school.

Jamie had said: What will I do then?

Eoin said sharply: Maybe try talking to them.

The Locker Hall was warm. There were three huge steps down into it and it felt like the bowels of a sub-marine. Everything hummed and his ears felt hot and wet inside. Jamie popped his jaw once or twice, and he gave some awkward side-eye to the bench he would need to sit on. He thought of how impossibly low it was to the ground, and considered taking off the school bag, but it was all too much for two hands at this juncture, so, instead, he leaned against the wall and left his head back. It was cold and damp, painted in a thick oil paint and not plas-tered. Jamie ran his head along it back and over where the grooves between the breeze blocks clicked with a rhythm he enjoyed. He closed his eyes and listened as boys bus-tled about.

One boy walked towards him.

Hey, Jamie, he said. And then he stood quietly beside him.

Terence, Jamie said, opening his eyes wide.

He liked to give him his full name, Terence because he shared a name with Terence Tao who won the Fields Medal in 2006. The same year Terry was born in the city of London.

4

Tess leaned across the staffroom sink and lifted a mug off a ledge. Another teacher was fussing about. Well, Tess, how was summer? he said.

Grand, Tess said: Seems so bloody long ago now, doesn't it, David? Always the same, first day back – like we never left. I almost forget but . . . usual. Baking, walking, beers, not in that order. Spend yours knee deep in calculus?

Knee deep in the sea more like, he said, smiled and walked off with his cup.

The staffroom was filled with the patter of people. Tess tore open the packet with her teeth and dropped the teabag into the cup, threading the string through the gold handle. She had occupied the same seat since she began teaching at the College, farthest from the door and underneath the windows that framed the Cloisters and the waterlogged pitches. A clunky scalloped table took up the room, it reeked of tobacco and stained your skin mustard. Mahogany chairs with carved armrests and deflated tapestry cushions were set about the table.

Heard there'll be changes, someone whispered.

There's always changes, Tess said.

More teachers arrived. Most kept to themselves, pushing yogurts and lunch boxes packed with greens into the humming fridge under the counter, then settled around the table and soon silence descended as they awaited the Principal's address.

Finally, Faulks stormed in, banging the door back against a poorly planned counter in his wake. He looked around fast, counting staff with head nods. He wore a harsh black bib under his shiny black blazer, a flash of white shirt gaped at the buttons. Faulks had a habit of putting on pounds over summer months.

In the Name of the Father and of the Son and of the Holy Spirit. Faulks prayed quickly.

Everyone was blessing themselves when a knock came to the door.

Yes! Faulks said. Come, come. He walked over and snapped the door in. Come, I said! His temper was stoked by the interruption.

A man stood in the door frame. Apologies, he said.

Yes, Faulks responded.

Am I late?

Faulks replied: I beg your pardon?

Your letter said nine-thirty a.m. He was specific with consonants as though English was a second language. I'm Mr Foley, Tadhg, he said, moving forward a pace to Faulks. I'm the new woodwork teacher. He inflected the end of the sentence and pulling his hand from his back pocket, outstretched it.

Ah, Mr Foley, in from the islands, Faulks said, grabbing

a tight hold of the man's hand. I have you now, you caught us all there for a minute. Welcome. Apologies if you thought the letter said nine-thirty. Take a seat like a good man.

Ellie Staunton, the music teacher, who sat opposite Tess at all meetings, beckoned Tadhg Foley to sit beside her. She was impulsive with greetings, tactile from spending her days showing boys how to press their finger pads on a string's instrument or clasp a drumstick.

Tadhg moved to the vacant seat and called back over his shoulder to Faulks: Again, apologies. I'm not noted for my tardiness. But here we both are, he said and he leaned back and opened the second button of his plaid shirt, fanned his hand out inside it, and then he fiddled with a ring on his finger.

The room was stifling with bodies warming up.

Tess felt her face flush.

Also, no jewellery, Faulks said, furtively glancing at his notes but he was distracted now and trying to figure out where he left off. Blue in the face telling the boys, but as your Welcome Pack was so . . . sparse.

No pack, Tadhg said, like I said, and he fixed himself in his seat. Then looking about, he pulled a Claddagh ring from his finger and left it down on the table for a brief moment. Faulks eyed the ring, and just as he was about to start up, Tadhg lifted it, flicked the silver and set it spinning it along the table. Everyone watched it looping and dancing in its own axis until, finally, it settled.

Faulks spoke quickly about some building works that would be going ahead late autumn, dates for PT meetings, mumbled on about inspections, warning everyone to be prepared on the off-chance the school was delivered a 'drive-by', before announcing that a whole school assembly in the Oratory would immediately follow the meeting.

Then: You should have your timetables just . . . about . . . now. On important matters he updated his staff via email when they were in his presence to gauge their reactions. Updates never went around on a break.

Everyone except Tadhg Foley scrambled to laptops and phones. A timetable could make or break your year. Faulks knew this, played them, picked his favourites for half-days – mostly those who turned a blind eye to his incompetence, people who helped him out, covered for him. It was customary to overload the hard-working.

Opening her timetable, Tess quickly noticed that her Additional Needs' base group was missing. She checked again, her mind racing, and though this was something she had predicted for some time might happen, she had failed to prepare a response. She checked again. Then she checked herself. She was prone to haste, Paul warned her against it. Warned her against her own state of mind, her lack of objectivity, and thinking of him berating her, she shot her hand into the air.

Mrs Mahon? Faulks said.

It's just . . . apologies, she said, clearing her throat. My AD class, they're not on my list.

My AD class? Faulks said.

Perhaps it's an administrative error. Should I talk to Ann in the office?

Faulks shook his head. That cohort of boys have left.

Tess's throat dried and closed. *Left?* she said.

Yes. Left, Faulks said.

So we have no Additional Needs students.

Correct and incorrect, Faulks said, gathering his papers. This is no longer a suitable . . . environment for some of them.

Them? Tess said, and stood up, and as she did, Faulks drew the tips of his fingers together and tapped them randomly off one another. Mrs Mahon, he said, catch a grip of yourself. It is a parent's right to send their children wherever they see fit – this, quite frankly, is none of our business. For the upcoming academic year you have a very full timetable.

Tess stopped herself from saying any more – she knew it was not due to time constraints. It was an ambitious load, he was correct in this, and she was relieved to see she had been given first years for English class.

Tadhg Foley picked up his ring and pushed it back on his finger before walking out.

5

The Oratory was claggy and stale. Mould patches crept along the walls where blackened spores speckled beneath windowpanes and water pockets bulged. The radiator heat rose, fogging over the window glass, and hanging over the altar was an emaciated Jesus, crucified from wire. The tabernacle was filled with grand spikes of things, glowing red hearts on candles, gold cups and two madly elaborate fresh flower baskets. The cavernous church was painted in royal blues, dashes of gold filigree, startling white wood-panelling and varnished floorboards.

The organ – an instrument tasked with getting souls into heaven by forcing air through the fipple – started up like a whale echolocation, and startled Tess, who sat up straight in the varnished pew. Churches made her feel inadequate, but this one made her also feel unwelcome.

Faulks pulled a cassock over his head.

The organ stopped suddenly and there was some awkward stifled coughing among the staff. Rows of first-year boys in grey blazers walked up the aisle, filing left and right into assigned pews.

Tess stood to greet them, as was the custom, but she

soon felt dizzy and acutely conscious of her body. She sat again and crossed her legs but it pinched, so she uncrossed them. Her father had rarely taken her to church, perhaps once or twice at Christmas, and she had some vague recall of washed-out sequences with Granny Liz dropping coins into a slit and lighting candles for Tess's mother. But Tess didn't trust memory. The Head Boys walked to the top of each row, twelve of them, distinguished by their gold pins and a sure-footedness; a certain undeniable attitude – so that even if you did not know their purpose – you knew their rank. In the town of Emory, Head Boys had preferential treatment – women with trolleys full of groceries stood back at checkout tills, children followed suit at the counters of sweet shops. Head Boys were served alcohol before their eighteenth birthday in Brooke's Hotel and out at the golf course, where they were also gifted memberships. And it was an open secret that they were encouraged by Faulks to snitch on teachers. Most obliged.

As the Oratory filled, Tess held her breath. O'Toole, the newest Head Boy, known as the Proc, stood at the end of her pew, his gangly arms hanging about his waist. He smiled widely at her, freckled lips revealing braces. He was accompanying a younger boy and Tess instantly recognised him. The auburn hair, the zigzagging.

Sit here, Jamie, yes, here. Good lad, O'Toole said, encouraging Jamie into the pew by the shoulder. Jamie stiffened, then shuffled in, his large shoes catching in the kneelers.

His eyes moved about as he scanned the church and then he sniffled: Allergies, he said.

Tess handed Jamie a tissue from up her sleeve. Don't worry about them, she said.

Thank you, he said, accepting the tissue, and wiped his nose.

That's Mrs Mahon, O'Toole said with a slight lisp. You might just keep an eye on him, miss. Won't lie, it's been a bit of a . . . busy morning. Don't just sit there, Jamie, say hello. Francis O'Toole was always eager. His life, so far, had been good.

Allergies, Jamie said again and sneezed into the crook of his arm.

We found him out on the Cloisters, wandering about and looking at trees, O'Toole said to Tess. You might be able to show him his classes. Won't lie, bit odd, he whispered. He turned to the student beside him. Never knew we had so many trees, did you, Jonesy?

Nope, Jonesy replied. Seems to really like trees, and appears there might be a crisis around Irish trees, something about oaks coming in from out foreign, and wasps in them, and that it could be an epidemic, Jonesy said, circling his index finger at his pimpled temple.

Can't be all as perfect as you two, now can we? Tess said as she leaned down and picked up the tissue.

True that, Jonesy said, smiling. They turned to take their own seats in front of the altar.

Jamie stared ahead as Tess shimmied over to sit closer to him. His name was displayed on a name-tag on the lapel of his blazer: Master James O'Neill 1A. He buttoned and unbuttoned his jacket methodically until he caught Tess staring and stopped dead.

Hello, James. I'm Ms Mahon, pleased to meet you, Tess said, dipping her head towards Jamie. You doing OK? Can be a lot these first few days, can't say I'm mad about them myself, hardly slept a wink last night. Never know what to wear for first day back.

Jamie nodded but was alert like a suburban fox and focused on Faulks. It was a strange thing for a teacher to say, to talk about her own worry, and he was unsure if there was an appropriate response.

Tess lifted her handbag from the leather kneeler, opened it and pulled out a tiny toy cat.

Jamie's eyes shot to her fingers. He smiled.

You want it? Tess said. Here, have it, I have loads. I love cats, I collect these ones. It's an affliction the way I collect these little guys in fact.

That is not a fact, Jamie said.

No? she said.

No, it is not, it is an opinion, Jamie said.

Frosted Flakes, Tess said, I've eaten my body weight in the bloody cereal to get them.

He was taken aback by the word *bloody*. But he loved cats.

So do I, Jamie said, I collect them. It is not my first day back, actually.

It's not? Tess said.

It is my first day period, he said, so no, as I have never attended this school, this is my first day. Also, this cereal cat offer is over in ten days. Just FYI.

Right, Tess said. I won't be giving any more cats away then.

Jamie said: I cannot have a real cat because Marie is allergic and besides, I am not quite convinced that I would like the responsibility. It is enough looking after Eoin.

Tess laughed. Eoin your brother?

Jamie sneezed again, distracted by a grotesque painting of Jesus with blood coming from his head. *Jesus Falls for the Third Time*, he read, dabbing his nose.

Eoin is not my brother, he said. I don't have a brother. Actually, Eoin does not have a brother either. Eoin's my father.

Right, Tess said, and I don't have a brother.

That makes three of us, Jamie said and smiled. I like threes. I was born at three p.m.

Really? Here, have this little guy, Tess said, I don't think Marie will be allergic to a rubber cat.

Correct, I don't think she is, Jamie said. Although it is a very common thing, a rubber allergy – did you know that? Far more common than people realise. The reaction is called an Immediate Hypersensitivity and it is a reaction often manifesting as hives. I have one here on the back of my hand, look, a hive or a little bite but it is not from rubber. I got it in the back garden, which is odd, because I rarely go out into the garden but recently I went out just for a breath of air. Eoin tells me I need to come down from my room and go outside for a breath of air.

Tess said: Good advice.

Yes, you would think so, Jamie said, but it can manifest in rhinitis – something I am also prone to. I am definitely allergic to something in this church. He put out his palm to accept the cat.

I hope you're not allergic to me? Tess said, and just another FYI – a rubber allergy is worrying if you're prone to mistakes in your copybook.

Jamie said: Is that a joke?

Yes, she said, but neither of them laughed.

My name is Jamie, he said to Tess. This badge is mistaken. Eoin never said we would be getting badges, perhaps he was not clear that I have a nickname . . . of sorts. Do you think Jamie is a nickname?

I think it's a lovely name, Jamie.

Right, he said. Another mistake. I've counted three already this morning, and though I like threes, I do not like mistakes. Eoin said I am not to talk in the Oratory, Jamie said and was now shifting in his seat looking about him. Eoin said that it was strictly a place of prayer and reflection and silence was observed at all times. Which is a ridiculous phrase if you think about it, to try and observe something non-existent.

It is, Tess said. But good advice from your dad.

He went here. Jamie said. He used to sleep here in the dorms.

Ah. Yes, he was a boarder.

Yes. Yes, he was. He hated it.

Did he? Tess said: I hope that it's changed a little since then. I'll sort a new badge when Father Faulks finishes.

Let us stand to greet the Lord, Faulks began, as he lifted his arms out like a great egret.

You are all very welcome today, boys. Generations of great men have sat on those seats. Christ's College is built on the tradition of Christ's journey and you are its newest soldiers. Welcome. Welcome.

Terry began clapping as was his habit in church when someone bellowed something uplifting. And Jamie watched him as he sat with the new boys, and they smirked and elbowed one another and Terry had a big broad grin on his face.

Faulks proceeded about John the Baptist washing the feet of Jesus and after a build-up full of gusto you'd expect on the sports field, or if someone was about to go to battle, the bad news came.

Caveat: Boys are not as successful as boys should be.

Mrs Barrett, the religion teacher, moved close by Terry's row and put her hand to her lip to stop them talking. They paid little heed to her, and soon, other teachers arrived with grave expressions and stood beside the row of excited boys, gesturing at them to put their hands into prayer.

Caveat: The girls in the school next to Christ's College were outdoing boys academically and they were also distracting – so for now, they need to be avoided. Boys were failing and this was having an effect on many facets of life, both public and private. Sciences, engineering, technology and mathematics are the domain for boys, strive to be top in these fields, he said.

Tess had heard it all before, the sweeping promises, the gross generalisations about gender, the misogyny, but no one cared, or no one seemed to care. The boys loved it. It was not their fault, what they heard, how all over the place they could be throughout their school life was because: Girls. She thought of Paul and felt her head spin. She wanted to get up and walk out, she wanted to disappear. But Tess just quietly berated herself for another lapsed summer without finding somewhere else to be. Another school. And yet, she thought, why should she move, why her, why not Faulks, or the three nodding teachers in their matching duck-down coats? Why not anyone else, but her?

Faulks grew louder now:

Caveat: If you are here for any other reason other than to be a great, find yourself a new school.

There was no other school for miles around.

Jamie stared at Tess. He had never heard someone shout out like this before. He didn't have a clue what Faulks was talking about, or if any of it actually mattered, and he felt that Faulks as leader of a college was very far from Mirzakhani and he had yet to say one thing with any specificity.

But he liked the way Tess's eyes were turquoise with a yellow fleck, the way she was wearing a navy jumper he swore Eoin also wore, the way she ran her tongue along her lips and pushed her index finger into the palm of her hand, like Jamie often did.

Caveat: Men do not have an inclination to humanities and social sciences. Failing at morality is the first stumbling block on a Boy's road to hellish self-loathing. The grooming of the self is the first place to start.

Tess felt herself hold her breath.

So to this end, he concluded –

Caveat: No runners, no hair dye, no piercings, no

T-shirts under shirts, no visible boxer shorts, no gaudy elastics on braces, no long hair, no shaved hair, no tattoos, no smoking, no drinking, no swearing, no ball sports indoors, no girls in chats, no girls, tie neat (Oxford knot), and nose rings are for dragging bulls, not gentlemen. And absolutely no uncouth behaviour. And he finished with the same remark he finished with every year: The door is there, and the gate is farther out, leave if you must, leave today, off you go, do not waste time if you are filled with cowardice, you are not bold girls, you are not locked in here. This is not a Magdalene Laundry.

Many boys sniggered, some clapped. Most boys had never heard of a Magdalene Laundry.

And just before the final blessing, Tadhg Foley unfolded his arms and walked out.

Tess let her breath go.

Jamie sat in the pew and waited for Tess to usher him about or to give him direct instructions. As he waited beside her, he could not understand why the cat lying in his palm had one ear that flopped forward and one ear that would not bend at all. It really was strange that a toy stuffed with gel would have different anatomical gel particle actions. Even the simplest of things like a toy you find in a claw machine or at the bottom of a bag of cereal was a scientific marvel.

Filing out after the Head Boys, most students appeared chipper than when they arrived and full up to their small chests with a new kind of courage. It was both distracting and powerful. And dangerous.

Jamie turned to give the cat to Tess, and ask what he

should do next, or perhaps talk about the differences between gaseous and liquid particles, or perhaps he would try to meet Faulks and see what exactly he meant about some of the more abstract comments.

But as for Tess,

well, she was bent double and crying like Marie, that way women cry when they do not want anyone to see them and they try to suck the water back in but it keeps coming coming coming.

And so Jamie understood that this was a time to say nothing.

6

Jamie left the Oratory alone.

Outside the church, some boys were gathered by the stained-glass window, where the last uncollected school bags waited on the tiles.

Hey, said Boy One, leaning against the wall. Did Teacher need to mind you? Eh?

Jamie paced about looking for his bag.

Hey, Boy Two said, coming out from behind Boy One, hey, you, he asked you a question.

He's talking to you, fucktard, Boy One said, crushing himself up into Jamie's face.

Boy One was by Jamie's estimation fifteen centimetres smaller than him, and wore a silver neck chain with a crucified Jesus around his neck that was turning his pale skin green. This was the third Jesus encounter today and though Jamie was fond of things in threes, the wiry green neck of Boy One was unappealing.

Heard you're thick, Boy One said.

Jamie thought this was a boy who might know very little about the human condition. Still, his armpits stung.

Like, I heard you're like, an *actual* fucking 'tard. Didn't think they were letting them in here no longer, least that's what my dad said, only reason they chose this place for me was because they're cleaning it up from all the immigrants and thick fucks, heard they're all gone on the fucktard bus. What happened, you miss your ride?

Jamie stared at Jesus hanging on the chain. It was strange to him that a boy who appeared to have a certain religiosity was so inarticulate about expressing himself. Jamie scanned his face, eye to eye, down along his nose, his lips, noted that the boy's top lip was childish and without hair and was also sweating. Neither Boy Two nor Boy Three had jewellery on, and neither had the school-sanctioned tie about their collar.

The hostility meant Jamie was hot and sweaty now, so he went still like a snail on the underneath of a windowsill. A snail that when poked, retreated its body back into its shell. One summer on the green at the Heights some boys had picked all the snails off the walls, gathered them in great fistfuls and crunched them under their feet in piles just to hear their shells crack. Jamie stayed indoors for weeks after, and the ordeal had stopped him eating crunchy cereal for months. Unnerved by the memory, he continued down the steps searching out his school bag – as this was the most pressing thing about the day at this exact moment – and he was going to focus on the most pressing thing in any given moment as a quickly-revised plan-of-action.

Who the fuck you think you are, walking off, eh? Boy Three shouted, his voice unreliable, deep and croaky, and then suddenly high-pitched.

Don't fucking walk away, Boy One said, we're talking to you . . .

Jamie visualised some odd shapes in odd places. The four of them like jelly snakes and the College like slime encroaching on them, moulding itself about them all. He then considered the circumference, the diameter and the area of the space of this latest encounter in his day, the route at which each move made by the boys would change their surface trajectory.

Jamie said: I could have sworn I left it down just here beside the door of the . . . the . . . church.

They were all around him in a ring now like hyenas.

Boy One imitated . . . *the . . . the . . . the . . . church?* You got a stutter too, faggot?

Jamie lifted up other bags, checking to see if his was buried beneath the bag rubble. He whispered quickly to himself now, then placed his hand against the wall to steady himself, head down, but Boy One kept repeating himself and Jamie couldn't block out sound, in fact it is a human impossibility he considered, and giving in, he turned and he said: Do you mean faggot meaning a bundle of sticks and / or a disparaging remark for a homosexual?

We mean you're a fucking *Gay Boy*, Boy Two said.

I've just entered puberty, Jamie said, loudly. So I'm actually like a volcano.

The boys fell quiet.

Take it from us, you're a fucking fag, Boy One said.

Jamie was thrusting bags about.

The boys laughed and nodded at each other.

It is not an insult if it proves itself true, Jamie said, and it is something that does not insult me in any case, the sexual preferences of humans.

Where was his bag though? He remembered getting a drink after being outside, then zipping it up, he remembered closing over the top flap – an emergency measure, but everything after that was a blur.

Jonesy or that Proc Boy had helped him zip it.

Yes, he thought, Jonesy had helped him, because now he remembered that he had stumbled when they had come back inside from looking at the oaks, and he was talking about the wasps spawning all over the countryside and how they were great beasts of colonisers but best avoided. And, yes, they had come back inside, and O'Toole was nearby, he was passing a football over and back to Jonesy, kicking it about, and then he remembered O'Toole telling Jonesy that Jamie should not leave his school bag right outside the Oratory or it might be *nicked* – he remembered this word as sometimes Eoin used it if Marie left her handbag in the front seat of the van – so he moved it, Jonesy, that's right: Jonesy moved the bag.

Jamie felt such an immense wave of relief, the senior boy moved it, the one with the train tracks, and left it closer to the President's office, that's what he said, *leave it nearer the President's office*, which made Jamie think of Donald Trump.

Jamie's thoughts fired like stars shooting in the night sky as the boys randomly spat insults at his back, disparaging words, mostly about homosexuals and sex acts which he would decipher later.

He was angry. Eoin hadn't explained how unfocused the morning would be.

He was scalding now, prickling all over, and he wished he was back in primary with Marianne the class assistant, and Ms Shea, who had a tent in the corner of the room behind the coat stands for just this very moment, a red tent that he could just crawl into and listen to anything at all, but mostly birdsong calling out from the large headphones with its cord like a swirly rubber band.

The morning had not gone to plan and was now, quite frankly, gone to the dogs.

He was sure Ms Shea would have welcomed him back and looked after him, but he knew this was not the done thing, to go back to primary on the first day of secondary and besides, Marie chimed on at great lengths about the *done thing*. And worse, what if some other new boy had taken refuge in the red tent and there certainly was not enough room inside for two?

Yeah, yeah, sure you fucking did, Boy One said. Maybe it just disappeared. I've heard rumours that bags here just disappear. Same shit can happen to boys too, like magic, and he clicked his fingers in Jamie's face but they just knocked off each other. Bet you believe in magic and wizards and shit like that? Bet you love that Harry Potter, you do know he's another fag?

Jamie had no interest whatsoever in Harry Potter and shook his head as he continued searching.

Seems like thick fuck's dead between the ears, boys. I reckon we shouldn't bother, Boy Three said, and was the first hyena to lose his appetite.

You fucking dead or just plain disrespectful? Boy Two said, not giving up, and he was up in Jamie's face now, shoving his head under Jamie's chin.

Boy One went on: Deffo looks dead . . . Heard you killed your mam, he said, and then he shouldered Jamie, hard.

Jamie fell and was slumped now on the other bags, clutching his face.

That's what me nan says when we pass you in town, Boy One continued. Me nan says: That boy killed his poor mam, only a kid, your mam too, I heard. Bet your dad's a fucken nonce.

Jamie bit his lip and pulled a loose piece of skin. It bled. I didn't kill her, he said, standing himself up.

That's not what I heard, big lummox like you, what you do? Knock her down the stairs?

No, this is . . . Jamie said . . . No. I didn't knock her. She got Hellp, he shouted.

She got help, did she? The three boys mocked and laughed with each other. Mustn't have been much fucking use your help, eh?

Boy One said: No *Yo Mamma* jokes for you then.

I'm not sure about that, Boy Three said. We could try . . . Yo Mamma is so dead . . . he paused. Then stopped.

Everything fell silent for a moment.

Yes, Jamie said, standing up quickly. He had spotted his bag farther down the corridor and was so relieved that the boys could say what they liked to him now. She is dead, he called out, and brushing himself off: She is dead, you are correct, but I didn't kill her. He was stood in the middle of the corridor now and noticed Boy Three and Boy One were rubbing along their arms and grimacing.

Jamie understood that the condition, Hellp, was an acronym easily misconstrued.

What he did not understand in that moment was his own physical power, for as he had pulled himself together to retrieve his bag at all costs, he shouldered Boy Three and Boy One in a clumsy but most effective act.

Thereby proving, if not to Jamie himself

but to the boy hyenas – that he could very easily over-power them.

Jamie's body was volcanic,

but even more powerful than he realised was his off-kilter way of dealing with the world.

He reached his bag and pulled the shoulder straps on and as he did, he turned to the boys and said loudly: H-E-L-L-P. That's what my mother had. It is a syndrome. It is a maternal syndrome after childbirth that raises . . .

The soles of his feet were on fire,

and then he suddenly felt as though a tap had been turned on and his whole body gushed.

The second boy looked at the others and said: The fuck's he on about?

Fucked if I know. Dumb fag.

. . . the blood pressure of the mother . . . in the inci-dence of Hellp, if preceded by eclampsia, begins to rise and the vascular . . . Jamie was stood staring at the ceil-ing and with his face wet with tears: It has entirely nothing, entirely nothing to do with the infant, he said. But his voice broke because this last piece of information was a sentence he had been told so often but he did not believe, in fact: he knew it was false.

Because it was simple – if Noelle Doyle had not had a baby, she would still be alive, and swimming.

Jamie then closed his eyes and sang an old rock song about a runaway bride in the rain in November.

The three boys bolted.

After waiting a while with his bag on his back, just stood in the middle of the corridor, Jamie decided the best way home was to simply walk. There was an emergency key in Marie's letterbox. This was an emergency.

He stood outside and continued singing. He was glad to be back out among the trees. He listened to a strange bird woot and he was sure he could feel the currents of the River Brú which were close by them both.

7

The lunchtime news was finishing up on the telly when Marie rapped hard on the front window of her house. Jamie was sat on the sofa, rigid in his blazer, and slowly turned to her.

Eh, let me in, she mouthed outside the window and was waving her thin arms. She still had her paisley cleaning apron on.

You have a key, Jamie said back, and fixed his eyes again on the news.

You have my key, Marie shouted, exaggerating the movements of her mouth.

Jamie got up and unlatched the front door and turned to catch the forecast. Marie followed him into the small sitting room.

You OK? she said.

Fine, Jamie said, eyes on an advertisement for pouring cream as a happy lady drizzled it over a slice of apple tart. This always preceded the weather reports and made Jamie hungry.

Eoin's on his way, love.

Why? Jamie said, puzzled.

He got a call from school, that Father . . .

. . . Faulks, Jamie said, and shot Marie a look.

Yes, yes, that one. He rang your dad. Are you sure you're OK? Marie said. And sat on the arm of the sofa.

Oh, Jamie said as he watched her sit down. Yes, I'm OK, I am OK . . . now.

Let's see, Marie said unwinding a scarf from around her neck, I think this calls for some tea. She rummaged about the kitchen for a while and called in to Jamie: Right, come on out here, sit at the counter and keep me company.

She clasped her hands around her teacup and leaned her elbows on the counter watching Jamie blowing into his mug. Eoin soon came rushing into the small dark hall, coughing. The radiator inside the front door was clicking as he unzipped his black fleece and hung it on the bottom of Marie's stairs. He threw his keys on the carpet of the bottom step.

What's all this . . . he said walking into the kitchen. He was about to berate the boy. He began again: So what's all this about Jamie? he said, softening. Eoin had practised his lines, what he wanted to say had been banging about in his head on the drive over from the hotel, someone had lost their wedding ring down in the U-bend of a bedroom sink. He was going to be firm and explain the dangers of bolting. How it showed a lack of respect. And it was not going to be tolerated. He planned on saying: This isn't primary, Jamie. He might even threaten an assistant like the primary had for kids who were 'flight risks'. He might ground him. He considered cancelling the internet. Or maybe he could cut off his Netflix subscription. But truthfully, he hadn't fully decided on anything by the time he pulled the van kerbside of his house in the Heights. Walking into Marie's kitchen, he was less sure.

I'll just put the kettle on, Marie said, despite a full teapot in the centre of the counter.

What's the matter, eh? Eoin said to Jamie as he leaned on the counter. And looked directly at the boy who was looking into his mug of tea. Jamie tapped the little rubber cat that was left down by the mug.

The weather forecast tune chimed. Both of them threw their eyes in to the big telly.

Now, what's up, lad?

Nothing. Jamie said.

You bolted out of school, Jamie, Eoin said, stretching back from the counter. He leaned against the sink, one foot crossed in front of the other, his trainer tipped downwards, so that to Jamie he looked a lot like a dancer. I had my hands halfway down a U-bend and my phone wouldn't stop ringing. That Faulks is not at all happy with you. Jesus, fuck, you gave us all a right fright.

Language, Marie snapped.

Jamie wasn't fully sure of what frightened Eoin. It was the middle of the day. Nothing happened to people on the streets of Emory in the middle of a random Monday, the corridors of school were where all the dangers lurked. Everyone was safer outside, surely Eoin knew this.

Sorry, Jamie said eventually. I am fine. And Marie started to talk loudly and fuss and bustle about making everyone a sandwich.

You should not, and I mean, do not *ever*, just walk out

of the College, *ever* and the thing is, Jamie, you knew this. We had been through this. So. Many. Fucking. Times.

Marie propped small triangle sandwiches in front of them both. Jamie drank in tiny sips and Eoin gulped his tea, having a second cup and eating the sandwiches in one bite.

So, did you meet Terry? Marie asked, eventually.

Yes, yes, I did. I met him in the Locker Hall in the morning, and I saw him once in the Oratory, and I met one teacher, Tess. But she started crying. She had a navy jumper on, and a long back. She was very nice actually. She gave me a cat.

Marie looked at Eoin.

OK, well, tomorrow's another day, isn't it? And no more running off, Eoin said grabbing Jamie by the head and rubbing his hair softly with his knuckles. Then he kissed him.

Jamie was more than willing to talk about Boys One and Two and Three, but no one spoke of them.

8

The next morning, Eoin drove Jamie to school in the van. Jamie didn't protest. Eoin also chatted in the yard with the only teacher that Jamie could identify, Ms Tess Mahon, and he spoke with her for some time before school began. Jamie could not make out what they were saying. Eoin knew it would have been proper to go and make an official appointment with Faulks, but he thought it was better if he relied on the kindness of someone Jamie trusted. Tess promised she'd keep an eye on Jamie. *Check in* were her exact words. And when she got into school, she filed a notice with Ann in the office, and sent about an email to all his teachers about the parental concerns and explained the 'flight risk nature' of 'aforementioned student now known as 1A12'.

Later that day in her first-year English class, Jamie sat at a double desk, alone, where he had plenty of room to sprawl out across (and under) a table. Tess gave the group fixed seating, which he liked. She started the year with poetry, and beginning with Simon Armitage's 'I am Very Bothered' was proving more challenging than she had predicted.

Jamie waited back after the lesson. I do not get it, he said again.

What? Tess said. What part?

All of it. It is a ridiculous poem. And you've set questions and they have no answers.

In your opinion, Jamie.

No, in general. How does the poet feel? That question. I cannot answer it.

Well, how do you think he feels? Tess said.

I do not know. He shrugged his shoulders.

How would you feel, Jamie, if you handed something hot to a friend and it burned them?

Jamie said: But did he?

Did he what? Tess said.

Did he actually do this, should we not separate the poet from the speaker?

Yes, she said, I suppose we should. Would it be easier if I reworked the question?

Yes. He thought for a moment. Here, this is a better question: How does the boy who holds the scissors under the Bunsen burner, then hands it to his friend, feel about causing a serious body injury to another peer? Jamie said as Tess wrote.

Right, so you can answer it that way then, Jamie? Tess asked.

Yes, of course, it is a better question, but frankly, I am no farther along.

What? Tess said.

Because I would never do it, Jamie said. It is cruel.

Yes, yes, but he wanted her attention, Tess said, read the

last line of the poem, she continued as she peeled the skin off a banana. She had left home again with nothing to eat.

He did, and then he should have just asked for it.

Indeed, Tess said, smiling. Right, you're late, for – and Tess leaned back on her swivel chair and ran her hand along a master timetable – for um, for art with Ms Dunbar. How lovely. So off you go.

He is trying to make amends, the poet or the speaker, whoever burned her, Jamie said, finally.

Yes, yes, he is, Tess said. Art now, she said, as a class of seniors bubbled up outside her room and the agricultural science teacher bellowed at them.

I do not know where I'm going, Jamie said, quietly.

Right, she said, and let the seniors file in. Jamie stood back. And when they were all seated, Ms Mahon bellowed: Not a sound when I'm gone. Jonesy nodded to her as he passed in last.

Tess walked Jamie the long way up four flights of stairs to the art room, where he continued his chat as they walked.

But he can't. He cannot make amends, Armitage . . . the speaker . . . whoever. She was possibly scarred for life, Jamie said.

Of course he can. Everyone can make amends, Tess replied.

Hmm, Jamie said, considering this. But he burned her fingers on purpose, to get her attention, in a situation that was highly dangerous in the first instance: a science laboratory. And it was foolish and horrible.

I know, yes, I get this, Jamie, but it happened and he reflected on it, and regretted it.

71

Yes, yes, that is all valid. But is the poet the speaker? Did he actually do it?

But does that matter, Jamie?

Of course it matters, everything else is wrongheaded, unless we can answer that.

Ah, here we are here, Tess said to Jamie and she knocked gently and opened the door of the art room. And Jamie stepped inside the classroom. It was filled with paintings and pots and ceramics and bones and skulls of dead animals. And all of his class group were stood about at easels and were rolling up their sleeves.

We have just sent two boys looking for you, Ms Dunbar said to Jamie. Glad you found us though. She had enormous earrings hanging from her small earlobes with Joan Miró prints and an elaborate skirt with splashes of paint.

Jamie, Tess called out as he walked to a free easel. Stay with your class now, just move with them for the rest of the day.

I'll see to it that he does, Ms Dunbar said to Tess.

Thanks, Claire, Tess said, turning to run back downstairs, shoving the rest of the banana in her mouth.

*

As the early weeks of term passed by, Jamie settled into a routine of sorts. Walking to school became less complicated and intrusive. He liked the pattern of it, especially because there was more rain now that autumn was leaving. This pleased him. And he had begun seeking out Ms Mahon, at other times of the day, and often waiting back during her lunch hour. David, his maths teacher, walked him to classes also, but was often silent and reserved, and was never drawn on chats about Maryam Mirzakhani or Terence Tao, and he showed little or no interest in building machines. Ms Dunbar sometimes had Art Club during lunchtimes and though Jamie often spent all of his lunch breaks alone, Art Club was boring. Ms Dunbar played Mozart and when Jamie or any student had a burning desire to ask a question they had to put up a little flag and sometimes Ms Dunbar dropped it down again, and that was that, and sometimes she attempted to answer their question, but it was rare she did so with any sort of intelligence. Terry was about the place too, but he liked to get involved in the debating club, as it was fierce and uncontrolled and basically you could say what you liked about anyone, particularly women. Terry said it was a riot when the house discussed things like *Feminism has the Place Ruined*, or *Cancel, Cancel Culture.* Everyone got so up in their feelings and shouted and no one listened. But Terry said it was great fun and was so glad that there were no girls present. Jamie went along for one session, which began with one of the school's rugby chants to the tune of 'Who Let the Dogs Out' but was worse, and in fact was 'Who Let Emory's Boys Out' which introduced extra beats. Jamie walked out of that session halfway, and later said to Terry in the jacks that the ensuing debate about media amounted to hate speech, and Terry told him to get a grip, that it was only banter. A word Jamie also hated. Almost as much as he hated the word uncouth.

*

Do you know what I really like, Ms Mahon? Jamie said one day.

What do you really like, Jamie? she said, as he ate his lunch and she marked papers on the role of the witches in the Scottish play.

I love that school starts at the same time every day.

It is useful, she replied and smiled at him as he ate a walnut whip with a tiny wooden spoon.

*

Soon, autumn had stripped everything bare. In this space of decay, Ms Mahon was growing and becoming many things to Jamie. An orientation, guide, driving force, counsellor, teacher, nature lover, and Jamie began to consider her a friend, perhaps, though he was unsure of how you went about putting the title of friend on another person, particularly a teacher. He wondered if there was some kind of a formality – did you ask them to befriend you or quietly infer it? The latter he felt was fraught with complexity and mind reading. What if they refused? After considering his options, Jamie decided friendship was not something that needed the acceptance of the other person, unlike marriage.

And in the evenings and on weekends, just before a

74

film would start, Eoin often asked if he had made any friends.

Yes, Jamie said, Terence, Terry. Though it was complicated, for after years together, Jamie was not sure if he was actually friends with Terry. They never did actual-friend-things together like eating lunch or back-slapping that seemed popular among the boys in Form 1A. But Terry always said *hello*, and borrowed a blue pen from Jamie's pencil case during every maths class. Sometimes they shared a calculator too which was a nuisance. But Terry was well positioned in Jamie's life, for he was often just standing there when Boys One to Three were acting like hyenas, and usually they left Jamie alone if Terry was close by. And vice versa.

Jamie might have included the senior boys O'Toole and Jonesy on his list of friends. They had proven kind and useful and said *howya, Jamie Lad* regularly to him when they passed in to Ms Mahon's room after his English lessons. But after that group, there was very little else to call a friendship, not like some boys in the Heights who shared all day long with one another cruising around on bicycles. He did spend the longest periods of time with Ms Mahon. She kept their room orderly and organised, even sometimes lighting oil burners that smelled of lemons, but mostly she kept the place as free as she could from sensory distractions. And she allowed him drop in for free classes, or when she was free. She was reliable too.

Monday was catching-up day. Tuesday was new-materials day. Wednesday was hump-day day. Thursday was pushing-on day and Friday was usually fun day, often incurring a nature walk with Ms Mahon where she would point out birds, finches and tits, and rooks and jackdaws to the class, and say lines of poetry about nature with her eyes closed.

Blackberry season is over, Jamie blurted out when she was reading aloud 'Blackberrying' by Sylvia Plath in class.

We stockpile and freeze them, one boy suddenly said aloud.

I don't believe in stockpiling, Tess said.

Jamie shrugged. I disagree. How can you plan if you don't?

Look at the bear in *The Jungle Book*, another boy said, look what happened with all the honey, that's a warning. And everyone laughed, except Jamie, who thought this was careless.

Maths class was Jamie's second-favourite part of the day, when he went to David. David was an odd gentleman, who allowed the class to call him by his first name, and was forever working things out on little pieces of paper and firing them into the wastepaper bin. Jamie wanted to encourage him to use a notebook, but something about David made Jamie cautious, and more silent than usual.

*

Soon September was over, the month that always brought an unusual energy, like January beginnings, but with more intensity. Everyone was fatigued by October, focused on their overloaded days while sneezing and coughing, and many were running low-grade fevers as was common this time of year.

The first two months had taken a toll on Tess. She was busy every evening planning classes. Jamie arrived for most of her breaks, and in this she felt less alone than she had in a very long time. She would correct her copies while listening to him, and sometimes Terry popped in too, and liked to recite bad rhyming poetry at will, and was thinking about becoming a slam poet in Chicago, or New York even, though Jamie cautioned against such whims.

She was more and more uncertain about her own future, and listening to Jamie rattle on about life and what everything in any given day might mean, his desire to find the interconnection in every random set of occurrences, made her realise how much she was missing out on – in an effort to keep peace, or to just avoid drama. She was beginning to realise that by avoiding drama she was headed for an almighty crash. And how she had switched off entirely from looking for any beauty in the world.

9

What is it? Jamie asked.

What's what? Tess replied, opening out windows on the last day before half-term.

Jamie said: That noise. He remembered hearing it on his first day, when he bolted.

What noise?

The *woo hoo hoo hoo* noise? Jamie said. Listen.

A bird, Jamie . . . it's a wood pigeon.

Jamie said: Strange how it is always hooting. Does it not ever tire?

Doesn't appear to.

Why can I never see it? Jamie said.

Perhaps it doesn't want to be seen?

Jamie considered this as Tess pulled off her heavy coat and hung it by the door.

Why would it not *want* to be seen?

Dunno, Tess said, fear maybe?

Is that a new coat, Ms Mahon? Jamie said.

It's not technically *new*, Tess said, perching on the corner of her desk. It's my winter coat so it's new to you. I take it out when the seasons change, she said, looking out the window at the sky.

Good idea, Jamie said, what with November coming, though looking into gardens on my way to school this morning, there are still some roses in bloom, the soil is still warm. I also panicked because: Global Warming.

Tess laughed and eased herself back fully on the desk, as she swung her legs around.

It's strange, Jamie said, fiddling with his jelly cat.

What?

You just laughed at catastrophe.

Tess said: Yes. Sorry, Jamie. Global Warming is no joke, just the way . . . you said it.

Women really are *ironic*?

Tess smiled. You mean *iconic*?

No. Ironic, Jamie said. I don't think you are taking me seriously?

Yes, of course I take you seriously, she said. But sometimes you take the whole world serious enough for everyone.

Jamie considered what Tess said. He trusted her. Do I?

Yes, she said, and tell me, why are women ironic?

That is a thing I need to figure out. I asked Terry and he said he has no clue about women, they are a mystery, despite actually living with one. It was something Eoin said, once, when I asked him what Noelle died from, and he said, *Hellp*, and then he said, *fucking ironic, eh*? So I consider that to be the reason women are ironic. I've googled it, but it doesn't fit.

Who's Noelle?

My mother. Eoin's . . . And then Jamie stopped talking.

I'm very sorry, Tess said. Jamie shot her a look. And she continued, I am very sorry when people have experienced loss. I mean, death. When someone dies.

Right, Jamie said. But it's hardly ironic. You could not call my mother's death ironic, could you?

No, it doesn't seem to fit, that's true, Tess said. But I think that perhaps Eoin just said it because he was hurt.

Hurt?

I guess irony is . . . Tess took a deep breath. The illness that your poor mum died from is called Hellp. And it affects the blood and liver.

Yes, Jamie said.

So, your dad said it was ironic because it didn't help your mam at all, in fact it killed her.

He was making a bad joke, Jamie said.

I think when people are hurt, they say things they don't mean.

That's absurd.

Yes, you're correct, well, a little bit, Jamie, and the irony here is the expression of one's meaning by using language that normally signifies the opposite – often to a cause humour or, sometimes, to make a point.

So he was making a joke about her? About her dying?

No.

That's what you said.

No, Jamie. He was using black humour.

What?

Sometimes hurt people use black humour. It's a dark or

morbid humour, that makes light of a subject matter that is generally taboo.

Taboo? Jamie said. The word tickled his lips.

A prohibition on something, something someone might say. In this case . . . Tess stopped dead.

What about this case? Jamie probed.

In this case, the death of your mam, but only, she said, quickly, I suspect he used it to deal with it. It can be very hard dealing with, you know, death, Jamie. And people have different ways of handling it. There's no right way.

Jamie hummed a moment. Thank you, he said, finally. I do understand iconic, and you are neither iconic, nor ironic.

Tess switched on her computer in an attempt to distract him: Right, let's see what's happening in this world today.

The world will be doing what it always does . . . rolling along like tumbleweed, Jamie said as he zigzagged to Tess's whiteboard.

Tess said: Jamie, what are you working on now?

I can't explain yet but it makes me happy and besides, you adults always say, *books good, screens bad*. Which is ironic considering there's no library in this school.

Tess laughed. That's a fact, Jamie. It was futile arguing. She had not slept the night before and had not the energy for verbal combat. Jamie needed a plan or he fell into solving numerous, complicated and infinite maths problems on the board. And she had failed in her morning's planning. He was strong-willed and independent in his own learning, though Tess had learned it was easy to distract him.

The wood pigeon hooted again.

Ms Mahon, Jamie said, the marker is running dry.

Jamie, how about you actually call me *Tess* now?

He looked at her aghast. Oh no, I don't think I can.

She was quiet for a while and finally said: Mrs Mahon is my mother-in-law and that makes me feel—

Old? Jamie interrupted.

Tess laughed. I've no problem with being old. But I'd rather not be the second Mrs Mahon.

Is it a trigger? Jamie said as he worked out on the board.

Trigger?

Jamie responded: Yes. An outburst in reaction to something personal, like trauma or abuse. You know, like trigger warnings for content on YouTube and at the beginning of university lectures, though most usually in humanities and social sciences such as English Literature or Gender Studies. Maths does not need trigger warnings for content. It's inoffensive, maybe the most universal language in the world. That might make it the most beautiful language, he said.

In your opinion, Jamie.

Yes, Jamie said. It is frustrating at times, progress in mathematics moves at a glacial pace, but it is inoffensive, correct. And as causing offence is so subjective, I'm sticking to a life of mathematics.

Tess laughed. What'll I do with you?

Tell me about the bird.

Tess pulled up the sleeves of her cardigan. Her elbows were a mottled blue. She was always cold, but this term she was unable to heat herself at all. She'd taken to heating her whole body with a hairdryer in bed after school for hours. Tess pulled a plastic spiral hair tie from her wrist and lifting her black hair up. She sealed it in a topknot.

The day's light had failed to illuminate the yard outside. The oak tree curled along the red fire escape that led to the workshop from a back entrance. Amber lights filled the top narrow windows of the wood workshop. Sometimes during summer months, when Tess had her windows ajar, she could hear the noise of the saw and the manic laughing that boys make when grouped together in a practical subject.

Go on, Jamie said.

Wood pigeons?

He nodded.

Tess read from the computer screen: Flight is quick, performed by regular beats, with an occasional sharp flick of the wings, characteristic of pigeons in general. It takes off with a loud clattering. It perches well, and in its nuptial display walks along horizontal branches with swelled neck, lowered wings, and fanned tail. During the display flight the bird climbs, the wings are smartly cracked like a whiplash, and the bird glides down on stiff wings. The common wood pigeon is gregarious, often forming very large flocks outside the breeding season. Like many species of pigeon, wood pigeons take advantage of trees and buildings to gain a vantage point over the surrounding area, and their distinctive call means that they are usually heard before they are seen.

What does *gregarious* mean?

Fond of company.

Like you?

No, she said. I'm not sociable.

You are.

But I stay in my room.

Yes, but you like company.

I do? she said.

Yes, you do, otherwise you wouldn't always have me in this room chatting, Jamie said, writing *Gregarious* in cursive on the top right-hand corner of the whiteboard, the space where Tess puts Objectives of Learning for a full class of students listening to Frank O'Hara reading about lovers or Yeats speak in riddles about politics.

Yes, Tess said.

Today I heard five Shakespearean insults walking along the corridor, and it is a first – five insults in quick succession, not five of my favourite, and if I hear one more, it will be a good day, an even day.

Oh now, maybe you'll be lucky and hear one last insult before the day ends.

We are lucky, Tess, Jamie said, her name awkward in his mouth.

Really? *Lucky?*

Yes, it is reported that those who have dead mothers, while the child is in infancy, are more likely to die in the first year of life, and neither of us did, that makes us both statistically *very lucky*. As far as my preparation for Shakespearean insults goes, I am not a fan of Shakespeare per se, I only read the insults as memes online. I've never read any of his plays. I used to read his sonnets when I was younger and Marie was weaning me off Poe.

Poe?

Yes, Poe. Edgar Allan.

I know who Poe is, Jamie.

I have heard mostly single-word insults here.

What? Tess said, slowly considering what he had told her.

Weedy, rank, scut, lout and *reek*, Jamie said. Then he repeated them counting out as he went.

Jamie! Tess said.

What?

Who uses these words?

I don't know, I don't know the boys' names in my class, except Terry and Piotr.

Terence, yes, who's Peter?

Piotr Pulaski. I hear *fag* also, and its plural, bundle-of-sticks variation, *faggot*, though the boys here tend to drop the last vowel sound on that word, and in fact many more words ending in that broad e / y sound. But that's not technically Shakespearean, that insult, *faggot,* at least I have no evidence to prove it is, Jamie said as he blew his fringe up.

Tess was silent.

I'm monologuing.

It's OK, she said, quietly.

Do you know another funny thing?

What?

You told me all about the wood pigeon who is perched in the wood workshop.

Yeah?

I have been thinking, neither the wood pigeon nor I can take part in woodwork. I can't be inside the room because of the saws, also more importantly because Father Faulks said that I am a danger to myself in that room, even though Mr Foley said firmly that I was not a danger to anyone. I have never been in that room, so it is puzzling to me as to how Father Faulks came to that hypothesis.

What? Tess said. When were you speaking with Faulks and Mr Foley?

Jamie was furiously writing now. He avoided Tess's eyes peering at the back of his head: Did I say something wrong?

No, no, Jamie.

Father Faulks talks with me lots in his office.

What? When?

Friday afternoons. He sometimes takes me out of religion class. I don't mind, I hate religion. That deacon from Harrisburg irritates me. Did you know there is not one provable fact discussed in that class with Logan? And what kind of name is Logan?

What? Tess was flustered now but panic would silence him. What do you and Father Faulks talk about?

He shrugged.

Surely you must talk about something.

School.

What about school?

Maths, Eoin, my future.

Your future?

He's always on about my future and wanting the best for me. I said the future is not a topic I like to discuss as it has so many variables at this time, and I am not encouraged to over-think variables, as it can lead to anxiety, and to–

How did he respond to that?

Laughed, Jamie said, quickly. He also asked if I preferred boys or girls.

What? Tess said.

Yes. Absurd.

What did you say?

I said that gender was forced on us but mostly that I pay it very little heed. It is a very old-fashioned approach to humans, much like religion – very unquantifiable.

How did he react to that?

He asked me which one I'd prefer to date. And was still going on about boys and girls. I said I do not date, as I am not sure what that means, and refer back to my answer in any case, to which he said I was exasperating, but I think he meant exciting.

Was Foley involved, Jamie?

Yes, Jamie said, putting the lid on the marker. It was Wednesday. I was coming out of the Oratory, I only know because this was the day you were late. Wednesday, the day you came in crying and your face red. This happens to all adults. Remember. That is what you said, remember, and I said, *Ms Mahon, you really are a mess* on Wednesday and you said, *oh that's OK, Jamie, sometimes people are busy and rushing, this happens to all adults.*

Foley . . . Mr Foley? Go back.

Mr Foley asked why you hadn't picked me up. I was looking around and waiting for you, and he comes up to me and said, *hello! Jamie O'Neill,* and I said, *hello! Mr Foley.*

Is that all?

No, Father Faulks was coming from the Oratory at great speed and Mr Foley puts out his right hand to stop Father Faulks.

He did what?

Yes, Jamie said. Just like this, re-enacting the scene with great gusto up and down the classroom. Then he said – and let me just say, Tess, he was cross – *Once again, I would like a word about why this fine young man isn't partaking in my woodwork class.* And then, confusingly, Mr Foley smiled at me. He has such red lips, Tess. I said that I was not a man yet and they both stared at me, and you have told me to go completely silent when all eyes are on me. Father Faulks can stare for so long without blinking. He just kept staring.

What happened then?

Father Faulks said, *we've been through this Foley*, in *that* exact voice, Jamie said, scrunching up his face. Foley said, *it's* Mr *Foley*. And then he said that I was not to go into the office ever again without a chaperone. He is always on about chaperones.

And how did Faulks respond?

He said, *how dare you accuse me . . .* Then Mr Foley stood out in front of him, and said, *I'm not accusing you of anything, but students should be chaperoned by an adult.* And I do not go into the office any more now. In fact, I am not to pass the threshold, that's what Mr Foley said. I had to google threshold which just means don't go into the office, again adults complicating everything.

The bell rang.

Jamie clicked the lid back onto the marker, turned to the whiteboard, scanning his work before he cleaned it, then rushed out, relieved the bell had stopped the conversation. Tess locked up her classroom, walking out into the autumn evening where the fallen leaves were yellow and mulchy underfoot. She was shattered, for as much as she liked Jamie, he could be absolutely exhausting, and now she was also filled with concern.

10

The garden gate clapped in the breeze as Tess approached her house. The day had brightened to a mellow light. Paul would already be home. Soon she would be sipping beers. After drinking, she would be unsettled. She might smoke cigarettes in the back garden. And she would obsess about Faulks and the boy, and then smoke another and smoke one from the warm amber hue of yet another in a steady cigarette continuum. After which she would fall asleep, most likely, outside, especially if the night sky was clear. And as she considered the week ahead, Tuesday, the Clinic, implantation day, she was filled with thoughts and stepped down to cross the road, failing to notice, or even looking to notice, a car fast approaching. The driver slammed on his brakes and so followed a loud screeching, and then a thrumming as the car stalled. The engine knocked off.

Tess froze.

Her bag was fallen down by her knees, her knees that had buckled like loose elastics and she collapsed on the road.

Shit, the driver said, jumping from his car and running

to her. Fuck, shitshitshit, I'm sorry . . . Tess! It was Tadhg. He crouched down beside her. I was watching you way back and I had you spotted and I saw you were . . . off in another world. I thought: she's going to walk out into the middle of the road.

Even in the drama he spoke with a certain exactitude.

But I never dreamed you would. Shit. Shit. You OK? He rubbed her between the shoulder blades, then suddenly he retreated, and picked up her bag, and shoved back in a wallet and two brown jars of pills that were rolling on the asphalt. He zipped it. I didn't expect you to step down like that, I was sure you'd look. Are you hurt?

Sorry, Tess said, quietly. And no, I don't think so. I'm sorry, she repeated staring at the road.

But poor timing for a death mission, eh?

Tess shook her head, narrowed her eyes. What? she said, dazed and looking directly at him now.

School break! he said. I mean, what teacher chooses to die on the holidays? If it was the first day back you pulled this stunt, I'd be impressed.

Tess laughed a little and tried standing up.

No, wait, hang on, don't move, Tadhg said. Stay still and feel it out. Are you sure you're not hurt?

I'm OK, you didn't actually hit me, Tess implored, I just fell with . . . fright. Jesus, we're making a scene.

Don't mind them, Tadhg said, eyeing some students gathered on the path. He took a white hanky from his pocket and wrapped it around her hand and tucked it in between her fingers.

If you sure you're OK I'll lift you, but only if you don't

think you've broken anything. Actually, might be best if we call an ambulance.

I'm fine, please, Jesus, Tess said. She was heavy with tears now and bit hard on her cheek to stop the water from coming. Thanks, she said, for this. She lifted her bandaged hand.

Sure? I mean, you seem a little dazed is all.

I'm sure.

Tadhg helped her to her feet and as soon as she stood up the adrenaline surged through her and she wanted to get inside. But then the thoughts of retreating into the house with Paul also filled her with dread. She wanted to speak. But her heart was flipping and her hand stung.

You sure you're OK? Tadhg said, looking under her hair towards her face.

I'm grand, she said, eventually.

Tess wanted to say: It's not you. She wanted to say, I cry all the time now, and wish I could stop it all, but it's so relentless. She wanted to say that even in her classroom she cries sometimes. And sometimes now, even sitting on the toilet, she can cry at her reflection in the ornate mirror across from the loo. Then she'll laugh at the idiot who hung a mirror opposite a loo.

Tadhg linked her to the path.

Really, I'm fine. I live just here. Now fuck off, Tess said, smiling.

OK, take it easy, a few painkillers, Netflix? I'd really rather bring you home.

No, Tess said, it's not a good idea.

Tadhg understood the tone. I'll head on, call me later,

let me know you're OK, and he pulled out a card and shoved it into her bag. She was surprised, he didn't seem like the kind of individual to carry business cards.

*

Paul Mahon finished early on Fridays. He loved a long weekend and had stopped off on the way home to pick up supplies for the bank holiday. He was busy about the kitchen when Tess returned. Jazz FM blared. Paul aired out spaces he lived in, wherever he found himself, he needed air, he said it was because he had no window in the bank. Despite the open door and the October breeze, despite awaiting Tess's return, he had missed the drama and was singing along to Nina Simone.

Tessy, ah, you're early, Paul said, checking his watch.

Hi, she said, hanging up her coat.

Good day? Paul asked, glancing over his shoulder, then back to food prepping. Rain's cleared.

Seems so, Tess said, sitting in the hallway as she unlaced her oxblood boots, and pulled them off. The hanky slipped.

Paul said: Early finish?

Early? Nonono, Tess replied, brusquely. She folded the white square that was dotted with her blood and shoved it into her pocket.

I wasn't expecting you so, well, so soon, Paul said. Wish I was more . . . prepared.

Her entrance seemed a trespass.

You OK? Paul said, wiping a knife through a tea towel.

Fine, yeah, Tess said. Her nerves and adrenaline were

replaced by a terrific need for solitude. Her return home filled with a friction re-entry that was common.

Paul glanced at his watch again. Righto, he said, breezily as he arranged cuts of soda bread in a walnut bowl. Here, he said, lifting his hands, no skin off my nose, Tessy, whatever time you're back at, I just like to be pre-warned, a text so I'd be more organised and maybe surprise you.

Tess stared at him.

Tess, I'm not complaining.

Paul, you're having an argument with yourself, she said. Besides, you could have been a teacher, it's not rocket science. But that's the time we finish at?

Who'd cover the bills? Paul said, laughing.

Honestly, she said. For fuck's sake. She was on the brink of tears again. Her hand stung.

Here, Paul said, quickly, startled by her anger. Let's start over. He pulled a high stool out from under the island and tapped it.

Tess sat.

I've food in the oven. Won't be long, he said, opening the door with oversized oven gloves and pulling a bubbling dish towards him. He stabbed a knife to its centre, then slid it back and closed up the door.

I'm not hungry, Tess said.

Really? Might be nice if we made the effort?

Sorry, it's just, I had lunch with Ellie, Tess lied.

Ellie?

Ellie Staunton.

Food won't be long and in the meantime . . . help yourself . . . Paul said, ignoring her. He waved his hand across olive leaves stuffed with pine nuts, sun-dried tomatoes, apricot shades of hummus, Parma hams. Then he sliced foil from the neck of a bottle of wine, uncorking a red.

Everything needs time to breathe, Tessy, he said to her as she watched him: You look pale. And then he suddenly began gently tapping her face with the back of his hand.

I'm fine.

Sure? You're sweaty.

I'm sure.

I was just thinking, Tessy–

Yeah? she said, scraping a thin layer of hummus onto the warm bread.

Just an idea.

Tess nodded.

Things are hectic at work, I won't go on about it over the weekend, but what if I drop you to the Clinic on Tuesday and I'll just swing by the office, tidy up some loose ends?

Fine, Tess said, biting her cheek again.

Great, that takes a load off, he said. We're prepping for the Amsterdam conference, and it's all hands on deck sorting out tech. He poured wine with his left arm behind his back, the way he poured for his parents, twisting the bottle clockwise at the end of the pour, and catching the drop in the last second. Meticulous.

Tess drank quickly, though she longed for a beer – not a craft beer, or an IPA, or a bottled beer or a beer infused with anything, just a pint of lager pulled from a tap in a pub with a sticky floor and filled with people shouting at televisions full of soccer players throwing their hands to their heads, humans drunk in dark corners, chatting as though the end of the world was coming, as though their lives depended on the conversation, and eating chips, places with madly patterned carpet and shiny walnut bars.

I'll have my phone on, Paul said as he opened the icebox, searching for frozen vegetables.

To the left, Tess said, faintly.

Tess thought of their embryo in the hospital somewhere as Paul poured the frozen peas into a saucepan. She picked an olive with her finger and thumb, rolled it, then nibbled at it, eventually freeing the tiny stone, and she continued, picking and nibbling, and placing the stones in front of her like abacus beads. Then she pulled more bread cuts, splurged a dollop of hummus on a small side plate, her stomach uneasy. Eating helped. But digestion hurt. She stood up and walked into the TV room where she put the plate down on the arm of the couch and flopped onto it. She unclipped her bra and pulled it through the sleeve of her jumper and then flung the bra across the room.

On the telly a chef was making bread and enthusiastically discussing yeast starts – it was a rerun where he emptied leftovers from his fridge and then pantry into a bowl; eggs, flour, water, milk, frothy yeast bubbling. Tess liked reruns. She liked playing the same song over and over. Or rereading a book. He shoved his arms deep into the bowl, squishing then suctioning the dough, and then scooping it from his thumbs and adding flour, said: *It's malleable now.* Elbows deep in the ceramic dish. She pulled Tadhg's hanky from her pocket and wrapped it around her hand, then used that hand to dip the bread generously into the hummus. As she ate, the cloth smelled of the outside; smoke and sea. Her appetite returned. The chef scattered in tiny black olives, sun-dried tomatoes, anchovies, cheese and chives and tossed the dough onto a wooden plinth that he had dusted in flour, and finally he moulded it in a circular dough plait.

Just chuck in your end-of-week leftovers from the average pantry.

Sure you're OK? Paul said, sticking his head around the door.

Yeah, sure, Tess said. Paul eyed the bra thrust across the room. Oh! he said, smirking.

Tess looked away.

I've been thinking, he said as he stared at the telly, you should think of up-skilling, this term has you in the worst form.

I like teaching, Tess replied, defensively.

There is a difference between liking something and being able for it and do you . . . actually, do you really like-like it?

Yes, Tess said.

There is no harm in looking, plenty of online work you'd be great at, where you could avoid people and you could work at your own pace.

I like people.

Don't they just irritate you?

No, she said, staring at the telly.

I would love to see you . . . happy, that's all. I'm heading up for a shower, food in thirty. Paul loved the regularity and routine of food.

Grand, Tess said finally.

She would go through the motions. Drink the wine. Forget. She was good at forgetting.

The last time she encountered her father on the street, he hadn't recognised her. *Girl,* he said loudly as she had dashed across the street to avoid him. *Good girl,* he called out after her. *Could you spare a fiver?* She had forgotten this.

Soon Paul was back downstairs in a bathrobe with a towel tucked on top of his head. She was finishing off the last of the wine. He switched the channel to a stand-up comedy gig in the Apollo with a thin guy making jokes about mothers. Paul laughed loudly. When the joke was over, he muted the telly and said: I feel we haven't had a proper chat in weeks.

The wine was effective and she was in the rare mood for a chat. I have this boy, she said, and you know, I have him for English and he's remarkable. He's hell-bent on building a machine of perpetual motion, and loves so many things, his energy is . . . so remarkable . . . and geo-desics, beginning with a doughnut, and working your way in or is it out? Today was explaining irony . . .

Sounds a little juvenile, Paul said. A perpetual-motion machine?

You think? Tess said.

Paul nodded, then he leaned in towards Tess on the couch, and slipping his hand around her waist, he started to kiss her neck. Then he put his fingers to her lips to per-suade her to stop talking. She was conscious of her black-ened wine teeth. But she didn't care. He put his finger up to her lips again, and said again: Sssshhh, please, no more talk of school or work, it's a bank holiday. And she was about to embrace him, or try, but the room was so silent and his breaths were loud and whistled.

This calls for music, Tess said, quickly, and now full of a desire to shift her body away. She jumped up and moved to the other side of the room, where she was suddenly conscious of her breasts. They felt heavy without a bra. Her stinging hand reminded her of Tadhg and the wine was making her light-headed. She flicked through Paul's vinyl collection. Let's have music! Tammy Wynette anyone? She said giggling manically. She looked around the room as she lifted one of Paul's mother's vinyls from the box and waved it about.

Tess, he said. Stop.

I mean, who listens to this shit? she said.

And he stood up and grabbed it from her, placing it back. Please stop. Tess went out to the kitchen to grab another bottle of wine. Oh, lighten up, she said to him as Paul followed her out, but his mood had changed. Tess was laughing hard now. He walked across the kitchen and ever so quietly he lifted the lasagne out of the oven, left it on a wooden board on the island and carefully covered it with tinfoil, then a tea towel.

Tess uncorked another bottle of red.

I thought that was dinner, she said, watching him covering it, as she held the side of the island with her hand. She poured some wine into her cloudy glass and drank it, but she was dehydrated now, and it felt dry and difficult to swallow.

I've lost my appetite, he said. And you're not hungry. Though food might help.

Oh, for fuck's sake Paul, surely you're not upset about me taking the piss out of your music?

He pulled the towel off his head and threw it to the base of the washing machine. No, he said, nope, just, I've just lost my appetite. And then he turned about and headed upstairs. I made a big effort this evening.

Stay, she said.

No, this is the laughing that turns, he said, and went upstairs.

Tess watched him go, pulled a face and gulped from her glass.

When she heard their bedroom door close tightly, she pulled a box of cigarettes from the back of a cupboard and went outside. There she lay on a damp sun lounger, lit a cigarette, and whirled it in red circles against the black sky. She continued for some time smoking and staring at the moon until she was giddy. She still wanted to dance.

She pulled the card from her pocket.

Tadhg Foley. And with a hand-sketched currach and his number in bold print.

She dialled.

He didn't answer and after some fails, she left a text message.

You like to call over? Bored. Xzxc

The message, read at 2.07 a.m., went unanswered.

11

Tess baulked on Tuesday morning just as she was about to leave for the Clinic. She re-washed cups, changed scarves, alternated between shoes, until she eventually stood in a pair that were neither practical nor pretty and were already causing her pain. Paul was sat outside their house in the driver's seat of the Honda. The engine was ticking over and once or twice he revved gently. Finally, Tess bolted the garden gate. Then she pushed the gate back in again to double-check. She re-bolted it. She opened the car door and shimmied into the seat, dragging her stilettos after her like a foal lunging over a stone gap.

You took your time, Paul said, checking the clock on the dashboard as he flicked through work notes. He slipped his conference papers under the driver's seat and sipped from his coffee. Don't want to be late.

Tess's skin was hot and sweaty in the fussy fabric of a layered dress, and pink splashes erupted across her neck and down her arms. Her scarf snatched in her earrings. She had drawn black eyeliner along her hooded eyes in a moment of haste, and she flicked open the visor mirror above her head to fix it. One line was thick and straight, and the other thin and flicked upwards. She began to smudge one with the finger pad of her index finger, then the other eyelid, until they matched and made her look depressed and sleepy.

Paul indicated to pull off. Shit, what happened your hand? he asked, as he was changing up gears.

Emory was scattered with pumpkins on pathways outside some town houses. Bright oranges, greens, apricots, some were carved with vicious smiles, some were left uncarved. Witches hung from porches on brooms with skinny faces and purple hands.

Nothing, Tess said, slipping off her shoes. She lifted her feet to the dash. The petrol station on the corner was doing an offer on devil doughnuts with a spiced green latte.

Doesn't look like nothing, Paul said.

I fell on the road on Friday, that's all.

What? Paul said. The road? You never said. You OK? He fiddled with the radio.

Fine. I just fell, Tess said, as Paul reached over and took her hand to inspect it.

Jeez, looks nasty, he said, then he jerked the steering wheel and swerved. Fuck sake, Paul, she said. Watch the road.

He slowed. Why didn't you say? His eyes were on her now. I thought you were weird on Friday. Maybe you had concussion?

She glared at him. Can't a person have the odd accident? You'd think I'd fucking know if I hurt my head. Jesus. She looked ahead.

They were silent for some time.

Sorry, Paul said.

Tess said: I'm just . . .

It's OK, he said, touching her leg.

Don't, she said. Just go. We will be late.

He pulled out and the main road narrowed just out past the town border.

The car in front of them said *Drive Slowly, Baby on Board*. Tess never understood those signs. A kid with spiral curls and a patch on one eye stuck her tongue out at them and Tess lifted her feet down, and stuck her tongue back.

The private clinics were at the back of the hospital, with their own drop-off. Paul drove around the back and Tess was sure he would enter the multistorey, park up, say something nice, go with her, but as he circled the drop-off waiting for an ambulance to pull out and let him in for a moment, Tess filled with rage.

You're feeling abandoned, Tess, but what you need to ask yourself is: is this reality or am I paranoid? Is this a rational response to Paul's actions?

He pulled in, hazards on again, and said something reassuring.

Tess got out, slamming the door. She was unsure if he would drive off, even when she was stood alone on the pavement, twirling the dumb scarf about herself and his car was long gone.

You have communication issues, Tess and Paul, deeply rooted communication issues, they need immediate attention.

Good morning. The receptionist was cheerful. Her dark

hair was split down the middle and tucked tight in behind her ears.

Tess, Tess Mahon. I have an appointment with Dr Green.

Nice to see you again, Mrs Mahon, she said. Here you go, my dear, and she handed Tess a clipboard. Please take a seat and fill this in.

Tess was irked at *dear*. At the hand displaying the directionality of the form. She filled in her details, and passed them back.

Thank you. All looks great, she said scanning over the document. Has the rain cleared?

Yes, Tess said, unsure. She hadn't noticed the day.

Won't be long now, Mrs Mahon. Quiet this morning, you're in luck. Dr Green will be with you in just a moment. Oh, just one more thing . . . she said, arching forward and lifting up off her swivel chair. She whispered: Are we still on the Zoloft?

Yes.

Xanax?

Yes.

How much?

As required.

OK. She scribbled. On average?

Maybe 0.5mg, maybe a little more, depending, you know. Tess paused.

The woman skilfully waited for an answer.

Depending on the day . . . Tess said, quietly.

She scribbled on the back of the form.

And did we manage to fully cut out the alcohol?

Yes.

Great, great. That's all great. Like I said, he won't be long.

Tess took a seat and pulled a book from her bag but before she could open it, Dr Green arrived to the waiting area. Small blue plastic sacks over his shoes crunched as he walked.

Tess, hi, good morning, you're welcome . . . back. The rain stopped? He said, extending an arm for a handshake. It was strange to see his bare arms in the short sleeves of his scrubs.

Hi, yes, yes, it has, Tess said, lying.

Would you like to come through? he said.

Tess fumbled about her and gathered up her bag and book and walked slowly. Sure, sure, she said. That *was* quick, she said to herself, but Green overheard.

You're one of the lucky ones, Dr Green said. Hectic here last week. You look lovely, he added as he walked down the corridor. Off somewhere nice?

Yes, I had a meeting this morning, Tess said, lying. I had to swing by the office.

School this early?

We work hard too, she said. It's a general misconception that we're all about holidays. She knew she had crossed a line. She didn't know why, but she felt compelled to lie. But no one understood her job.

I didn't mean . . . it's just . . . tough job, teaching. Have you exam classes this year? Green said a little flustered now as he walked ahead down a narrow corridor. He turned in to one of the examination rooms.

Yes, Tess said.

Dr Green's room was a dark mulch of bog yellows, greens and mahogany woods. A window was covered with a heavy blind. Green took a seat behind his desk. It was unusual to see a desk so empty.

So, please, take a seat, Tess.

Tess sat.

We'll talk you through this again, although you're a pro, Green said, turning on his computer screen.

A nurse was stood by the wall. Tess jumped, startled by her. Hi, she mouthed.

The nurse smiled.

So we've no Daddy today then? Green said.

No. Tess paused. No husband either.

Apologies. He clicked the mouse and read her details. Paul, pardon me, he said, eyeing the screen. He coughed gently. No Paul?

No, Paul also had to swing by the office.

Green said: Right, busy time, end of quarter. You're a busy pair!

Is it? Tess said, flatly. A busy time?

You OK, Tess? Green said dropping his hands on his lap and dipping his head to the side. He swivelled his chair towards her.

Yes. I'm fine, Tess said, quietly. A little . . . no, no, I'm fine.

Yellow paint was fresh on the walls dotted with some laminated notices: Fresh Paint, Do Not Touch. Tess reached into her bag for a tissue. Her book fell out.

At . . . wood, Green said, reading upside down and he picked it up, my wife loved her other one . . .

The Edible Woman, Tess offered, though she has written many, she said, thinking it unlikely he knew what his wife read.

Yes. Yes. That one. Perhaps.

Yeah, she's great, Tess said holding the book and rubbing her hand over the front cover.

So my wife says.

Right, Tess said. You read them?

No, not my kind of thing, Green said.

How d'you know?

Pardon? He said, swivelling towards her with a cuff and battling with the sleeve of the dress until eventually he had enough arm. The cuff tightened and Tess began to panic, sure there was a fault in the blood pressure machine. Her hand swelled, the skin was so tight she felt it would tear.

If you've never read them, how do you know? she said.

Green laughed. I see, good point.

An elaborate plant in a huge terracotta pot stood in a water tray with its leaves carefully oiled. Ivory certificates with faux wax seals were framed and hung on the walls and a black seat like a sun lounger was plonked in the middle of the room with a gigantic microscope clutched to the ceiling overhead.

The right arm of god.

All the dark cavernous spaces of women, Tess thought, all the rooms they hide in, having procedures, all the placing and misplacing, entering and exiting of embryos, like you might plant a geranium in spring in a small pot, or rinse one out of last year's compost come next spring, all the little bird nesting boxes on the gable ends of houses with last year's nests abandoned, ready for cleaning, or cleansing, to welcome blue tits back, who feed their hatched young up to five hundred times a day. But no one ever sees them, or watches this closely.

So. Let's get moving, Green said, swivelling about to her on the seat again. Would you like sedation?

Yes, Tess said, I need . . . I mean I want it, she said, correcting herself. *Need* sounded addictive. She wanted to sound like it was a whim.

Your blood pressure is a little high, Green said, as he un-Velcroed a black cuff from her arm. We'll take it again in a while. Take a few deep breaths, Tess. Just try to relax.

The nurse left a small plastic container with pills in front of her and a tiny cupful of water. Tess quickly swallowed them back without water.

So, Tess, Green said, as you know, this, well, it's a fifty–fifty at very best.

The Clinic had a fifty-seven per cent success rate but there was a marketing prowess in a fifty. And there was, extraordinarily, only one embryo. Green had trained in America where patients were different. In America, they were *in on it*, in on the emotion of it. Americans were all about emotions. Quick release. The Irish were all about emotion suppression. Slow release.

And Tess, we were all so sorry about the last time, Green went on.

She nodded.

But here's the thing . . . Green said. There's *no difficulty* with implantation, it's just . . . he said, swivelling about again on the chair, he threw up his hands, one of these mysteries. *So* tonight you need to be kind to yourself. No stress, OK? Nice meal maybe?

She soldier saluted.

OK. I'll step out, Green said. Jane here will gown you.

Tess nodded.

You sure you're OK? Green asked again.

I'm fine.

Would you like us to call Paul?

Tess was pale now. The red flushing had dissipated.

No.

Sure?

Yes, quite. Quite sure. Thank you.

Just as he was about to leave, he swung back: Full bladder?

She nodded and then she cracked the water cup as the nurse came towards her with a green gown, hanging loosely in front of her.

Here, let me help you, if it's OK with you, Tess, I'm just going to unzip you, she said, as she rummaged about the back of Tess's dress. Oh, is this one of those hidden zips? Hate these, she said, fumbling about the fabric and pinching Tess's hip, then prodding her with her thumb. She then tried to figure out the costume jewellery.

Maybe best if I just leave this to you, Tess. I wouldn't like to break it. It's . . . it's pretty.

Is it? I think it's a lot . . . like everything right now, all a lot, don't you think? Tess said, clutching the garish necklace. I really don't know what I was thinking. I find it so hard to dress for occasions. This is an occasion, isn't it? Would you call this an occasion? She spoke fast now.

I think you're overwhelmed, Tess, the nurse replied. Why don't we . . . let's see if I can't . . . just, she said, pinching the clasp on the big necklace, trying to unclip it. Tess, would you like to talk about it?

Tess shook her head.

It's natural to feel overwhelmed.

But Tess had stopped listening now . . . Shit, I'm sorry, Tess said, grabbing the necklace. I can't, I just. No, I don't, I'm sorry, I have no idea how to open it. It's a stupid fuck of a dress. It makes me feel all . . . ridiculous . . . I can't go ahead with it. It's not right, it's just, no . . . I can't . . . Tess said again as she pulled her dress fabric from Jane's hands.

It's all OK, Tess, try to relax, maybe sit back down and wait a while, give the medication time to work, it's natural to be like this. If we got a penny every time in here that someone . . .

. . . No, fuck, you don't understand, see, Tess said, sorry, or . . . thing is . . . I don't want one. I don't know why I'm even here . . . on my own . . . Do you have many women come here alone?

Yes, of course. Sometimes.

I don't think that I actually *want* a baby. I don't think I do.

Tess! she said, just take a few deep breaths. This might be your last shot. What's the harm?

What's the harm? Tess thought to herself, what harm, and who will be harmed?

It was such an utterly mad fucking word, harm. It was harm.

What harm. What harm. Try again.
You won't be harmed. Were you harmed?
Who harmed you?
Did you cause harm? It's harmless.
Implant it, it'll probably not hold. You're hostile.

The room spun fast now. It is only harmful if it holds. But what if it *is* you, Tess, that is harmful, full of badness, no good whatsoever to this embryo, that has defrosted. Then she thought of chicken fillets in a dish in a grocery bag on the windowsill at home. And of Paul and the peas. You see it might be all the harm in the world, Tess said, finally, after the room stopped spinning. Gathering her belongings, she bolted, and running fast out into the car park, she was unsure of where she was going to go next.

Outside, Tess gulped lungfuls of air. She noted that it was not raining. She noted that the sun had come out. She also noted that her body was on fire now. She was running hard until she noted that the arches of her feet were burning, and she was carrying the stilettos in her hand, and in the other, she had the little plastic pill jar. She noted her breathing, and then panting deeply she slowed and tried to control it, and eventually, stopping, she stared directly up at the October sun, and then she noted that she was smiling.

*

Paul hadn't expected her call so soon and was over an hour returning the five-minute spin back to the Clinic. In the meantime, Tess strolled to a small grocery shop opposite the hospital and flicked through some magazines and was licking an ice cream when he pulled kerbside, hazards bleating faintly in the sun.

Hi, he said, smiling as Tess sat in to the car.

Hi, she said, her mouth full of cold vanilla as she dropped her shoes and bag in the back seat.

You OK? He leaned in and kissed her. How'd that go? He looked at her bare feet.

Bit stoned, she said, quietly.

Paul laughed. A bit late in the year for an ice cream, he said nodding at the cone. Jesus, work was mad, and he dipped down to check his mirrors.

Or a bit early, Tess said as she lifted the last bite to her mouth. She licked her thumb and her index finger.

Paul passed her a tissue.

And as she pulled the seat belt over her breasts, she thought of them full. All the times her body got ready, filled up, then her empty breasts days after, as the blood that had pooled inside her, to grow and nourish, rushed from her over and over. And on into all the long months spent pushing her body to unbearable limits, for herself. For her just to say, *Here is my body and it is working like yours, I, too, can be a mother.*

Yeah, good, she said, rubbing her sticky fingers with the tissue.

All go OK? Paul said.

Yes, fine.

I've been thinking, Paul said, I'll take the afternoon off, so how about we get takeaway, watch a film, or something?

Great, Tess said.

There's a new documentary on Netflix – a guy who takes a car trip across America.

OK, Tess replied as she gazed out the window at the lolling hills passing by, clouds billowing fast over them, rain soon. When?

It just dropped today. Ninety-two on Rotten Tomatoes.

No, when was it set, Tess said, this trip across America?

She watched as his freckled hand changed gear. The neck of his blue cotton shirt was wide open. Then his whole body arched forward from the waist as he set about checking mirrors again. She noted the accidental authoritarian way of him, how sometimes he moved in desirable ways. He was once so fuckable, she thought, as she watched his thigh muscle contract when he pressed on the clutch.

Once she had also loved him. She noted this too.

During the Sixties, Paul said. Guy and his crew, they drove across all the states, him and just a cameraman, sounds great, someone risking their life to document inhumanity, any interest?

Paul was always inclined towards revolution at a distance.

Sure, Tess replied. And then she sang along to a song from the nineties that played out on the radio. Something about it set her to remembering Jennings playing songs in the kitchen as he cooked her dinner. A band she could sing along with but couldn't name.

You're in good form, Paul said. Sleep if you like. Maybe you should.

But Tess was wide awake now, sleep wasn't coming.

Paul said: You want to talk about it?

No, Tess said, quickly. Let's just wait and see what happens.

OK, Paul said.

They continued in a more relaxed silence and when they arrived home, Paul waited for her, and closed the car door gently after her. He opened the front door so quietly, afraid he'd wake somebody, afraid he'd startle his wife's body.

I'm heading up for a nap, she said.

12

Tess changed quickly in the upstairs bedroom and she ripped the dress from her, stuffing it into the waste bin in the corner of the room on top of empty cups and tights with ladders. Her skin relaxed and soon the hot redness faded completely. She stood in her bra and knickers in front of the mirror, lifted her shoulders and dropped them suddenly. She repeated this a few times. When she shook her head, the Clinic's smell lingered in her hair. She threw herself down onto the bed, and pulled a coverlet over her. She felt between her legs, ran her hand across her flat stomach, considered medical waste, and then imagined a man dressed like a beekeeper disposing of the embryo in an incinerator, reminded of a queen bee she once watched on a documentary, shoving males from the hive, nosing them out, sometimes alone or often two or three females working together, until the male was exhausted and eventually fell to his death.

It was some hours before she woke. She listened, and the house was silent save the noises and groans and whirrs houses make. She dressed herself to go downstairs, where she pulled on her rain mac and stepped out into the evening.

Outside was filled with a smell of peat fires, people

were just arriving home from work. Settling in. Tess turned left to the woods, and walked on until she reached the wall with the stile, and climbed over. A laminated sign was nailed to a tree: *Leave No Trace* and some lost-and-found items were left carefully by the entrance: short gum boots covered in daisies, a pair of sunglasses, a gnarled dog leash and a baby's bottle full of milk.

Autumn's sun threw the last shards of the day's light through the trees. Soon the clocks would fall back and people's rhythms would be off kilter. Some would even die in the early morning, their hearts confused by new routine. The dark of winter was a challenge. Bareness arrived like a death, though it balanced with a lack of expectation of the season. People had permission to hibernate too, bed earlier, go slowly about life for a little while. Go off grid.

Tess had grown up in an estate on the opposite side of the woods, out near the Old Forge which was shut for years. No one now brought horses up the streets of Emory and through the woods for a set of new shoes on large working hooves. The forest had become its own beast, pushing in on what was once well maintained.

Tess walked on faster as the rain began, plashing quietly on the river. She thought about turning back, but instead started to jog. Soon she was sprinting for the second time that day. The moss, strewn with crackling twigs, crunched underfoot as she hopped crude gaps in the low stone walls and little bog holes: the twigs reminding her that spring would come again and they'd be gathered by swallows returning to build nests in the rafters of houses. Tess missed the swallows when they left her gables, flying south: watching them leave, she felt an immense loneliness. Then an undeniable envy at their freedom. The crows never seemed to leave.

The tall trees offered canopy from the rain. Sitka spruce – popular in the nineties during a time of concentrated reforestation – were now a great threat to indigenous Irish trees. There were some willow and hazel trees farther in near the Forge, sown by fishermen over a century before for boatbuilding. And while the evergreens offered advantages, the deciduous trees were full of a story of survival, of cycles.

From a clearing, Tess slipped along a lush bank and side-footed to the river's edge.

The rain stopped. Tess was sweating now and out of breath. She had been running hard.

Tadhg Foley was stood at the edge of the river on a small inlet beside a low boat, squared off at the back, a proud bow and inside was weaved like a basket. Tess leaned by the trunk of a tree, watching him for a while, then becoming conscious of herself. She lifted her matted hair up, and pulled it onto the top of her head.

Tadhg bent one knee and twisted his waist to the river. He flicked his hand, releasing a stone from his grip. As it skimmed, he ducked, and dropped his shoulder just before he cast another.

Six, seven, eight hops, followed by ripples on the dusk-grey water. He pulled a third stone from his pocket, edged sideways, and thrust again. Eight. Then he dipped down and threw a final stone.

Hey! he said, spotting Tess and shouting up to her.

Hi, Tess said, shyly.

He beckoned at her to come and she sidestepped down the rest of the bank.

Fuck fuck fuck, she thought, her heart pounding. Her clothes wet.

What're you doing out here in the dark? Well, almost dark, Tadhg said as he threw his head back and looked up to the sky.

Hi . . . Tess said again. It's not *so* dark yet, not really.

Until someone turns a light on, Tadhg said.

Yes, indeed, Tess said smiling. But what's the likelihood of someone turning on a light?

Tadhg smiled. Surely you should be on a holiday, or working on a Halloween costume?

Halloween's not my thing, Tess said, fixing her topknot and pulling a few strands loose around her face.

No kids? he said, throwing a rope behind him onto the boat.

No.

Ah, well, that's the difference. Halloween and kids seems a busy time, sounds fierce competitive from what I hear – my friends always give out about it. Kids seem to have turned them off many of life's events.

Whole fucking world's obsessed with kids, Tess said, suddenly with force. She found it hard to imagine Tadhg having many friends.

Sorry, Tadhg said. I didn't mean to – he stopped for a moment and stared at her –

cause offence.

They both fell quiet now. Tadhg fussed with cords in his pockets, pulling them out one by one and knotting them to each other.

You come down here often? Tess said, in the end.

Every day.

Missing home?

A little, Tadhg said, shrugging his shoulders. He turned his back to her and lifting his arm, he thrust another flat stone to the sea. I miss it in the summer, you know, it's busy then, but fuck me, winter is depressing out there, he said. You ever been?

Summers, Irish college – the Gaeltacht, Tess said, but never in winter time.

Bleak, he said. But summer . . . summer's nice.

Summers were filled with young students over from the mainland to learn Gaeilge. He remembered swimming at dusk, their bodies lashing in the cold water, legs tucked around him. All the first experiences.

You OK? Tess said.

Yes. I'm fine, he said.

Tess reminded him of one girl. Her dark hair, or the exacting way she spoke.

When the girl's last day on the island came, after they had spent the entire summer together, Tadhg made an excuse to take the ferry to the mainland to see her off. He found it hard to let her go, and realised in time that maybe he loved her. That maybe this was what love was. But he could never tell her, it was so exposing. And so he pretended on the day she was leaving, that he had to help with cargo, that something was coming back out from the city of Galway, a cow he had said, and he had to help men bring it back to the island. Perhaps he would pluck up the courage to tell her something about his feelings on the ferry.

Down on the island's pier was busy and full of students with rucksacks, crying and saying goodbye to a freedom that would likely never return. Back in their own world, with their own people, and the competition that comes with the young and affluent, life would always be different. This summer was an experience for her, not a life she would live.

Her father had come from Dublin to collect her. When the ferry docked on the mainland, he ran to her and quickly scooped her in to him, kissing her, affection Tadhg was unfamiliar with. He was dressed in garish shorts and big Oakley sunglasses on his face, his round chest zipped into a Helly Hansen jacket, busy cologne, and he kissed her again before he put her down. Then he lifted her backpack onto his shoulder and took her guitar case and they walked back to his Range Rover. Tadhg remembered cream seats, and an angry dog in the back in a bassinette. When her two worlds met, she reverted to a child, muttering something about how Tadhg had come over to bring a cow back from Galway. He remembers her saying he was a farmhand, or something like it, *a hand* in some way, which was entirely incorrect, he was a student, just like her. Her father laughed. She sat into the Range Rover without waving, and just as he thought she was about to lift her hand to wave, she pulled out big sunglasses from the glove box and put them on her small face.

Tadhg had hoped he would keep going then, maybe

leave the island, open up a little. Maybe keep on going to Dublin, leave the island to fuck. He was always going to meet people at the ferry, arrivals, departures – it seemed most likely that the baulks, the stop/starts were to test himself. He didn't realise he had been doing it for so many years, until eventually he understood that no one was coming to save him. He didn't know what he expected. That man had hardly looked at him, did not shake his hand, did not offer his hand, had never made eye contact with him, only embraced his daughter, packed up his jeep and reversed out, driving eastwards.

Tadhg never heard from her again.

He missed the last ferry back to the island that night. It was coming autumn, not a cloud in the sky, and he had slept rough, waited for morning.

He flicked another stone to the river. It sank. The boat rocked on the water.

Yours? Tess said.

Yeah.

Are you not freezing? Tess asked, eyeing his buttoned-down shirt. She leaned down and ran her hand along the boat.

No, Tadhg said, I don't feel the cold. Or at least I don't think I do.

This is beautiful, she said, running her hand along the side of the hull, over its smooth tarred edges. The *Joan of Arc*.

Thanks.

Joan of Arc? Tess said.

How's the hand? he said.

Oh stop, I'm mortally embarrassed, Tess said and winced. I'd forgotten all about that. Maybe my brain has done me a favour – overwritten it?

Not sure it works like that, he said, laughing.

So mortified, she said again. And about . . .

Don't. Don't mention it, Tadhg said quickly, please don't, avoiding embarrassment for both of them. He cracked a twig. So you had a good weekend.

Look, I'm sorry, about the text . . . I was . . .

Don't mention it, Tadhg said quickly again, we've all been there.

How're you settling in at the College? Tess said.

He threw the twig to the clearing . . . It's grand, you know for the most part. I've been very busy. But here – that Faulks is . . . a little unusual.

He's a force, Tess said.

And then some.

I can't manage him at all, she said. Anyway, fuck him, we're on our holidays, tell me about this boat.

Currach, Tadhg said.

Did you make it?

Yes.

You sail back home in it?

Sometimes.

That's amazing, Tess said. Looks fragile.

Ah yeah, but mostly I take the ferry, I have many modes of transportation, he said.

So very modern! Tess said as she sat beside the boat on the damp grass. Tadhg wasn't expecting it and something about seeing Tess on the ground panicked him.

Here, you want to go out for a spin? he offered.

Bit late, no? Tess said looking up at the darkness that was covering now. But then she was on her feet without thinking. Tadhg looked at her shoes. Flat, and rubbery.

Just careful, they're vulnerable, he said. You could put your foot through, OK? Step onto the foot boards.

Tess nodded. I did notice, she said, gingerly stepping in. It felt unsteady beneath her. They sat on two seats, Tess ahead, both facing out to the water.

You really go all the way to the island on this? Tess said back to him. She was even more surprised at how fragile it all seemed from inside.

Yes, but here's a hack, helps if you pick up the oars.

Oh right, sorry, she said, I've never . . .

Tadhg nodded as he pushed off from the bank with one oar. They were very long, and thin.

The boat glided out on the river.

Drop your shoulders down, he said, now lift the oars, right, yeah, like that, one slightly about the other, yes, that's it and Tess began to row the river too, and soon her arms felt heavy and her lower back ached.

Do you jog late every evening?

No, not so much, Tess said. I've just had a fuck of a day.

Shit, Tadhg said. Here you can drop them, they're secure, and he continued to row, as she sat back. It's really not been your week, he said. You OK?

The reflection of his headlight threw strips of white light out on the river.

Yes, Tess said. No. Actually no, I'm not.

The river whooshed and the boat felt inclined to topple.

Don't worry, you'll get used to it, Tadhg said, watching her hold the side. It's best if you don't make any sudden movements, least not with the bad luck streak following you about.

She laughed.

Tadhg dropped his oars, and leaned forward to her, and she felt him at her back and thought he might reach out to her. But nothing. They both watched as the oars dragged on their thole pins and a rat rustled near a tree on a tiny island they passed, its green eyes glowing in the dark.

Then in a moment of awkward silence, Tess told Tadhg about the Clinic.

I hate lying, Tess said, picking the oars back up after.

Is that a question?

No. Yes, maybe. Do you think it's a question?

If it's a question, the answer is, yes, you should hate it, you're being dishonest.

Harsh, Tess said.

You are being dishonest, Tadhg said again, and he leaned forward on his seat. But you know you are and I don't think you need me to tell you.

Tadhg's oar cut the water.

Everyone keeps secrets.

Does that make you feel better? The *everyone-else-does-it-why-can't-I-whataboutery?*

Yes, Tess said. Bet you have secrets.

Tadhg said: Yes, of course. Everyone does, but this isn't about me.

123

Tess said: Ever been in a long-term relationship?

No.

Really?

I've had casual relationships.

Right.

They fell silent again.

Lift the oars out of the water, Tadhg said, reasserting himself. And he turned the boat around, began to row back. I'm not going to give advice, Tadhg said, rowing quickly now, his breaths even and intense. Because no one listens to advice. Not really, the *why* of things are impossible, most benign, it's no great importance, sometimes searching out answers, or worse, allowances is dangerous. You did it, bolted from the Clinic. Walked out. Walked out along a river and jumped in a boat with a randomer.

Hardly a randomer, Tess said.

You know what I mean. People change, Tess.

Back on land the atmosphere felt suddenly formal. Tess was mulling through her rolling regrets. Regret at the morning, her dishonesty, at confiding in a practical stranger.

I'll walk you to the road, Tadhg said.

Are you not out this way?

No, I live up in the Old Forge.

No way, Tess said. You can't live there, surely it's uninhabitable?

The Forge was shut for years now. Tess hung out there as a teenager before the council blocked it up.

I thought that place was a shambles?

It was, Tadhg said.

But why? Why are you living there? That's fucking crazy.

Why not? It's free. And I have no interruptions, Tadhg said and he walked her out to the stile, and helped her over.

Tess! He shouted to her when she was on the footpath and faced for home.

Yeah? she called out, hand behind her ear.

Text when you're home safe.

She lifted her hand in the air as the rain pelted down now.

Oh and bring Jamie to the workshop Monday, let's see if he might like to build something.

Paul was sat in the kitchen, scrolling, when Tess walked back in.

Ah hey, you're back, he said.

Hi. I went for some air, she said, I needed air.

Oh Christ, Tessy, you're soaked. He stood up but she turned to the stairs.

I'm heading up for a shower, she said and stood a moment at the jamb of the door watching a choir of boys sing out on the TV.

Food? Paul asked.

No thanks, not hungry, Tess called back as she climbed the stairs. Soon she lay floating in a bath filled with lemongrass salts and as the water turned cold, her narrow body felt heavy yet buoyant.

Paul was snoring softly when she slipped into their bed.

In the dark, she started to compose / delete texts to Tadhg . . .

. . . Thanks for the chat
Thanks for talk
Thanks . . . I needed that . . .
Look I must have sounded . . .
Sorry . . .
Enjoyed the boat, nice surprise . . .
Appreciated the chat, Goodnight. X delete X –
Ta. X
Ta. X
Boat emoji. Red Heart emoji . . .
FUCK.

Finally, the text read:

Thanks, Tx.

Instant response . . .

You're more than welcome . . .
It was nice to see you.

. . .

Followed by a return text:

Sleep well. T

13

Jamie was pleased when Monday came around. School days were structured, unlike hanging out at half-term. But there was a change to this Monday, and to all Mondays for the new term. Ms Mahon was taking Jamie for some support work to organise his week. Faulks had requested extra organisation time.

Welcome back, Tess said, have a nice break? Jamie took short steps into the room, his feet turned out as he crossed the linoleum, red bag high on his back. His body was fixed into a new red anorak that was zipped to his chin.

Father Faulks said I have a double class with you now on Mondays. Is that correct?

Just for a little while, Jamie. Is that OK? Tess said.

Yes.

Tess smiled.

I got a winter coat, he said lifting off the bag and unzipping the anorak.

I can see, it's lovely.

Did you have a nice break? Jamie asked.

Yes, I did, Tess said.

Jamie didn't reply. He understood a finite statement.

He lifted a marker from the board tray, playing it like a majorette's baton between his fingers, but Tess plucked it quickly from him: You won't need that, exciting news, change of plan, she said. Mr Foley has asked that we go to the workshop.

Really? Jamie asked. Why?

I guess to make something, and how about we seek out that wood pigeon?

Jamie said: What should I make?

Mr Foley will give you guidance.

Like you do, Tess?

Is that a joke, Jamie?

Yes.

Tess laughed.

You want to hear another joke? Jamie said.

Yes, but, Tess said, lifting her bag and water bottle, tell me on the way. And she switched off the classroom lights fast before he changed his mind.

They walked the dim corridors past the Oratory, past Faulks's office until they reached the landing by the old swimming pool that was filled in and repurposed as the wood workshop.

Jamie said: This was written on the toilet door, Tess: *Polish! Go home but leave us your women.*

Jamie! That's not funny.

Jamie continued: *And take ours.*

JAMIE! Tess said sternly, ssshhh. That's really not funny.

No? he asked, hopping from foot to foot.

No, Tess said sharply.

Sorry, I didn't mean to offend you, he said, looking at

his feet. It is written on the toilet door, and so I thought that perhaps it was funny. The boys in class say they love Polish girls so if the men went home then the women would be left as wives for the Irish men.

I understand the joke. And left *as wives*? Tess said, crossly – we're not chattels, Jamie. They stopped outside Foley's workshop.

Do you know Piotr? Jamie said.

Piotr?

Piotr Pulaski. He's very smart, Tess. Very good at maths. He is from Poland.

Tess smiled.

Tadhg had a free period on Monday mornings through to break, as practical classes were left for the afternoon sessions when students were full of distraction and sugar. Faulks prioritised maths, Latin, Classics, applied maths, chemistry and physics on the morning's timetable. Tess was uncertain if Tadhg had arrived at work yet, and for a moment she panicked. Jamie sensed it.

What is the matter? Jamie said.

Faulks's office door opened and quickly Tess shouldered the double doors of the workshop, and they gave way.

Inside was filled with wafts of timber and petrol, a numb coldness clinging to the air. The doors swung back quickly and Jamie saved his face with his two arms outstretched – a habit he developed for protection in the toilet cubicles.

Jamie was nervously chatty, unsure about the radical

Monday deviation. Above them the high ceilings teemed with timber objects, finished and unfinished, some varnished, others painted. Lamp bases, wooden aeroplanes, chess boards, skeletal boat frames, mirror frames, wooden dream-catchers with bright feathers and entangled in colourful ribbons, coffee tables and bar stools with missing legs. Wooden birds flitted about on strings. The windows were tall and touched the ceiling, relics of the pool that was once full of water, boys thrashing about in the cold. Twenty-four work benches were arranged in rows with large blue clamps on their edges and tools neatly laid on each bench: jigs, saws, hand-planes and chisels. Up against the breeze-blocked walls were large cabinets, caverns filled with old uncollected projects; eggcups, mug trees, one unstrung harp, one painted Spanish guitar and a scattering of chairs in various stages of completion.

Jamie walked by a slim café chair. It was fragile and light and carved from a wood Tess wasn't familiar with. Jamie sat heavily on it, dragging it along under the workbench with his tiptoes. He prepped his tie.

Hey, Tess, Jamie said in a deep American accent as his eyes darted around, *I ain't eating nothing that don't have enough sense to disregard its own faeces.*

Jamie! Tess said. What has gotten into you?

Pulp Fiction. Diner scene, Tadhg said, walking up behind her.

Tess was startled.

Correct, Jamie said, turning about.

Great movie, now pull off the tie, Jamie.

Jamie nodded and pulled the tie's knot. Greys and reds unravelling. He rolled it up.

A Tarantino fan, Tadhg said. He unzipped his coat, unwound his scarf and stuffed it into the arm, before rolling up the sleeves of his checked shirt and tucking them in above his tanned elbows.

Nice surprise, he said, smiling at Tess.

Yes. I like Tarantino. I'm not a complete fan, per se, Jamie said in unusually excited articulation. And some of it is gratuitous. Style over substance. Besides, it is very dated now.

Dated? Tadhg said.

Yes, dated, Jamie said, unsure of how to expand on the why of all of that. Eoin had said this over the holidays, when, instead of celebrating Halloween, they stayed in bed, hiding out from bangers and masks, fireworks and hauntings, eating noodles from tubs, and again they binged Tarantino's movies in chronological order.

Have a favourite? Tadhg asked him.

I don't do favourites.

Not true, Tess said, what about . . . red?

Jamie eyeballed her.

The colour, Tess added.

I know what red is, Tess, Jamie said, defensively. It's a habit I try to avoid now. Having favourite colours is childish.

It is? Tess said, playfully.

Yes.

Tess, Tadhg said. First names?

Ms Mahon is a mouthful when you see each other as much as we do, Jamie offered.

I can imagine, Tadhg replied. *Jackie Brown* is my favourite. Did you see it? Also green, my favourite colour.

Predictable, Jamie said, expecting Tadhg to press him on it, but he didn't. Jamie didn't want the conversation to end. He realised he had been finite in his opinion on favourites and colours.

He liked Foley. He pushed: Yes. I have watched *Jackie Brown.*

Tadhg said: *Well, you can't trust Melanie, but you can always trust Melanie to be Melanie.*

Who's Melanie? Jamie said.

Kid, who's Melanie? I thought you were a fan. Tadhg said and laughed.

Jamie was confused and he hated making a mistake: Yes. You're quoting. You're quoting from *Jackie Brown.*

Tadhg laughed gently. Why do you avoid favourites? he said, changing course.

It leads to fixation and that stops me sleeping.

Fixation? Tadhg said.

Yes. The art teacher taught me about it, mostly how to recognise it. It can lead to compulsion. Though I do not know why – as far as I can tell she has developed her own compulsions.

She has? Tess asked.

Yes, she is obsessed with Mozart.

Really? Tadhg said. Surely there's a lot to be said for compulsion, no? Firing yourself headlong into something?

Tess ran her slim hand along the frame of a half-made chair and followed along on its underside. Is this oak?

Larch, Tadhg said.

I have a favourite book, Jamie said, interrupting Tess. Not sure you will have read it.

Try me, Tadhg said, vaulting his body onto the bench.

The Complete Tales and Poems of Edgar Allan Poe, Jamie said.

I have not read it. Correct.

Jamie prickled under his arms. This was not a statement he could easily respond to.

Tess said: I hope you don't mind us being here. Jamie was eager to get out this morning. We're always stuck in. And we love listening to your wood pigeon through the windows so we thought, why not go and find him.

Jamie shot Tess a look.

You were eager, Jamie? Tadhg said. First thing after a week off and you're bored with Ms Mahon? That won't do her confidence any good. Teachers are sensitive creatures.

No, Jamie said. I wasn't bored. I love her . . . classroom. I like her ideas mostly. And she is kind, you might not always think that, because she sometimes shouts. But she is great at explaining poetry, and sometimes, though I like poetry, it can be frustrating.

Frustrating?

Yes. Trying to figure out the feelings of the poet, and if he's the speaker, and if they are the same person. And there are some clues, but no real answers. Not really.

Is English your favourite class?

Yes. No, Jamie said quickly correcting himself. Maths is. Well, maths should be.

Really? Tadhg said.

Humans can survive without poems. It is nice to have them, but without them no one suffers, whereas the world *needs* maths.

Why?

To help people to develop machines. And I have a great ambition to build a machine this year. A perpetual-motion machine.

Why? Tadhg said, again.

For personal reasons.

In that case you'll be investigating nature and mathematics and science? They can go together very well, much like jelly and ice cream. Tadhg was bustling about and looked at Jamie as the boy made an odd face, scrunching his nose, and then lifting his eyebrows.

Tadhg went on: No subject can work without another – systems, patterns, it's all one big loop. For the most part. So in this way there is a certain interconnectedness to everything. Excluding those parts we don't fully know.

Yet. Don't fully know *yet*, Jamie said. These unknown parts are what we must figure out. And I'm not sure that woodwork is useful for this purpose.

It's a cross between design, art and nature, Tadhg said.

But art isn't important, it's nice for people who like to be stimulated . . . Jamie said, trailing off, thinking of the art deco on the Odeon, and the colours he loved most in the world. OK. I do love colours, he said, quickly. Certain ones.

I think art is a way of figuring the world out, Jamie,

and it's all trial and error, figuring out what's important. Film is art too.

But it is passive entertainment, Jamie said. Sometimes it is a waste of time better spent doing something else. And really, look, Mr Foley, I am not in school to figure out what is important. I already know that. I do not need school for the machine, it is a personal project.

Right, Tadhg said and he looked at Tess. She held his stare.

Maybe you could show us some of the tools we will be working with, she said.

Tadhg started handing items to Jamie, and explaining each – types of woods, sandpaper grain – but Jamie was not listening now. He was stimulated by the pieces of wood in the rafters. By the way something could move for ever. He was thinking of Noelle in the blue water. Busy.

I am thinking how there are good people working your Venn diagram approach to world design, Jamie said, idly holding a screwdriver.

Like? Tadhg said.

Jamie thought a moment. Sabrina Gonzalez Pasterski is one, the theoretical physicist . . .

Ah yes, she built a plane when she was about your age?

Yes, Jamie said, but she is far more complex than that, she is always full of good ideas.

Surely no one can have good ideas all the time, there has to be room for errors, even Pasterski will have bad days.

There should be no room for errors, Jamie said. Especially as an adult. If everyone paid attention to their day . . . it would be all a lot better.

But that would be exhausting, Tess said.

Not as exhausting as things falling apart, Jamie said. There are some things that can be pre-empted and in that case, avoided. But people, they are statistically so . . . so . . .

Accident prone? Tadhg said.

Negligent. Accident prone. Prone to chaos.

Chaos Theory? Tadhg asked.

Yes. This, and also chance, and I feel it in your workshop, Jamie said eyeing the ceiling. It's unnerving – this whole place . . . is chaotic.

What is?

The way, it is so . . . random. I can't find a pattern.

There might not be one, Tadhg said.

There is always one, Jamie said. I just need to find it. But right now it looks like a place where . . .

. . . Things fall apart? Tadhg said.

Yes! Jamie said.

Now that's a good book Jamie, have you read it?

What?

Things Fall Apart.

No.

By Chinua Achebe, Tadhg said.

I know by the title that your book will be about things falling apart and besides I am going off fiction. I think now it might be a waste of time. Things always fall apart . . . it is . . . thing is, I live in fiction. My life is the plot of a bad book and therefore I have no interest in reading fiction . . . it won't . . . help me. Jamie was breathing fast now.

Tess interjected: Maybe we should decide on a project?

So what you're really saying is you have no interest in

suspending reality? Tadhg said, ignoring Tess. Is it because of some physics theory you believe that things fall apart? Does this make you afraid?

Yes and Yes and No, Jamie said, quickly.

Things really can fall apart, you're right, but you can't live your life by disproven physics theories. Do you not want to know about how to put them back together again? All the pieces of chaos?

No, Jamie said.

No? Tadhg asked.

No. You can't. And I do not need to know how to put things back together again if I live in before, the before they fall, that's where I stay, in that moment, planning, before things fall apart. That is the safest place to be.

But you can't always protect yourself, Jamie – this is about protection? Tadhg said, wandering around the workshop now.

Jamie shrugged.

Right, this machine, talk to me.

Go on, Jamie, Tess said. Why do you want to build one? She moved closer to him.

I am trying to build a machine for before the falling apart, Jamie said, staring at the ceiling. A perpetual-motion machine. I have some plans, but the idea is, it will never ever stop moving, and it will bring me closer . . . and then he stopped himself dead.

Your machine needs to exist in a single moment?

Jamie was quiet. He looked directly at Tess: Yes, she said. With a constant energy.

But we can't live in single moments for ever, Tadhg

said, and lifting a canvas apron from a nail, he lassoed it over the boy's head. Or be constantly *on.*

Jamie said: I want a machine that is propelled by the perfect sequence of events, a machine that begins to move until it builds its own energy, relies on nothing, and the sequence of events leading to its propelling itself is so perfect that it stays moving for ever, and then, when I create the perfect volume of energy—

Can other people use it? Tadhg interrupted.

It was something that had never crossed Jamie's mind.

Why would they? Jamie asked.

I'm trying to figure out *the why.* Think of Pasterski's plane? If I could do that, figure out why you are so keen on building it, maybe . . . Tadhg said, as he started to move pieces of wood about the bench, and he locked one into the bench vice.

Suddenly Jamie began laughing.

Why are you laughing?

I'm not building it out of wood, Jamie said, it's not that kind of thing, they are just objects, this will be an actual machine.

So it needs to follow no other function than never to stop moving?

Yes.

But why?

I want it to be a constant source of energy.

But you're a source of energy, Jamie, isn't that enough? Tadhg said.

No! It needs to . . . have its own ability to be . . . to . . . He stopped again. It will be anti-fragile, Jamie said, eventually.

Anti-fragile?

Yes, like humans.

We're fragile, Tadhg said, softly, machines might be anti-fragile, but not us. And what I'm hearing is, you want a machine that's full of energy and anti-fragile. You want it to outlast you? Then what of it?

Wait, what is this for? Jamie said, suddenly taken by surprise and aware of the apron he was wearing.

To protect your clothes. There's goggles in the pocket, put them on too, good man.

Tadhg walked gingerly around the workshop, picking up solid pieces of wood, and finally he settled on one.

Eoin would laugh if he saw me wearing an apron.

Eoin?

My dad, Jamie said.

Eoin must have a tough time trying to save you from things falling apart. Just one thing, Tadhg said, you haven't told me why you need this machine to never stop.

Jamie was scalding all over. He stopped for a moment, then started talking quickly and loudly,

the sensation of the sandpaper was upsetting him

he took a long deep breath and spoke, quickly:

When Noelle swims, she is always on my screen, I want her in my head, and I like watching her, it makes everything slow down, and if a machine runs at the same time she's on screen I am hoping they energise each other,

he took a short breath and was loud now:

this machine, I have all of this . . . all of this in me, curves and loops and Maryam, and yet I just can't . . . I cannot feel her, anywhere, no one tells me about her, or talks about her, and I can't feel her . . . I can't—

Tadhg laid his hands on Jamie's shoulders. The boy had his eyes squeezed shut now.

OK, we'll build a machine, Tadhg whispered, we'll build something, don't worry. Then to Tess he mouthed: *Noelle?*

His mam, Tess said, quietly.

She is dead, Jamie said, his eyes shut tight.

14

Jamie visited Tadhg's workshop every school day after that first time. They often worked side by side in complete silence making objects, and they worked with very little purpose other than feeling the woods and relaxing the boy. First, he carved and assembled a mug stand. But Jamie thought the ergonomics of Tadhg's design were poor; the stand was reliant on every mug being the same weight and size, so Jamie designed a mug stand like a menorah, but with six prongs and not seven – for balance. Then he made an aeroplane model with a small engine. Suspended from the workshop, it went around in the same circle for weeks, and for those weeks their time went thus: Jamie drew plans, Tadhg cut wood, and together they assembled. Jamie learned about dove-tail joints, hinge joints, woods, deforestation, sustainability; the way redwood was unforgiving, ash sensitive, and pine could fall apart. They spoke about rainforests, gorse and forest fires, of Tadhg's plans for biological farming. Of Tadhg's childhood on an island. Tadhg learned about loops, curves, geodesics, M-theory, cats, the soundtracks to a plethora of films, and every Spielberg Easter egg. Tess continued to take Jamie to the woods, often, and looked at the last few giant Irish oaks, and later, they potted some acorns with Tadhg. And soon they were sanding long thin laths of wood, and cutting another important piece out of oak. And Jamie had no idea what was important about it, but he started to just go along with it all, because he accepted Mr Foley liked to work in silence sometimes.

You'll be in an exam year when these are ready to plant, Jamie, Tadhg said.

Jamie nodded, busy mushing seaweed compost down on the acorns.

He carved a TIE fighter from *Star Wars* and as the wood turned, Tadhg watched how handy Jamie had gotten, how effortless he made carving look. Jamie painted the TIE fighter as close to Vantablack as he could find, and when it dried, they suspended it with twine from the rafters, close by the plane, and Jamie built a little motor for this one, different to the aeroplane engine, and it twirled about the workshop.

Then one day when Jamie came to the workshop, there was another TIE fighter beside it.

Terry made it to match yours, Tadhg said.

Jamie inspected it, it stung a little, but it was excellent, he thought, better than his own.

Easy to copy someone, Tadhg said.

Sometimes the workshop was filled with a class, but Jamie had stopped taking notice, except once when Terry had a rotten banana in his bag, and that day, he chatted at Terry about the clamps on a wood turner, and they talked about Imperial Stormtroopers, Terry called them Space

142

Nazis. He told Jamie stories about his life in London but Jamie, exhausted by all the detail, asked him to stop telling personal business and so they carved a Darth Vader head and painted it in silence.

Jamie made a chess board, a wooden flute and a key rack. He drew designs of Mirzakhani's, loops and shapes and triple spirals, and Tadhg helped him carve some that were tricky and Jamie wanted them to be exact, and Tadhg commended him on getting closer to some kind of continuum, at least of shape.

Maybe that's what you're looking for with the machine, continuum?

Other boys often worked alongside them in the workshop, and sometimes it went late into the evening with seniors busy prepping projects for exams.

On a dark gloomy Friday, the day they turned the College's Christmas tree lights on, a day that lacked structure with boys rushing about on errands, excited with the promise of a break, Tadhg was heading out for the weekend when he came upon Jamie crouched outside the workshop. His hands were clasped over his head.

Shitshitshit. Jamie! What's happened? Tadhg said, rushing to him and kneeling down in line with Jamie's face. The boy's lip was swollen and a purple clot was forming and he was sucking in some blood and gagging. Shit, Tadhg said, searching his pockets for a hanky. What happened? Here, put a bit of pressure on it, good lad.

They were locked, Jamie said, the doors. He was sobbing hard. The doors, they were locked, and I thought, maybe that you had gone . . . for the weekend. That you were gone. Because, he said, because you rarely lock them. He snorted hard.

I had locked up, I wasn't expecting you, I was just on my way out. Shit. How're your teeth? Take a breath, kiddo, have you broken any?

Jamie was bewildered. Yes, this *is* unexpected, he lisped, as he stared at Tadhg. Blood dried around the corner of his mouth and the sides of his face were flushed red with white blotches.

Open up, let's see if you need a dentist.

Jamie sat on the edge of the café chair and opened his mouth wide, though his lips throbbed. Tadhg jumped on the bench opposite him.

Looks OK to me, I think, but you got a right bang, kiddo. Or two. And, Tadhg said, straining to see into the boy's mouth, I think you've put your teeth through your tongue. Feel around, make sure nothing's chipped.

Jamie felt around his mouth with his tongue, and thought he was suffocating. He gagged as Tadhg unscrewed his water bottle and handing it to him, said: Don't drink until you're sure nothing's loose.

Jamie nodded up and down and pink froth dripped on his uniform.

Take a gulp now, that's it, Tadhg said, putting some tissues under his chin. Right, a few deep breaths now – you're in a bit of shock, is all. Who did this, Jamie? Tadhg said.

Jamie shook his head. It is not . . . important, Jamie said. The skin on his lip was hot and thick and felt foreign.

It is. Tadhg said, quietly.

No . . . it's not . . . it is just . . . that is not what has me upset . . . his lip bled again, they shoved in the toilet door, but they always do it. I am used to it.

Who? Who shoves in . . . what door? What boys?

Other boys from Form 1A, Jamie sobbed. It is usually Boy One, sometimes Boy Two. Boy Three does not seem to hang out with them any more. But Boy Nine has started joining in. He is bad news.

Boy One? Boy Two? Nine? What are you talking about? Tadhg said. You're making no sense.

The locks are not fit for purpose . . . the locks on the . . . on the . . . they kick the door in when I'm sitting on the toilet. I usually only use urinals, but I . . . I was crying and I needed . . . to be alone. Cubicles. There are no . . .

Jamie's nose was bleeding and instinctively and without asking, Tadhg squeezed the bridge of it. Those doors should have proper strong bolts, you should have said something to me, or David.

David? Jamie said, nasally. I'd rather die.

Ms Mahon then, Tadhg said. Right, right, fuck this, I'll sort them.

The bolts or the boys?

Both.

You can't Mr Foley.

See if I can't.

I don't like the sight of blood, I will faint, Jamie shouted suddenly.

Put your head between your legs, kiddo, here, let the blood flow, you've had a shock is all. It happens.

145

But you are not listening, Jamie said from between his legs, I was crying going *in* to the toilets.

What?

I'm not crying because I'm bleeding, he said, as though he were underwater, head clamped between his knees. So: chaos is a branch of maths that proves dynamical systems whose random states of disorder and irregularities are governed by determined laws that are highly sensitive to initial conditions, right?

Shush, Jamie. Take a breath, kiddo.

Jamie was crying hard now.

. . . It is interdisciplinary, Mr Foley, he muffled, and you are always speaking about this, and then he lifted his head up and his face was all a red flush: and so, Jamie continued, within the apparent randomness of chaotic complex systems, there are underlying patterns, interconnectedness, constant feedback loops, repetition, self-similarity, and the basis of which is self-organisation—

Jamie, look at me, Tadhg said.

Jamie lifted his head slowly.

Watch my mouth, carefully, watch my lips move.

Jamie froze, looked at Tadhg's red lips.

You are not OK. Crying is good but you need to get something off your chest? I'm here. And for fuck's sake if a door needs a bolt, I need to know.

You absolutely should not curse, Mr Foley. That is twice now.

Sorry, correct, I shouldn't.

I didn't win, Jamie said, getting up and pacing about. You see, that is the problem, I did not win, and now nothing, *nothing* will connect.

Win? What?

I didn't win the Maths Award. Father Faulks gave the award to Piotr.

Piotr?

YES! Pulaski, he's good at mathematics, but mostly calculations. Piotr, he is one of the best in class at crude mathematics, but I cannot prove I am the absolute best if Tess is always taking me out for extra classes to talk about stuff I have no interest in. He was crying again now. And she knows nothing about mathematics. It is not right. And no offence, Jamie said, I don't want to build out of wood, I don't need a mug holder, or a TIE fighter. I only live with Eoin, we only have two mugs.

. . . I know, I know there's your machine to consider . . . but the two things aren't mutually exclusive, one could lead to the other. Building solves problems, Tadhg said. Small fires lead to big ones, yeah?

Maybe, Jamie said, sobbing into the grey sleeve of his blazer.

But you're correct, Jamie. It seems very unfair, though I don't know your results compared to . . .

. . . Piotr.

Yes, Piotr. I can't imagine what you are feeling.

It is a miscarriage of justice.

Ah here, bit dramatic!

Jamie was stung.

As regards the award, these things happen all the time, Tadhg said.

David loves Piotr. And I can't explain why, you know I'm in that class, like a . . . fish out of water.

Tadhg laughed.

This place is so disjointed. I do not know why you're laughing. Father Faulks spoke about the need for uniforms and for grooming and was caring for our parents this morning. That is what we need to do, he said. And if building things from wood were as important as mathematics, then there would also be an award for this subject. Which goes some way into proving that building something great as you suggested the first time I came into your workshop is a big waste of my time.

Jamie, people like Faulks don't understand.

It isn't fair.

Fairness is subjective, Tadhg said.

But that is preposterous and the mathematics department is not fit for purpose.

Tadhg said: Right, I think we need to get out of here.

You know what, Tadhg?

What?

It makes me furious, Jamie said, sucking in his fat lip.

Right, let's go, we need to get out, air might help.

Jamie followed Tadhg out of the school building. Tadhg was approving a nature walk by calling Tess, and was talking fast as Jamie ran skip-stepping to keep up. Tadhg was in a temper. Jamie had two white pieces of tissue blocked up his nose and they walked out into the crisp winter air,

past the pitches, moving deeper into the green under-
growth that would take them to the river.

Tess was waiting for them down by the river. The thrumming day had brought on a headache, and she ran to them
and called out: Jamie, I'm sorry, I had no idea.

What? Jamie shouted across the distance between them.

I'm sorry, Tess said. I will try and sort something on
Monday.

Don't, Jamie said. You cannot redact a prize, and Tess,
you cannot fix it. David forgot all about me because I'm
always with you. I don't want to exaggerate my capabilities, but he doesn't have a clue. As for Piotr, being adept at
calculations, and neat in your copy, is not award-winning.

Jamie, enough, Tadhg said. It's not Tess's fault. Or Piotr's.

I disagree, Jamie said. I'm taken out for classes here
and there without any planning, almost every school day
now. Eoin says I need support, but it's absurd, Boy Seventeen can't even read. Everyone going on about me need-
ing support. Absurd.

It might help if you could name the kids in your class
and not just number them, Tadhg said, bluntly.

Tadhg! Tess said.

Why? Jamie said.

Because it's polite, Tadhg said, and normal.

Who cares about being polite? No one cares, Jamie said.

Tadhg turned to Tess: Thanks for coming. So that we
don't all bring this . . . mood onto my boat . . . let's forage.

Forage? Jamie said.

Yes, *rods*, Tadhg answered. Let's get some rods.

Rods? Jamie said.

What's with the echo? Tadhg asked.

Yes. Most likely there would be an echo. I'm surprised, Jamie said, because I've had this awful day and now you want me to work.

It's prep work, Tadhg said, sarcastically, your favourite.

But it is freezing, Jamie said, shivering, and preparation for what? He stuffed his face into his collars that were zipped up to his chin.

Just for a surprise, Tadhg said, I have a plan, and it might quiet that mind of yours for a while. They neared the icehouse and ran up one muddy trodden side of it, that was well overgrown with brambles, and Jamie helped Tess. Standing on top of it, they could see out to the river and farther.

They had a long way to come from the Bishop's Palace for some ice, Tess said, laughing.

They did, Tadhg said. No one worries about hard work when they have someone else to do it for them.

Hate surprises, Jamie said.

Tadhg was silent.

Thanks for doing this, Mr Foley, Tess said, shivering.

I don't even know what we are looking for and I am very cold, Jamie said.

I thought you loved winter? said Tadhg. We are looking for rods, look, just like these. He held up a hazel rod that he had sliced.

I like winter from inside looking out, Jamie said, skipping again to keep up.

Here, Tess interjected. Follow me, and she took them to a clearing filled with willow: I think these are white willows and by spring they will flourish, don't they look kind of feminine? The male and female flowers grow on separate trees.

How can a tree *look* feminine? Jamie said, and shook his head.

The willow was straight and thinner than hazel.

Here. Watch, Jamie, Tadhg said, first showing him slowly how to cut, and then he passed the knife to him. Give it a go.

What are they used for? Jamie asked, catching some in his fist to cut.

Building boats, or baskets now, mostly, Tadhg said, for tourists.

Jamie stared at the reeds.

Slice like this, Tadhg said and he gave Jamie a glove for his left hand, mind your thumb, tuck like this and just a quick slice, again, there, see, pick ones without much growth, the fewer buds the better. The first boats were built thousands of years ago with these.

I've never been on a boat, Jamie said.

First time for everything, Tadhg said. Emory was a busy fishing port once, hard to believe that now that it's all so overgrown.

What did they need so many boats for? Jamie asked.

To fish, Tadhg said, mostly. Or bring supplies in to Emory from bigger ships – currachs carried live animals from the ferries into the town, and supplies, and more importantly carried them from here to the islands, tables, chairs, cattle, barrels of gas. Ferries often waited out by the estuary as the river is too shallow to dock big boats.

Jamie said: But you said yours was a vulnerable boat, that if we jumped too hard, you'd push your foot to the water.

Yes, Tadhg said, they are vulnerable, but powerful.

Jamie hummed. He paused a minute to think about this.

Tess said: Really, cattle?

Yes, they'd arch the animal upside down and they'd fit it into the shape of the boat, legs often tied, or drag it behind the currach. Horses are much harder, too skittish and unpredictable. And the rods, Tadhg said, lifting one up, are light and fine, they're the very beginning, so when you're cutting, the younger the better, leave the thicker ones, they can be very stubborn. The energy of the rods; the give; I figure this all out first before I can nail the frame. You need to work with the rods first, that's how I build my boats. By feeling. Always started by bending rods.

By feeling a boat? Seems careless, Jamie said, rummaging about the bushes.

Thinner rods, Jamie, Tadhg called out as Jamie sliced, remember, the thicker, the less pliable.

Pliable? Jamie said looking back at Tadhg.

Bendy.

I know what it means, I just don't know why we have to cut so many.

They went along the river and Jamie played with a rod, bending it backwards and crossing it with another.

The rod's natural inclination is to bend to a bow, Jamie, look, Tadhg said as he pulled one and with some twine, he made a bow.

I always wanted a bow and arrow, Jamie said. He sped

up again, conscious of himself: Did you know the Scots pine tree has a bitumen that is the most powerful arrow top you can use and it can kill?

No way? Tadhg said, tying the rods in bundles with twine from his pocket.

They walked on to his currach, and when they got there, Tadhg leaned into the boat and lifted out two life jackets from under the seats. Jamie had grown tall during first term, the zip catching his chin.

We're actually getting on . . . going on the boat . . . Tess said, surprised. Then she laughed, cautiously.

Yes, Tadhg said.

I thought you were . . .

Tadhg said: You thought I was what?

Distracting. She pointed at Jamie. I thought it was a joke.

Do I look like I am in the habit of joking, Tess?

There was an intensity to Tadhg today that Tess was unsure of. He released the ropes from the pier, repeating it for Jamie in turn. Jamie practised tying and releasing, and after some time of miming a quick-release knot, he got the hang of it.

Joan, Jamie whispered, tracing his hand along the bronze plaque. *Joan of Arc*?

Maid of Orléans. Who believed god had chosen her to lead France in a victory against the English, Tess said as Tadhg looped rope.

Tadhg said: And after the moment of victorious battle at Orléans, was captured.

And tried for witchcraft and heresy, Tess said, as Tadhg helped Jamie onto the currach.

Tadhg curled rope between his elbow and his palm. He took the back of the currach, lifted the handle of one oar. Tess and Jamie sat side by side, in front of him, facing the river.

This currach is named after Joan, my mother, he said as he pushed off. And it's definitely my favourite.

Why? Tess said, running her hand along the gunwales.

I have good memories of the summer I made her. It was a few years ago, I took the whole long summer with her and I built her on my own, which isn't usually the way I do it. Usually to build our currachs, we do it with a meitheal.

A meitheal? Tess asked.

A group that come together, for a harvest, or to cut turf, anything really that involves many hands making light work.

Like a co-op? Tess asked.

Pretty much, Tadhg said.

Jamie was anxious with the unsteady current under the boat. Rivers are dynamic and moody like people, he thought.

Why don't you wear a life jacket? Tess said.

Old habit, Tadhg said.

Bad habit, Jamie said.

Yes, sure, but it's an old island thing, fishermen respect the sea so they don't learn to swim, it's a superstition.

Maybe they *want* to die fast? Jamie said.

Tadhg said: Maybe, makes sense then, I suppose.

Can you swim? Jamie said.

Tadhg replied: Yes, I can.

Then it makes no sense. My mother was an excellent swimmer, Jamie said.

Was she? Tess said.

Yes, she was, a champion swimmer. Eoin said she wanted to be an Olympian. But she cannot be one now. As she's dead. And I think that Mirzakhani was lucky to be alive when they gave her the Fields Medal. Better to know you were being honoured, I think.

They both nodded as Jamie looked to the horizon. And I'm also a very good swimmer, but I hate pools so it is a Catch-22.

They rowed on to the middle of the river, and then towards the estuary, and in the distance the trees blurred, fuzzy now, indistinguishable from each another, until they were one great forest, then a dark line and eventually faded from the horizon altogether, so they were surrounded only by dark water.

Tadhg handed Jamie a plastic map and a pair of binoculars.

We're here, Tadhg said, and headed here. Then he pointed to where the river enters the sea. Sometimes in the evening I go as far as here, sit in the energy a while.

Out to the estuary? Jamie said, looking back.

Tadhg nodded.

Can we go out now? Jamie asked looking into the binoculars towards the horizon.

It's a bit far, another time, Tess said. Your dad will be waiting for you.

Tadhg pointed out a spot in the distance where he said

the Atlantic Ocean began and then they turned back. Tadhg showed Jamie how to row, and for some time they went about in circles, but then they were moving in a straight line and Jamie was filled with a sense of relief. His mouth had stopped throbbing. The spire of the cathedral came into view over the tall trees.

You know, Tadhg said, as he watched Jamie looking up at the spire, I heard that at the turn of the last millennium, they began to build elaborate churches all across Europe so that the poor in medieval towns who knew nothing but poverty, when the day of reckoning would come, could climb the spire of the tallest church nearby, and during their Armageddon they could span out their hands and beg their god to take them up to him, into the clouds, heaven, so far they had moved these people from believing in the currents, and the harvest and . . .

. . . And? Jamie said.

The end wasn't upon them. But they believed it was and that belief was enough for them to climb up steeples to get to their god, actually physically scramble into heaven.

What happened? Jamie said.

Many fell to their deaths. Whether they ever met a god or not, who knows?

They fell quiet for a time, watching the lights.

Here's the thing, Jamie, Tadhg said, helping him from the currach out onto the bank. I think we should make one.

One what?

A machine, a thing that never stops.

Jamie stared at him: Yes, I am doing it.

I think it should be a boat, Tadhg said.

No, Jamie said, firmly.

No? Tadhg asked.

Boats stop. No, Jamie said. It is not right. Besides, I don't know how to design one. And they are not original. It must be original.

Yes, they are, Tadhg said. They are all original. Like you, made from scratch.

But they stop moving. They are not always in motion, Jamie said.

They never stop. Wood never rests. It is always seasoning. And moving. And besides, the boat will be left on the water, and on the currents. I don't need to explain the lunar effects on currents.

But your boat is stationary now, I don't mean to offend, but it doesn't work.

Watch it.

And Jamie stared at the small currach as it rocked from side to side on the gentle ripples of the river, unimpressed and thinking how crude it was.

15

This is the best concrete example I have of a meitheal: When Maryam Mirzakhani was awarded the Fields Medal for her achievement in Simple Geodesics on Hyperbolic Surfaces and the Volume of Moduli Spaces in 2014, the year I turned eight years of age, Mirzakhani already knew she had cancer. And when she was considering travelling to Seoul to collect the medal in person and due to the exhaustion that cancer has on a body, some distinguished academics acted as the 'MM Human Shield' to help her.

Our meitheal is happening today. We have been planning since November, and the frame is complete after Mr Foley bolted the gunwales and transom bars with the seniors and Terry and I sanded oars and laths, polished the seat after suddenly realising what I had been working on, we have all been busy bending rods for the couples, to get it into shape, and then to the water, to use a direct phrase of Mr Foley. He likes direct phrases.

The fact that Mirzakhani survived a terrible bus crash but later died of illness is, I think, coincidental. Her survival of the accident had much to do with the laws of luck and chance. Which I am beginning to accept as a thing-thing. I am also spiralling into a space where things are chaotic because I know I can destroy them. How easily I could tear a leaf into two because I have broken many rods trying to bend them. How I can twist things to the point of destruction. How on some nights instead of my mind pacing about the streets of Emory, it dreams vividly about twisting Boys One and Two until their eyes pop out, as this is a very real phenomenon, popping out eyes = exophthalmos. What is of a great surprise to me, is that Mr Foley is encouraging this. (The rod breaking, not the Boys' strangulation.)

After our trip out on the currach, he would not let it go. He's had me out so many times now, rowing, rowing. If I think back to the very beginning, it all seemed to begin with chopsticks. Mr Foley had me snap a few sets of the sticks that he got in the Chinese takeaway in town. The breaks trigger a snap-back effect, and sap-filled rods have a wild natural tension to them, to use Mr Foley's phrase. He spoke about coaxing and not forcing, and in the early stages Jonesy and O'Toole were there, helping.

The rods will go into the gunwales and this will form the skeleton. We have spent a lot of time drawing out on white sheets of paper, and I found this enjoyable. But Jonesy and O'Toole might, I think, have developed a fixation with the boat. I am concerned about this. They keep arguing now over steamed laths or rods, and if we are, being from Galway, too inspired by Donegal currachs and coracles, the latter which looks very much like a soup bowl you get in the hotel. I do not think I have seen a soup-bowl-type boat on water for any reason, so I am glad Mr

Foley has shot this idea down. That said, he keeps saying we are going to feel our way through the construction. A hybrid. And as I know, feelings are often very wrong-headed. I have voiced this opinion many times. Now, I think it is no exaggeration to say that Mr Foley is ignoring my warnings.

Good things are vulnerable and powerful, Jamie, he says back to me. Eoin says I should take a back seat, which was also stupid, as we have not even carved a back seat, and it is a one-seater boat we have decided on. I think this is due in fact to everyone's exhaustion over arguing about plans, and not indeed about any grand engineering ambition. None whatsoever.

Therefore, I have packed my notebook with all sorts of information; gunwales, laths, arches, ribs, thole pin designs, skin hides versus canvas. I have also sketched some Paul Henry paintings, without the colours, but just the moment of launching the currach to water. It seems a very great ordeal, and I note that he launched to the sea and I am not entirely sure of this river idea. Surely it will need salt buoyancy?

Marie tells me to listen to Mr Foley, he is the craftsman. But I am cautious.

I do not believe in divine intervention, though I have begun research on luck and chance theories that I will begin properly after we create the currach. Mr Foley has great hopes that it will solve or resolve something in me, but I do not think it is going to come close to the plans I have for my perpetual-motion machine. However, as Eoin and Marie say, Mr Foley is putting a lot of time into me, so I better have manners. Which I do. But Marie says things like, *don't talk back,* and *have respect.* Which I can manage with Tess and David (now I am almost over the maths fiasco, though I do think about it, and have unfortunately added it to my list of things I consider before falling asleep) and Mr Foley. But I cannot bring myself to have anything but a dislike of Father Faulks.

His weekly talks in the Oratory have grown more unsettling, much now about divine intervention and prayer, and manhood, and for a grown adult, he makes very little sense. What is becoming very clear is how he often thinks about gender, and about it as having huge implications for all of mankind (mostly about how much maligned boys are). It is also clear he is influenced by (if not plagiarising entirely) the Canadian psychologist, Jordan Peterson, whom I find a bore, but an articulate one, and I know that Terry has begun reading his book about being a better man in twelve easy steps, and something to do with chaos, and has started telling me things like *keep your shoulders back,* and that being precise in speech and taking action are important. But he also goes on about being the reliable person at a funeral, especially one of a parent, and especially your father. Peterson does say to pet a cat. I like this step.

I paraphrase.

But Terry never met his dad, who stayed on in London after Terry travelled with his mam to Emory. Actually, Terry has no idea who his father is. Marie says not to ask questions about this, but if he does not figure it out, it is most unlikely he will ever attend his father's funeral so he has worked himself into a state at being able to be reliable at this time, like Peterson suggests. Terry lives alone with his mother, Abba, and Jordan Peterson's YouTube clips that he is obsessing about have made him worried now that living alone with his mother might turn him into a half a man, not directly any theory of Mr Peterson's but combined with Father Faulks who warned us of the length of time we spend in women / female / girl company, and Terry has grown worried. I suggested we swap houses for a few weeks as Terry mostly has only a woman's influence and I thought it would be good for us both. But Eoin was uncertain and went on at great length about my routine. This set me thinking frantically about myself, and how it is unlikely I will need this twelve-step book as I live alone with my father, and I probably am over-saturated with male influence which is a close shave for me. But I am thinking that Marie is next door, and I will probably have to curtail my visits, until I become a full man, and also all the time with Tess, I need to be very guarded, so I will be cautious about their influence.

Terry asked lots of questions in religion class about his soul, because it is the one class you have free time to talk, it is actively encouraged by this young deacon from Harrisburg, who goes by the name of Logan, and allows (demands) a lot of enquiry. Logan goes on at great length about celibacy, the sanctity of marriage, and the destruction of the world due to abortion and also yoga, that seems to be a big nonono, as it lets in things we cannot control (no idea yet about what they are but will find out, and as a male I won't need an abortion, so I do not need to over-concern myself with worry about that) and it seems terrifying in his class. On holy days we have prayed for the souls of the dead babies for the entire class, encouraged to visualise them. Which was an image that lasted all week when I closed my eyes.

I have done some research, and yoga seems like a very happy and bendy place (for most people, and one very happy woman with a dog on YouTube seemed very friendly and kind). I am not at all flexible either, but this is the make-up of the male body apparently, so I am re-assured by this at the very least. That said, I don't know when it happened that I could no longer touch my toes. And I did try some of the yoga stretches, and I got closer, to the big toe, but I noted it too had begun sprouting hair, and might be the most crazy location of hair to date on my body. But maybe this will work in time. I am not sure why Father Faulks needed to mention it as being sinful, yoga, but again, I have more research to do here, and abortion seems far different from the perspective of the broader medical community. There is a lot, and I mean a lot, of information on it. And a lot of emotion. Logan also, like Father Faulks, seems full up with emotion and tales, and has few quantifiable tips to go on to protect us from becoming emasculated and I looked this up, and I am in grave danger of emasculation. So I spoke with Terry who encouraged me to join in the chants for the rugby team again this week at lunchtime and it was ferocious roaring. But I could see that everyone was very engaged.

I too have watched some of Mr Peterson's clips on You-Tube but he mostly seems to obsess about input output and the inclinations of the male brain versus the female brain, and he goes on about lipstick in the workplace, and Marie doesn't wear any. He does sound at first very intelligent, and even more so than Mirzakhani (at a stretch) his articulate enunciation is excellent, and he dresses very well, sometimes he wears two microphones on a suit, which is good preparation. But then I get really confused. He seems to have no space for outliers. I have no doubt that maybe he is intelligent, but again, I find myself at a place where I would like some practical application of what I should actually do to safeguard myself and to enter manhood fully formed. Most pressing is Terry, he needs to know *urgently* what *taking action* really means. We think he should get someone to set an alarm system in his home maybe, for when he's at school, and perhaps he should sit in another room at night to his mother with her soap dramas, and not be influenced by them. He hates soap operas.

We learned about chivalry in the Middle Ages with Mr Sweeney, who laughed about chivalry and said who needs to worry about women and children when they took him to the cleaners when his wife left him last year. This is a metaphor, Terry said, for her taking all his money. But how much money can a teacher really have? They always seem concerned about money.

Harrisburg Logan answers all our enquiries by telling us to put our faith in god, and he does much smiling, and dipping his head to one side. He is a small man, and bald, and though he is only in his twenties he wears giant shoes with Velcro. Maybe Terry can have faith in his god, as Terry really believes in a god and goes to church all dressed up at the weekends, the church next door to the Turkish kebab house. I told Harrisburg Logan that I don't believe in god, and he smiled and dipped his head to the side, and told me to put my faith in the journey. And that he was very sorry. I said I was OK, that when I die I am donating my body to medical science. And he told me that I would be taken up to heaven anyway. I told him that I would rather not be, and he said, *ah, well, it is not a choice you have, young man,* and he dipped his head to one side again, and said, *no choice at all.* And when I asked about free will, he groaned, dipped his head and made no sound whatsoever. He did not even smile. And then asked, *what will I do with you?* I suggested I go to Mr Foley's workshop to continue on the boat, and he shouted and said, *it is not a question.* So I think there are finite questions too. Not just statements.

Father Faulks carries on talking with great gusto as though no research has been done on the human condition since the Middle Ages (which it has in abundance), though I have yet to start my research into it fully, but this obsession with one perspective is often the way of adults who I now know are closed-minded. From investigation with Terry (on Google) we know that Father Faulks went to school in this very College, and then on to a seminary (a school with only boys who learn about theology, which is a subject based almost entirely on fiction; allegory and opinion) and then he was sent back here as a teacher of Latin and religion and then he became the President. So Faulks is, by very definition of being enclosed for a lifetime in one space – closed-minded, though he tells us about his life as though he has been on one big mad adventure. And if we look at it objectively – it is not his fault.

For an alternative perspective, Father Faulks is wealthy, and Eoin says that he has never has to work a proper day in his life, or ever had his arm down a drain. Marie agrees and she keeps his big house and cleans it, and she says that he does none of his own laundry or cleaning or cooking, and he has a car with a really huge bonnet, an import, Eoin says, and I wonder at how unfairly the world distributes wealth, often to the most stupid of people, like Father Faulks and Donald Trump.

I think how fragile everything seems now, that I know nothing of what will become of me, and if I'm even on the right tracks at all to become a man.

16

The workshop is dark and feels strange because it is strange to be in school on a Saturday.

Tess stands by Mr Foley in runners that are bright yellow and exuberant and off-putting. Her dark hair is tied up and her face is pale. She is wearing a hoody that says I ❤ *New York* and I wonder if I will also love New York when I get there. I think from all the films I've watched that it is loud and dirty and brown and Marie says it is stuck in 1988, though she has never been, so I am unsure how she arrived at this opinion.

My favourite New York film is *West Side Story* and I have no doubt the city has undergone inevitable change since that time.

Today, even the wood pigeon is louder. I wonder if he is more playful and persistent on Saturdays as he is left all alone in the workshop, and I also wonder what he does for three months of the summer holidays – trying to find someone to listen to him. I would lose my mind if I was all alone like this, and though I like to be on my own, I like to know that there is someone in the house. And now I am wondering if he also gets bored.

Mr Foley says he likes Christmas and has lights and tinsel up around the workshop to prove this, but they look out of place among the natural woodcuts. Mr Foley asked that Eoin also come in for the building of the currach this weekend, as the lashing is a big job (that's tying knots with twine I think) but I know that Eoin has no time to be building a boat so I declined his offer. Eoin is a practical person, and this is one of his busiest months of the year, every year, the weekend before Christmas, which is odd. Christmas comes every year and I wish people were more prepared with their plumbing needs, but Eoin says it doesn't always work like this, people can only handle so many thoughts at any one time. And they panic. Marie and I agree that it is not necessary to be planning and panicking the weekend before Christmas, and Marie says people put themselves into a lot of debt at this time of year, often just for a sofa,

which is absurd

but it always seems like a time of tension, and a time when people need the sink unblocked or an extra shower fitted for a house full of relatives which I am not familiar with but I see it on the advertisements.

I am anxious waiting for Jonesy and O'Toole to arrive, because Mr Foley has invited them even though he built the *Joan of Arc* on his own. I would like that solitude for this boat, so

I resisted their invitation

but Mr Foley passed no notice.

I protested and said I want the machine to be mine and mine alone, even if it is a boat and not technically a machine.

Tadhg said: It's not the way of the currach – it is a communal boat,

and I've noticed people popping in and out of his workshop cutting and sanding and bolting and it is now happening so often that I wished I had never taken up his offer to build this boat,

they come in and out as they please

to check the scaffolds and to run their hand along pieces of timber and ask Mr Foley what each piece is, and he goes to great length to tell what tree it came from. He points to the laminated *Trees of Ireland* poster he has on the wall, beside *Birds of the Wild*, and loads of other things to let everyone know about the outdoors, though I wish these were just our secrets, like they were at the beginning. He keeps this wall separate from the paintings' wall, on the other side, he has so much clutter, he is definitely a hoarder, and I thought then that perhaps this is all a mistake,

but he is insistent on this boat.

I should have continued to invent something alone, a boat is not an invention of any kind, really, if you think about it, and no matter how many times Mr Foley has tried to convince me it is, I remain unconvinced. I am also annoyed at my lack of originality, and this one that we are to create the back on today (as opposed to break the back) seems ancient, which is definitely not an invention.

Jonesy and O'Toole walk in before the ordinary school day would start. This shows they are eager and they are smiling and eating out of a bag of crisps, salt and vinegar that make my eyes water. Jonesy and O'Toole are also dressed in hoodies and trainers that make them look young and not at all in charge like when they are the official Head Boys on school days.

Terry is going to arrive soon to help,

and the seniors will shout out, *Our Man Terry*, as if they own him,

and I'm to blame for this awful mishap,

because Mr Foley asked what friend I'd like for this weekend;

I was immediately perplexed at the question,

and said, *I am not interested in friendships of my peers, I find them boring at best and anxiety-inducing.*

Mr Foley told me to stop with talk about anxiety and not to let crazy ideas like that into my head,

and he is right,

but it is very hard to stop ideas in your head, fleeting around,

but as I wait for Terry to walk through the doors I keep hearing lines from an Eminem song over and over. (Terry hates Eminem, and especially when I hum it.)

I try to think of something clever and smart to say to Terry when he arrives, as boys do when they meet one another. They say clever things and often slap one another. Jonesy is excellent at it, these simple gestures, and making boys laugh, it's a great skill that I must research, and as Terry is technically my guest for these days, I will need to greet him properly. I am not sure hitting him is the right approach.

Mr Foley said the craft of the boat would not be a problem for me, it would be the originality of design where I might come undone: as I like to stick to tried-and-tested measures of design in most facets of my life. I could not disagree, and he insisted that I had one original facet to my design, as we drew up all the plans.

Mr Foley was correct. I am finding it difficult to decide on one original thing for the boat. Mr Foley suggested something about Vikings and a head of something at the bow, but it set me to thinking about Mr Sweeney and I do not want my boat associated with him. Mr Foley has given me some time to think about it, that I must think of something truly original to make the machine mine. And I'm running out of time. *Bespoke* was what he said.

Back to Terry.

I chose Terry when Mr Foley asked me to bring along a friend, as simply as that, I was so nonchalant about the whole thing, and I blurted out Terry's name, which was a good thing because Piotr Pulaski was on the tip of my tongue, and I do not know why I was thinking of him at that moment, but I was. And I can only imagine what a travesty that would be. In all likelihood, Piotr would take over like he does in maths class without turn-taking, or allowing space for other boys to answer. He's infuriating, Piotr. And as he's a whizz at most things, I think Tadhg would really let himself down with his crude currach-building blueprint in front of a boy like Piotr.

Terry has just arrived and I pretend not to notice because he's followed in by his mother, Abba, who looks like she's about to take part in an aerobics class that Marie sometimes does in her small room in front of her big telly. Abba really has very little to offer this weekend, except taking people's attention and soon she is going on about that Joe Wicks off the TV.

Nice threads, Jamie, she says.

I look baffled.

Your clothes, she says.

I look down at my clothes; red hoody and cargo pants that Eoin gave me, which pinch and sting as I am larger about the waist than Eoin.

Tadhg begins the day with a welcome, and I'm unsure as to whether this was necessary as he's not a great orator, unlike Father Faulks who speaks so well about things that make no sense. Tadhg knows a lot of very interesting things, but is not likely to help people understand them without showing them with his hands.

He is upbeat and serious: Today is all about flexibility and adaptability, he says, and we need to keep an open mind as we build . . .

and he goes on,

the place is buzzing now.

Mr Foley looks directly at me as he has a good and fierce instinct when he's lost my attention. So I look at Tess. Tess looks at Abba because,

Terry has a drill in his hand now and he has turned it on, and the noise startles me,

he just picked the drill up at the direction of no adult whatsoever,

and everyone begins chattering,

and my heart is racing, but no one seems to care, as though it's no big deal that Terry has this tool whizzing in his hands, and I would like to know exactly what we are doing. Terry is being very confident, getting on with things that sound important, and running things by Mr

Foley, and Mr Foley is pointing out along the gunwale the marks he has made that need to be drilled, and he fixes Terry's goggles on him, and they begin with a pencil, and a tape, moving it across the frame between them.

A currach is a strange boat.

It's built upside-down,

and this one is a hybrid currach and the ribs don't need to be steamed, and Mr Foley favours the rods for the ribs over steamed laths, it's also going to have a paddle as well as oars like the old coracle boat, the one like a soup bowl, that was invented to catch salmon, but now the fisheries, since the 1980s, have put a ban on that, so it is not a popular model at all any more.

Our design is a little like the Aran Island version, we will stick the canvas, and we will tack it first. The tarring will happen last, (and it won't be tar, it's a paint Mr Foley is getting, as tar is too dangerous in a school, and I am pleased he is showing some health and safety concerns) and we have also taken our inspiration from the Donegal currachs, and not from Kerry's naomhóg. I read that the latter is considered the very best currach in Ireland. But when I said it to Mr Foley he said, *that is because Kerry people are very ferocious in putting their point across unlike his people from the Aran Islands.* And if Mr Foley's people are anything like him, I agree.

We are all instructed by Mr Foley to tease the pared rods, and slot them into the holes that Terry has drilled all along the gunwales so quickly that he is making me nervous, and everyone is fussing about, and blowing into the holes to release sawdust, and joining the rods side by side like couples, this will give it a nice shape Mr Foley says, and they all seem confident

except me

I keep going back and forth to the bench and feeling them all, running them through my hands,

and Tess comes over and shoves a couple of rods into my hands, and she stands over me and makes me slot them into a hole.

Come on, Jamie, she says,

it is all very haphazard, I say back.

But I slot one in a hole behind the seat space, behind the splice, and we loosely twine them, as Mr Foley will do the lashing himself, and here it's different from out at the bow, where we just place single rods.

And throughout Saturday Mr Foley keeps saying: Very nice, kiddo, remember, pull it half a foot through.

A foot? I say. This seems to make sense to everyone, except me. And I designed it.

Yes, you know, things at the end of your legs, Jamie, feet, Mr Foley replies,

and I look down at my trainers, and they are much bigger than Tess's, and Jonesy has the largest feet of us all, they're gigantic like trains and I just think:

this is a stupid rule of thumb,

it is not uniform,

and it will surely all go belly up.

Which reminds me of the zip pinching my belly skin.

This boat will never float if they all continue on not

adhering to the blueprint Mr Foley has up on the wall, crude as it is.

It's crude, I shout out, loudly. It will never float.

I am starting to panic now, but no one is listening and Terry is taking rods out of my hand and says: It's fine, Jamie, it'll be great, don't you think this is great?

Mr Foley shows us how to pull the rods tight through the holes in the gunwales, Jonesy is re-drilling some holes that aren't wide enough and Mr Foley says: Take it handy, Jonesy, not too wide, we need them pinched, can't have them flopping about. O'Toole is nailing things haphazardly.

It is the first time he takes control and I calm a little and move away from it all to look at the new art prints stuck up on the wall.

Jonesy and O'Toole are being sent on the lunch run, which Abba is complicating with talk about allergies and her pescetarianism.

Mr Foley is laughing.

It is a moment of great tension and I lose my appetite.

Mr Foley notices me stood over by the Paul Henry pictures for a breather as Tess would encourage, and there's a new art piece beside it, half man half grotesque monster, oranges and purples, it's all pinks and pale flesh colours about the hanging skin, and the piece looks like it is on fire. I know it's a Francis Bacon because I watched a documentary once on his workshop in the Hugh Lane Gallery, and I remember that Francis Bacon shredded art pieces that he needed to dump, because people were taking them out of his bins outside his workshop,

which is recreated in that gallery,

but what is pressing about him,

is this: He brought his friend George to Paris for the Grand Palais, and I don't know what terrified me more, that the man he brought along as his friend, and I think he might have died sat on the toilet (like Elvis), and the practicalities of how that could ergonomically happen, or that Bacon pretended as though it didn't happen at all,

and Mr Foley says: Do you want a longer break, Jamie?

I'd have really liked a break in this moment, to get Mr Foley to myself and away from everyone, but I knew the whole machine could crumble without Mr Foley there with his pencil and dipping-down eye, on his knees now, so I say: No.

And I thought it might be finite.

But it wasn't –

It's your boat, Jamie, your machine, get stuck in.

I know, I am just worried, I reply, and by the way it is not a machine. I am just appeasing the whole lot of them.

Try not to worry. Relax, kiddo.

It's just so . . . haphazard.

But it's not, not really, and it has many stages to go through, we'll iron out all the creases. If something is wrong, the next layer will catch it, I promise, Mr Foley says. Feel where the wood wants to go, and if you need it to resist it can do that too, challenges to the natural movement are good, it'll keep your boat alive.

I do not understand what Mr Foley is saying, so instead I say: I don't like Francis Bacon, not one bit.

Right, Mr Foley says.

He is horrible, a cruel man, and I do not know why you have hung up one of these paintings prints, it is grotesque beside Paul Henry's currach.

Bacon or the painting? Who's horrible?

Same thing, I say, and Mr Foley opens his mouth and closes it,

and this is finite.

After lunch everything picks up, which is strange because on a normal school day, after lunch is a *slump*, the processing of breaking down carbohydrates coupled with boredom,

and

soon we have all the rods in and the shape of a boat is there if you can imagine the world upside down and the boat plonked on it.

And it is dark outside, and the windows up above us turn to black, like black tiles, and there are twelve on each side, like the twelve Head Boys, and I think of a game of draughts I once played with Marie. Mr Foley and Tess are going about the workshop tidying up and she is even paler now than when we arrived, but this might be to do with the luminous lights that are on, that drain a person due to the refraction of the bulbs Mr Foley uses. We work on for hours.

Finally, back home in my room upstairs in the Heights, I fall asleep fast and I do not dream.

17

On Sunday I am the first student into the workshop at dawn. Mr Foley is here. He stayed the night, fixing things, and he says: Sleep well, kiddo?

I say: Yes, like a log,

which is insane, I know,

it is one of these ridiculous idioms that I'm learning, and like saying I slept like a baby, which Eoin thinks is madness as babies do not sleep (I was a *terror* apparently).

O'Toole arrives at the same time as Terry and this strikes me as odd, just seeing the two of them arrive in together talking quickly like people who know each other, which they do not, not really. Not like friend-friends.

I have never seen them talk before,

and now Abba is coming in clattering bags and talking incessantly to Tess

who is carrying baskets of food,

for perhaps after yesterday's chaos, Abba wants to be prepared. She has a Christmas jumper on with tinsel and a polar bear sitting on an ice cap, which makes me think of Global Warming, and the state of life now for polar bears.

The currach's skeleton of sally and hazel rods is in the

middle of the workshop floor and it really does look alive, and the centre lath makes it look like a boat now, I will admit this, and I admit to feelings of excitement just looking at it, maybe a mixture of nerves and excitement, which are perhaps the same thing, and the vast expanse, all the huge space its frame is taking up,

it's greater than all of us.

I have not been this excited since thinking I could at least disprove Hodge Conjecture, but I'm finding that the closer I get to Hodge Conjecture, the more of a vacuous space it is taking up in my world, and the way I'm thinking of it now is like a bad critic, instead of adding anything, furthering the conversation, I am just hostile to it,

and I have my plan now to make the boat original,

but I'm not telling Mr Foley today as it is not the right time.

I am also not sure what to do with excitement.

I hate to admit this, for some reason, as admitting it might make the project weaker, but I was eager all this morning, though also concerned with Mr Foley's measurements which have gone by the wayside. (His words not mine.)

The currach now looks like Gulliver flat down on the sand, and that makes us Lilliputians.

Mr Foley and Tess are in deep conversation around the Francis Bacon print. I cannot imagine Tess leaving anyone dead on a toilet and I know quite categorically that she would have cancelled attending the Grand Palais. The Grand Palais is certainly not the same as winning the Fields Medal. If I won the Fields Medal I would make sure not to conflate the event with any notion of romance, or romantic love. When I win it, I will bring Eoin, though I already know that he will be out of place, nevertheless he is very good at directions and trains so if it was to be per-haps in a European country, I will definitely bring him to navigate with me, not maps or plans, but to navigate the people.

Tadhg stands by the currach and says: The last four rods are the most important. He says again: Only single rods here, then we will place laths.

How will we place them? I say,

and then I say: To be honest (although I am always honest), these rods are at uneven intervals, Mr Foley –

and Jonesy agrees with me,

we are all stood about and *finally* Mr Foley has a meas-uring tape, I feel reassured,

and

he is squinting down and looking at the intervals that *our man Terry* has drilled the holes at,

and

in some parts he has missed the markings altogether with his drilling for the rods.

I am learning that Jonesy is a rule-book person too, and I am flustered and it is an immensely tense moment,

but now everyone has started to talk again.

Abba is going on about Christmas pyjamas,

and

the noise is so loud now with all the people chattering again and because the place was once an old swimming pool, it takes very little to fill it with sound especially when Abba starts singing. Her voice takes over.

Terry was very impulsive all right, but it's not important, kiddo, Mr Foley says back to Jonesy, after a lot of one-shut-eye-going-on-about-all-sides-of-the-boat, it'll all be grand.

Mr Foley is speaking so low now that I would not be able to hear him at all, except I have excellent hearing,

right,

the intervals of the rods, they are fine, Mr Foley says slowly, leaving his hand on my shoulder, which is nice (but also not allowed),

but I do not tell him,

and besides,

squinting again now, and bouncing back down on his hunkers and casting his eyes across the boat, he says, the laths will steady them.

The laths are all up against the breeze blocks and they look even and identical in size and are sanded,

and I know O'Toole and Jonesy took great care with them, I like them both very much at this juncture.

Mr Foley crunches down again with one eye squinting and Terry copies him, and I am doing it too. I am unsure as to what else to do, and considering I brought the problem to the table in the first instance, I kneel on both of my knees as I unbalance quickly,

and at first I was not sure what I was looking at, or for.

Mr Foley and Terry place a weight on the bow, that looks like a bag of flour Marie would use baking in our kitchen and Mr Foley says: That'll prevent the nose from lifting.

And everyone nods.

And we start together out at the bow, Mr Foley and I, and he goes dead quiet, and we set two short rods into the bow and stern, and Mr Foley ties the laths at either side with a long spool of twine that is black, and oily.

And he says: Run your hand along these rods now, kiddo,

as he ties almost a dozen laths to rods with the roll so quickly,

and

I feel a great tension with some of them when I leave my palm down, there is heat coming from them when I place my hands on the laths and the rods are being pushed back to the palm of my hand,

I say: It is very tense, Tadhg. I really surprised myself at using his first name, and so I go quiet, and I really need to tell him that it is my opinion that they are tied too tightly, but I don't know where to look now, and I squirm a little,

but he takes no notice that I have used his first name,

and he replies: No, no, they're grand, Jamie, just check that none has snapped,

and I do.

And none has snapped.

Jonesy and O'Toole drill each rod and place a long nail in each, and O'Toole is passing them to Jonesy now,

and

I voice another concern and Mr Foley says: This is not an exact science, currachs are built by ordinary men.

And women, Abba says. She is at the end of the workshop with Tess and they are drawing out on the canvas,
and Mr Foley goes to them now, and they are lifting and
gathering the canvas in great handfuls,

and

I am concerned now that Mr Foley has left the boat
to go to the end of the workshop and he stands with his
hands on his chin, and tells Tess to come to my aid, and
Tadhg needs to tie the rest of the rods to the laths, and it
will take him days I think. He is showing Tess how to do
it, only cross it twice, Tadhg says and Tess pulls the twine
now, and she thinks it is OK to release a little, give in to
the action and Tadhg agrees.

Some of these are very tight, Tadhg, Tess said, and I
really wonder what Tess could possibly know about tying
sally rods to laths on a boat, and I wish that Faulks would
come in and shout at everyone and only let Mr Foley speak,
and how Tess even noticed the tension, is most perplexing.
I have underestimated her.

Mr Foley says that maybe we will have to leave some
laths without rods, and everyone nods in agreement, and
Terry sets about doing this, and I admire his confidence,
for a first year.

The laths are two fingers apart,

you can use your own fingers like Tadhg Foley does
to measure this.

This should widen at the gunwale, to maybe two and
a half.

Perhaps three fingers here, this is OK too.

Tess Mahon's fingers with red nail varnish are used to

measure this. She has slim and very beautiful hands and I wonder how I never noticed them before. Or perhaps it is because she has her nails painted for Christmas like women sometimes do for a big occasion.

There is no strict length to a currach, ours is eight feet, Mr Foley says,

I say it is two hundred and forty three point eighty-four centimetres, this is a small currach, but it is a one-person machine, Tadhg says (technically he says it's a one-*man* machine, this is a habit that is proving hard to break),

and I can always build another one as I grow up, he says, or perhaps he said grow out as I have grown up quite substantially to date,

but I know he means in my sailing capabilities,

as I am learning to row the *Joan of Arc*.

This currach is modelled for me, for I am six foot tall, which Jonesy and O'Toole agree is big for a first year, and this makes me happy that they have noticed,

then

Jonesy says to O'Toole: Remember how small you were in first year, you poor fucker? We could fit you into a coral bowl and push you up the Brú in that. And the boys laugh at each other. And none of the teachers correct the use of profanity.

Mr Foley is exactly six foot also and so he lies on the ground to show me the length of the currach with his arms over his head and then Tess draws his figure around him in chalk as Jonesy and O'Toole hold him down, and everyone laughs, except me.

It's like a scene from *Line of Duty*, Jonesy says, when Mr Foley stands up and his figure is left on the dusty ground like a criminal – it's a predictable joke, but everyone laughs (except me).

And Abba says, Jesus, Mary and Joseph and the wee donkey, and everyone laughs, (except me again – because I am an atheist).

The currach has a depth of fifty-seven centimetres, which is the only correct measurement I am given today,

and

I welcome it,

though apparently it means nothing if I am not trawling for lobster.

So I say (to defend the measurements): I like lobster tails covered in butter, and everyone agrees except Terry, because Terry lives on sausages and beans and oven chips.

The angle of the joint from the gunwale up to the shoulder, or the splice angle of the currach is approximately five centimetres,

and

this is one-fifteenth as tall as Verne Troyer (famous for his role as mini-me in *Austin Powers* – also it is a funny fact that his first role was as a stunt double for a baby in the 1994 dreadful film, *Baby's Day Out*).

I digress.

There is space for a fixed seat and a small moving seat in this currach.

Mr Foley made the fixed seat from oak (the laths are ash, the frame and gunwales redwood, the thole pins are beech and the moving seat is from a piece of driftwood, because Mr Foley is most interested in upcycling).

The seniors are pretending to test out the moving seat and see if it will carry my weight. It is not in the least scientific because we have no idea of the strength of the seniors in comparison to the strength of the laths under the gunwales.

And then suddenly Boys One and Two are at the door looking in, even though it's Sunday – how did they get into school? – and they are laughing. I am the first to notice them, and my skin prickles, and Jonesy shouts to them to come in and help, and I say: No, no, no, no, quickly, and I have my arms around Jonesy and O'Toole to lift me to the seat, but my legs are gone weak now, and fizzy, and Mr Foley comes rushing to me, and watches my face, and leaves the back of his hand on it.

And Jonesy looks at me too, it is just those Boys, I say, they just, they said . . . And I stop.

What did they say? Jonesy asks.

And I blurt out fast about them blaming me for killing my mother. Jonesy drops the seat to the ground, and it crashes down and O'Toole is pulling him back now, and Jonesy pulls away and sprints to the door, and grabs Boy One by his hoody and calls him a fucking little prick, and Mr Foley and Tess are running out now. And calling out after Jonesy, saying: No, Jonesy, come back, but they are all out on the corridor now, and there is much shouting.

Jonesy is back in now, his face is red, and O'Toole says: That was foolish, and Jonesy says: No, no, it wasn't,

Francis, and I am struck as no one ever said O'Toole's first name before,

and

now I see O'Toole as the painter who left his friend dead on a toilet.

But again, they want to test a seat, and Jonesy lifts me from one side and O'Toole is the other and now they are carrying me around the workshop, it is sloppy, but fun, and they say it is amazing that I'm so stocky and well-built for a first year, and they leave me down, because they might put out their backs. Jonesy says: You could take that little cunt, Jamie. And I nod. Because I am at his mercy sat on the seat.

They carry Terry next and Terry loves it, and is smiling like a maniac, all excited about my boat, which I find interesting as I do not think I would care so much if this was his boat, and he says he feels like the king of England. I don't want to burst his bubble and tell him it is a queen as head of the royal family in the UK now. Marie is always looking at her on the covers of magazines she gets in the hairdresser's and seems to think of them as her own family.

Mr Foley has his hand under his chin now, and I wonder what's the matter.

And Mr Foley says: No, no, kiddo, don't worry.

I'm beginning to think nothing matters on this build. It is all arbitrary.

I will never live like this when I grow up and have independence.

The bull holes, canvas, skinning, tarring (he means

painting) and thole pins and many more bits and bobs are a job for another day, Mr Foley says.

Everyone eventually finishes what they are doing and Tess puts on some Christmas music on a little portable sound box and it is irritating.

Jonesy starts to laugh and pulls O'Toole up and they dance, and Tess and Abba dance like crazy people around the currach as Tadhg keeps creeping low and closing one eye and watching the boat. He spots me away from the group and comes to me and says:

You know the nylon twine is one point five millimetres, Jamie?

Really? I say.

I bought this in Greencastle in Co. Donegal, it's the only place that sells this tarred twine, you know where that is?

Yes. I say, though I don't, but I am trying to curtail my use of the word no. As I note it is an abrupt way to stop a chat.

And once I went there, you know, Tadhg says, smiling, and lifted himself onto a bench now, yeah, I went up on a date with this girl from Arranmore Island and I picked her up to bring her for a spin in my car. Of course, I was a long way from home. Anyway, she was nice, the girl, a bit hyper and a bit erratic though, and wilder than me.

Under my arms begins to prickle at the thoughts of an erratic girl from Donegal in Mr Foley's car.

He picks up sandpaper, chases it across the laths: But I liked her energy, and I went in to the small shop in Greencastle to get this special twine because I had two currachs to build that summer, and I thought when I was out and about I'd stock up. She wasn't happy – my date – with the deviation. I remember her face in the front seat of my car.

Mr Foley is laughing loudly now,

and I remember back and remember the shop I bought it in, but not for the life of me can I remember who served it to me.

What's Greencastle in the county of Donegal like? I say, quite officially to get the giggling girl out of my head. I make a mental note to go and visit and find the shop that sells the twine and buy it as a gift for Mr Foley when I am older.

Tell you the truth, kiddo, I don't remember much about the place, even though it's full of seamen and good advice on fishing and boating.

People . . . I say.

Well, yes, sea people, and I wasn't paying attention, how could I? I was on a date with a beautiful girl.

Must be very distracting – a date, I say.

Yes, it is, Tadhg says.

Hmmm, I say, dipping down, closing one eye, and I look across the body of the currach, scan it, and it almost looks like it is moving already, that the wall of its chest is lifting up and down, like Eoin asleep on the couch on nights when I creep up to bed.

18

Tess dressed in nude Spanx and a silk jumpsuit on Christmas Eve. Then she layered make-up on her face. She finished by spraying herself with setting spray to the voice of George Bailey on the bedroom telly. It was unlike her, the lime jumpsuit, setting her make-up so vigorously, but she was tired and gaunt, and Mrs Mahon would ask about her pallor. It was also an impractical ensemble for the wild December night howling outside, one of those jumpsuit affairs that you have to pull completely off your body in the loo, so you must plan to arrive there at the right moment, and if you were drunk and careless, the material flooded the floor and soaked in moisture. But the idea of church made Tess want to be outrageous. She had thrashed around upstairs for most of the afternoon, drinking cold mulled wine and watching *It's a Wonderful Life*. It was a day she hated, a film she loathed, but a film that was better to watch before Christmas, not after, like so many others that watched after Christmas filled her with sadness. Tess despised the attention George Bailey was given, despised his ridiculous teeth, despised how his suffering wife smiled throughout the madness of marriage with the same startled expression, saying, oh George, oh *George Bailey*, neat and well-kept, neat and homely, and oddly sexy, yet permanently shocked from over-plucked eyebrows. No one gets a second chance like that, and Tess considered Bailey's wife to be a fool of a woman, even if she looked neat as a pin. She hated Christmas, Paul's family with new haircuts and new cologne and new round-necked Hilfiger jumpers.

Paul arrived on the stairs landing. Ready, Tessy?

Yeah, just a sec, Tess said.

Look, he said, walking into the room. Tessy, he grabbed her hand, now this is, a lot, he said, smiling at her outfit.

Too much?

Maybe, he said. Look, I know we thought things would be, well, different now, you know with the baby and all.

But there was no baby, Tess said, not this time. She pulled her hand away.

Yes, I know, and I'm sorry. He sat on the bed a minute. I think maybe we should chat about it. We haven't talked, you know, properly.

Tess looked at her watch. It was half-past nine. She knew telling him the truth now would blow up the whole night. She swept some more bronzer across her forehead.

Thanks, she said. But not now, not tonight.

Paul and Tess left the house at ten for midnight mass, which started at half-past ten. Actual midnight masses had brought drunk people from the pub, so the church banned the late gathering. Tess was slightly drunk in any case and felt giddy as she walked up the path to the cathedral. Paul was a step ahead on the narrow path, hands deep in the pockets of a new herringbone affair. Tess noted that his freshly shorn hair was squared off at the back of his head like a Marine, and where his neck thickened, some child-like pimples had appeared.

He was in good form from afternoon drinking, another of his Christmas Eve traditions, barbers in town with his brothers, pints, then evening supper with his family – roast goose. But this year Tess had asked not to join the supper, and Paul had panicked and made an excuse and said they would all meet at midnight mass instead.

Tess and Paul had sidestepped each other for weeks, both of them creeping about the house since Tess quietly mentioned her period late November, whispering it like an adolescent, and promptly jumped into the bath, locking the door. After which, they both manoeuvred their lives so that neither interrupted the other for anything more than a practical question about a blocked sink or a life-insurance premium or a documentary on the telly that someone in Paul's work had recommended.

Emory was busy.

Inside, the cathedral was humming of myrrh and tonka. The advent candles were alight and flickering. Jesus was not in the crib, his porcelain-white face would arrive later in the night when Marie would finish polishing and hoovering, and she'd lift him from a cardboard box and place him on the straw. A shepherd had fallen over, the cow was missing a leg and was propped up by the leg of a table. There was no donkey. It was muggy and airless. Granny Liz's fur coat that Tess wore each year felt out of place once again, and the silk lime affair stuck to the backs of her legs. Tess recognised some boys from school. She looked about for Jamie, hoping that she would she spot him. But he wasn't there. The boys looked odd out of uniform, sat with their families. Jonesy stood at the back of the cathedral near some posters for *Special* – a Catholic crisis pregnancy agency – his arms folded and side-talking with old men. O'Toole sat at the front seat with his father, the local court judge, beside a line of brothers, and a thin mother lost in an oversized red coat was perched at the end of the seat. Tess had often passed by her jogging in the woods, a woman who was always moving, and though they shared a drink every year, they had never spoken directly to each other. Mrs Mahon leaned in to her son in the pew, embraced him and kissed him on both cheeks. He shook hands with his father as Mrs Mahon leaned across him to welcome Tess, who tapped her hand in return. She had lashings of perfume on and Tess started to get a headache. A brass plaque was screwed to the oak, and read: *For all the Deceased of the Mahon Family, Cathedral Road, Emory. May their Gentle Souls Rest in Peace.*

A seat of their own.

Rain pelted the roof. The College choir sang 'Joy to the World' and Faulks was attentive on the altar, polishing a silver chalice with a white napkin. The boys' choir voices were beautiful and moved Tess. Christmas brought Granny Liz alive to her. Now her body sweated, so that by the time of the second reading, light-headed, she put her head between her legs.

Mrs Mahon whispered to Paul: Tell her to go out and get air.

Mother said go out . . . Now, Paul whispered to Tess.

The congregation stood for the gospel.

Faulks was giving it gusto on the altar, something from Matthew and the virgin birth. Tess stood up and as the church spun, she walked quickly down the aisle holding each pew as she went, and on out into the night.

Outside, she was glad of the cold air. Watching her from under the cathedral arches, Tadhg Foley, who was growing angry that he was in the church in the first place, and noting Tess leave, ducked out the side entrance traditionally used by labourers in unclean boots and parents with whingeing children.

Happy Christmas! he said, running towards Tess as she propped herself up at the holy water font.

Oh! Tadhg. Hi! Tess said. Jesus, fuck me but the heat really got to me. Fucking churches, I hate them. Happy Christmas, she said as she leaned in and kissed him.

Tadhg laughed. I'm not surprised, he said, you've quite the . . . ensemble . . . on . . . looks like something from *Saturday Night Fever*. He leaned in again and kissed her back, twice, and she caught wafts of wood or smoke from the stubble on his jaw.

I'd hate to blend in, she said. In Emory of all places.

Little fear, Tadhg replied. He nodded towards the church, stuffing his hands in his pockets. Are you going to brave it?

Brave what? Tess said.

The final blessing.

No, she said smirking. I don't think I've ever finished a full mass.

They both laughed and then fell quiet and Tadhg kicked a loose piece of paving on the ground.

Here, Tadhg said, I'll walk you home, I'm headed that way anyway.

No, no, I'm heading up town actually, Tess said. We're going to Brooke's for a drink with the O'Tooles.

Right, he said.

Would you like to join us? You're very welcome, Tess said.

I'm grand, thanks, Tadhg said. But here, I'll walk you up.

It's been so wild out, Tess said. I was sure you would go home. You should have said you'd be on your own, you could join us for dinner.

I'm grand. It's strange, isn't it though?

What?

How concerned we get about people alone at Christmas. I like being alone.

Me too, Tess said.

There were blue and white Christmas lights hanging from gutter to gutter overhead, bright and alive. A young woman hugged an older woman on the street, and together they knocked on the door of a town house next to the pharmacy. An estate car passed them both by with a huge evergreen tree tied to the roof.

Bit late, Tess said. For a tree.

Tadhg said: They'll only have it up to take it down.

Could you build a boat out of that kind of wood?

Tadhg laughed.

I'm serious.

No, well, technically, maybe. But it would rot.

It would smell great though, Tess said. She loved the smell of a real tree at Christmas. And as they turned the corner onto the Square she stopped suddenly. Her head spun and she could feel her chest redden and expand and sting.

Her father was stood there, bent over, swaying.

You OK? Tadhg said turning back to her.

Tess nodded as she watched Jennings. For a minute, she thought he was about to fall in a heap, or collapse, but Jennings steadied and was dragging himself along the corner of Cinema Lane to the Square by clawing along the wall, one lame leg dragging after him. He stopped to suck on a cigarette in a closed fist, a rolled-up magazine in the other. He stumbled again and the magazine slipped from his hand and fell onto the road.

Fuck, Jennings said.

A stack of magazines were tied in a bundle outside the bookshop. Tess pulled out a copy and pushed it to his hand. Adam Driver was sullen and edgy on the cover. Here, take it, she said. Happy Christmas, Dad. The fricative quality of the words. He smiled. The raw pink arc of his bottom gum looked vulnerable as he straightened, exaggerating a sobriety. He shook out the magazine.

Mr Mahon, Tadhg said, nodding and then, quickly, putting out his hand.

It's Jennings, Tess said, quietly.

Of course, sorry, shit, Happy Christmas, Mr Jennings, Tadhg said shaking the man's hand once more. Jennings's shoelaces were missing, his bare feet were red and blistered in the open shoes.

Cathy! Jennings cried out.

Tess's head throbbed and she had cotton mouth. Cathy, Jennings said again. His pale fleece was unzipped and streaked with an oily liquid. His arms were fully out-stretched towards her.

Tess regretted stopping.

But she would regret not stopping, and so she put out her own arms, grabbed him at the forearms gently and held him back at his elbows. His arms were thinner than she'd remembered.

Tess knew that soon the Mahons would follow and call late orders in Brooke's Hotel on the Square. Mrs Mahon would have a sweet sherry. Mr Mahon would have French brandy with Judge O'Toole, someone would likely order champagne. Mrs Mahon would fuss and go on at great length about how her husband doesn't like to drink on an empty stomach with his ulcer and talk on incessantly about dinner timings for the next day's Christmas lunch. Mrs O'Toole would agree to whatever drink her husband ordered for them both, as was their tradition.

This is . . . well, isn't this, quite lovely, Jennings said. He was pissed and yet perfectly articulate. He rubbed Tess's wet fur. I love this colour on you. It matches you. I can't for the life of me remember where she said she got it . . .

Tess said: How are you? Where about are you living?

Jennings looked at her blankly.

Across the street Paul was hurrying towards them, his herringbone buttoned to his chin.

Have you gone fucking mad? he said, reaching her. He eyed Jennings and Tadhg in turn and then grabbed Tess by the arm. What the fuck are you playing at? Paul turned to his father-in-law. Come on, move along now, we've got nothing for you. Scram. He turned to his wife: Tess, the

O'Tooles are on their way. We'll be a holy show. Let's go. Fuck, what's on his coat? Paul said and rubbed his hands off his thighs.

Scram? Tess said, bewildered.

Hi, Tadhg said, interrupting them both and he put out his hand, you must be Paul. Pleased to meet you. I'm Tadhg, Tadhg Foley.

Yes, yes, right, Paul said, unconvinced. Sorry, who?

The new woodwork teacher up at the College.

Oh right, Happy Christmas, Paul said. Tess never said. Didn't know they offer woodwork now. Lot's changed since my time, guess there's loads of new estates now.

Tadhg nodded. He knew what the estate comment meant. Many happy returns, he said.

Paul turned to Tess: I was sure you had collapsed outside the church. I didn't know you were in such . . . having such a . . . he looked about . . . gathering.

Tadhg Foley turned to Tess: I'll head on, he said. And then he kissed Tess quickly and slipped away. Tess felt a flash of excitement followed by anger at him for just walking off, and she was left confused. She was startled, too, startled by her desire to follow him.

Mrs Mahon approached in Tadhg's wake, chattering like a hysterical bird and wishing all about her a Happy Christmas. She was telling Mrs O'Toole that she had forgotten to steep the marrowfats for tomorrow and would only wait for one drink. And again, she repeated herself, just one drink. Because: again, peas.

You didn't see Cathy? Jennings said.

Tess shook her head. No, sorry.

I'm kilt looking for her. I've been looking all week . . . all, yes, all of the time. And no, I can't seem to . . .

. . . find her? Tess offered.

Yes, he said. No. No, it's . . . I can't get her. He waved his hand about. I can't *get* her. You know? It's just, I'm always trying, you know . . . he trailed off, his glassy eyes were hooded over. Stood there, Tess thought about Tadhg walking out to the Forge, alone, about Jamie and his machine, about how fulfilled she was being among them and how naively Jamie was hoping, the bright hope he had, that the energy, wherever it would manifest from, would be enough to connect everyone, the living and the dead. But there was nothing for the half-living, Tess thought –

nothing at all for the dead walking among them.

Tess said: No, I haven't seen her, I haven't seen Cathy, I'm afraid.

He stared at her, blankly.

Tess said it again, and then said: I'm so sorry, really I am.

And then all of a sudden, Jennings threw his head back and began laughing manically: What is wrong with you? Oh my, but she's not lost, love. See, she was just with me . . . we went to the cinema together. We just went to see . . . my god, for the life of me I can't remember . . .

A film? Tess said.

Yes, yes, that's it, very good, the very thing, a film . . . a very good picture altogether . . . *On Golden Pond.* Great flick that one, ever see it? That Hepburn, well, she looks great in it, the eyes, just like Cathy. You won't know that . . . but she does. Dead fucking ringer for her, so she is, that's what I say, dead fucking ringer for Hepburn.

Judge O'Toole was stood a short distance away, beside the party and next to a large Santa Claus with puffed-out cheeks.

What do you think you're playing at? Paul whispered. Just leave him. You're making a show of yourself. Of us.

Terrible, Mrs Mahon said, and there's nowhere to put them.

Too much given to them now, medical cards . . . dole, Judge O'Toole said, pulling a scarf around his neck tighter until it made the jowls of his face bloat.

Might be an idea to extend their powers to on-the-spot arrests, Mr Mahon said, stop and search is so weak, now, guards just don't seem to have the stomach for it. O'Toole's sons nodded, all except the youngest.

Can we order for you, Ms Mahon? Francis O'Toole asked Tess. He remained formal outside of school.

I'll be there in a minute, she said.

And then suddenly, Tess leaned in and hugged her father so tight, it knocked him a little, and he slipped off the pavement, and then he cursed.

Fuck, he shouted, ankle-deep in the gulley's water.

She was with me, Cathy was, Jennings said into Tess's ear. She could feel his breath warm on her. And she's just disappeared. Did I tell you we went to the flicks? Just like that, he said. Gone. She's always at it, just upping and leaving me, you know? She's an awful woman. She's gone a long time, this time.

Paul checked his phone.

Go on, I'll catch up, Tess said, conscious she was holding everyone up. I can't just *leave* him here.

It's where he fucking lives, Paul said.

Does she know him? Mrs O'Toole asked loudly and indiscriminately and Mrs Mahon pulled her along by linking her wool coat: No, no, of course she doesn't, Margie, it's just teachers, isn't it?

How so? Mrs O'Toole asked.

Mrs Mahon said: They pick up strays. It's all that caring, at least that's what my Paul says, he's exasperated with her, she whispered. If you ask me she'd be as well give up that job and start on a family.

The group walked on into the hotel all except Francis O'Toole who lingered outside by Tess.

Ah, Cathy . . . Jennings cried out: Here she is now, told you she'd come. He waved enthusiastically as a woman staggered up Cinema Lane who turned into vantage under the lights at the Square. He turned back to Tess: She was probably waiting for me at the cinema. You wouldn't have the price of a pint, love, would you?

Tess opened the clutch of her bag.

Fuck this, Paul said sharply and he turned and walked off.

He's a nasty one. Ah, you're here. I was worried about you, Cathy, Jennings said, turning his attention to the woman.

It's Rosanne. It's fucking Rosanne. Always *Cathy? Cathy. Cathy*, she said, swaying, and then grabbed Jennings's arm, she attempted to slap him about the face. Jennings faux-winced as Rosanne stumbled, trying to loop her arm inside his, but she gave up and ended up leaving her narrow hand on the small of his back. It steadied her. Forgetting Tess, they walked to the side-gate of the bar and banged loudly. Every so often they'd lean on it, stare at each other – startle momentarily – then recognise one another again and laugh. Jennings grabbed Rosanne's narrow face between his hands and he kissed her forehead. They pushed hard on the pub gate until it gave way and the alarm began blaring.

Tess stood watching.

You sure you're OK? O'Toole said over to her, sure I can't order for you?

No, no, head in, I'll catch up.

But he waited.

That's my dad, she said.

I know, O'Toole said. Sorry.

There were more men in the alley and they lifted a keg upside down and Rosanne held glasses underneath, and they set to singing again, and one of them wolf-howled at the moon, that set a chain reaction. O'Toole watched Tess watching Jennings watching Rosanne. And every so often, Rosanne would sing one of those sad songs of loneliness and boats leaving, but she would only manage one or two lines. And all the while they stopped, started, and swayed, and sometimes they fell over, and now and then they'd hold each other up. Rosanne took a cigarette from the sleeve of a long, flimsy coat and tried to light it.

Tess stood up, her heart racing, and walking to them, said: Here, she said, here, take it some . . . money for pints and she pressed notes into Jennings's hand.

Who's this? Rosanne said, coming between them both.

Ah love, no . . . Jennings said to Tess, struck by her face now.

The rain had started to come down hard, dragging his eyebrows with it and when Jennings closed his mouth, he resembled her father – the memory she had, the shape, the jaw so familiar, angular, and he pulled that face he made when he was waiting a telling-off the morning after the night before. Now he lived in the night before. There were no sudden repercussions. His existence was repercussion enough.

Ah love, he said, don't cry, keep it, keep your money, buy yourself something. I didn't . . . he said, get a chance . . . you know . . .

Happy Christmas, Dad, Tess said, again, interrupting him as she leaned in and kissed his jaw.

Happy Christmas, he said, and called out.

But Tess was gone now and walking on across to Brooke's with her shaking hands stuffed into the pockets of the fur coat. She thumbed through a hole in the satin lining.

O'Toole followed her.

Great flick that one, you should go catch it, Jennings shouted in their wake: Don't bring that other fella though. Nasty lad.

The party were seated inside the door by the dying fire. It was empty, as most people were home with family. An officious hotel manager was busy about the dark space, opening champagne by their table, and bowing and scraping with an elaborate knife, and then talking about the weather and the courts in a high and excitable pitch, fussing as he lifted table candles over to them. Tess stood by the door and watched everyone busy in conversation. A boy she recognised from the College was holding glass flutes in his hands and the manager kept insisting he leave them down *here here here*, but the boy didn't know how to disentangle the narrow stems. He had black rims around his eyes and pimples dotted about his chin and under his neck where he had just started shaving.

Tess gently pulled one of the glasses free, like a Jenga brick, and then another, and finally they were all set down on the shiny table. Mr O'Toole and Mr Mahon thanked Tess as though she were also wait staff.

Did that terrible man stop bothering you, Tess? Mrs O'Toole called out.

Yes. Tess said. TriggerResponseActionConsequence, she said to herself and took a deep breath.

Did you see Paul? she asked.

In the jacks, O'Toole said, and he lifted his champagne flute and raised to his father's toast.

Lavatory. Mrs O'Toole. He's in the lavatory.

With panic rising in her, Tess bolted from the hotel.

TriggerResponseActionConsequence, she said loudly to herself as she walked fast past the bar where sheets of rain were rushing into the gulley and the crowd were shouting. All except Rosanne who was asleep perched against a faded John Player's sign.

A siren rang out.

19

Tess ran along Emory Woods Road. She stopped at the gate of her home and leaned on the wall to catch her breath, her mind racing. The artificial Christmas tree was alight in the bay window and looking at it, she felt nothing. It was as though she was looking through the window of any house, of any couple she did not know. She leaned over, unclipped her shoes, pulled them off her and ran barefoot towards the woods where she climbed the stile, not thinking, two stones at a time, and she slipped on the other side, quickly picked herself up. Her ears whoosh-whooshing with blood pumping as she ran on in the half-light, the path lit by the moon and some street lights. Soon it was completely black and so she used her phone light, breathless now. She was at the ice-house and she climbed up onto the mound on her hands and knees and sat there, her foot stinging.

It was almost midnight. She pulled the soaking fur around her and called Tadhg.

I'm sorry, Tess said. For calling so late.

It was impulsive, she knew, but she was so relieved to hear his voice. And now she was sobbing. I'm at the

ice-house . . . I'm OK . . . No. Look, I'm in the woods . . .
I'm alone. Thanks.

Tess lifted her knees up, tucked them under her wet
coat.

The town's lights reflected faintly out on the river, and
every so often another light would extinguish as a family
unplugged a tree or outdoor lights went off for the night.

Tadhg called out as he approached so not to startle her.
He leaned heavily on a hawthorn stick and his head torch
dipped through the clearing, spots on the ground and the
bare branches of the tree illuminating and darkening with
every pace.

Tess stood up.

Tess, Tess, what . . . what happened? he said. Are you
hurt? Did anyone . . .

No . . . no . . . I'm OK. Just wet.

Wait, I'll come up. Or no, just sit, you can slide down,
that's uneven there. And he climbed along the side of
the small hillock, heels deep into the mud. Jesus fucking
Christ, Tess, you're soaked, he said, and he put his arm
around her. Look at your face.

I'd rather not, she said.

What happened? Was it Jennings? Where's Paul?

Up in the hotel. Tess paused. Drinking champagne.

Jennings?

Drinking slops.

Tadhg leaned in and hugged her tightly. You'll catch a
death, we need to move.

I'm so sorry for calling you, Tadhg.

Shush, stop with all the sorrys. Mind your foot, here,

you can't trust . . . it's taken in a lot of water, he said as they moved down a little.

You can't trust anyone, she said.

OK, give yourself a second to settle down, take a breath. Tess, you're absolutely soaked. I'll walk you home.

No. No. Please no, she said, no, eyes wild in her head. I won't go home, I can't.

OK, that's OK, Tadhg said, softly, looking about as though the dark might offer him a solution. Just take a breath, this crying is no good at all.

It was pitch dark now almost save the moon and Tadhg's head torch.

Right, we can go to the Forge, sort out something there.

Ouch, fuck . . . Tess said as they began to walk.

Christ, Tess, you're barefoot, are you hurt?

I just took off my shoes, I couldn't walk . . . look, if I'm a bother, I can . . .

You're no bother, Tadhg said. But you must sit a minute. He lifted Tess's foot like a farrier might lift a horse hoof and pull a thorn from the sole. You're cut, Tess. It's bad.

Shit. Am I? I didn't even feel it.

It's bleeding, right, best if I carry you.

No. NO. No fucking way. I can walk.

It felt farther to the Forge than Tess remembered.

A horseshoe hung upright over the door and Tadhg touched off it as he unlatched it.

Tess waited. When she stopped her foot throbbed hard.

Come in, Tadhg said, beckoning. I don't bite – looks like you're bitten enough. Your feet must be in ribbons.

Tess entered. Crouching under the low door, she touched the shoe in turn and she was filled with an old familiar smell, smoke and leather.

Here, *sitsitsit*, just give me a minute, Tadhg said, looking about him. He began sorting lights. Sorry, I'd actually gone to bed.

Who owns it? Tess said, looking about.

The Forge?

Tess nodded.

The church, I guess, Tadhg said, like everything else in this town.

You not worried they'll evict you? She laughed, and then she started crying again.

You know what they say about possession. Oh Tess, fuck, I hate seeing you like this.

The fireplace was blackened and empty, a huge hollow space now with a tiny wrought-iron stove. Leathers and horseshoes hung where the forge fire would once have raged. There was an old table sat by a window with two plastic school chairs.

These look comfortable, Tess said, smiling.

Found them in a skip at the back of the College.

Tess took off her coat as Tadhg lit the stove, adding kindling and paper and then filling a kettle in the small dark galley.

Running water . . . Tess called out. Impressive.

I'm not a savage, Tadhg said.

Secretive, Tess said.

Private, he said, there's a difference. She nodded as he

handed her a jumper and some jog pants. Water might take a while.

Tadhg poured some whiskey into glasses in the kitchen as she peeled the green silk layer off her, and dressed in his clothes.

Sorry the place . . . is not more . . . festive, Tadhg said, handing her a glass as he looked about, suddenly conscious of the place.

It's fine – I hate Christmas, Tess said.

You do? Christmas and Halloween, Tess, so mystery is, do you like anything? he said, and sipped his drink.

It's a bad time of the year to have an alcoholic in the family, she said.

True, poor Jennings, he said. Can't be much of an existence.

She wrapped the woollen blanket around her. It was scratchy.

I have a first-aid kit, he said. I'll need to clean and dress that foot. Sorry. And you should really text Paul, let him know you're safe.

Tess groaned.

One text, he said as he disappeared again, dipping under the alcove, and he returned carrying a first-aid box. The galley kitchen was once where horses waited their turn, anxious and fretful of the flames, the narrow space once filled with their hysterical energy.

Here, he said, lift your foot again.

Tess did and winced.

This needs a stitch, Tadhg said.

No, Tess said and then she drank the whiskey quickly. It burned her throat, and her eyes watered as Tadhg hunkered down and tweezered out glass and some brambles from her foot. He put steri-strips on the deeper laceration. Finally, he wrapped it securely in a bandage. This will do for a while.

She liked the feel of his hand holding the foot with firm pressure, and she started to relax.

He poured two more whiskey fingers into their empty glasses. The second shot didn't burn, and Tess could taste vanilla.

So, what happened? Tadhg said, softly. The shards of burning wood in the stove glowed.

Tess said: You don't need to hear it. Honestly, I'll be grand. I don't know why I even ran out here.

Tadhg said: If that's for the best.

And they were quiet for some time. Tadhg drank and tended the fire as they watched the fuel burn and disappear to ash.

It's strange, Tess said, finally breaking the silence.

What is? Tadhg asked as he opened the stove door.

I can't hear the rain on the tin roof. I could have sworn it was still raining, she said, absently.

I thatched it.

Of course you did, Tess said. I remember coming here as kids.

You come here a lot?

A bit, you know . . . drinking, hanging out, boys, dope . . . the Ouija board.

Tadhg laughed: What is it with girls and the Ouija

board? Back on the islands the students were always at it, then freaking out if they contacted a spirit.

Tess laughed. I never took it seriously. I was the only one of my friends with a dead mother. But I never wanted to contact her.

Right, Tadhg said, quietly.

You were the same. Your father?

Yes.

How old were you when he died?

Seventeen. He drowned.

That's tough. My mother died before I knew her, you know, that is a whole different thing. Right?

Sounds like a rough deal to me, to never know her. I don't know if losing a parent is OK at any age – Tadhg took a deep inhale – goes against the order of things. He left the poker down.

True, she said. But losing your dad when you knew him all your life, surely that's life-changing? Tess said.

He was my stepfather.

Sorry.

No, don't be, he was great, there was no difference – he coughed gently – but for me, I thought for years it was different. I was different. That made everything different. I felt, I don't know, out of place maybe. In the way?

Did he make you feel like this?

God no, Tadhg said. I was the same to him, it didn't seem as though I was different, but I felt it, you know? Thing is, he was softer on me, let me away with more, no, he was a good man. But I never felt . . . I had issues

211

with my own father, unresolved, and they clouded every-thing . . . ah, it's nothing.

It can't be *nothing.*

I overthink – a habit from my mother's side, Tadhg said. He got up suddenly, uncomfortable now, and turned on a radio transistor. A voice recited a poem about child-hood, a repeat show, one they had run through the night. Then a poem about two lovers. After the poet, country songs. Tess stared out of the tiny window. It was two a.m.

Do you think he remembers the story *of* it, the singer, or the way people told it to him, or the actual event? Tess said.

We know only the story of a story, said Tadhg. The last memory of the thing is the memory. It's always a fucking subjective mess, memory – no? He paused. Did you text Paul?

The unexpected explosion of his name irked Tess. Fuck, stop, please, she said.

Just think the man has a right to know you're safe is all.

I've messaged him, Tess said.

Tadhg turned up the radio, and an American song filled the dark space with an unnerving loneliness.

Eventually Tess fell to sleep in the chair and some time later, she woke with a fright.

It was five-thirty a.m.

You should head back maybe? It's now, Tadhg said, peering out the little window into the dark, Christmas.

Tess stretched. Happy Christmas, she said, yawning.

Coffee? he asked.

Yes, Tess nodded. They'll be getting up for break-fast soon, she said. He'll have all of his family and their

212

children – she looked at him – in our house. I've been thinking of the baby, and what you said in October on the river. I wanted a baby, I did, but I think I wanted to have someone, someone for me. It's the loneliness that fucking kills me. But I couldn't do that to a child.

Were you arguing? Tadhg called out. Last night?

Fuck no, Tess said. I was thinking about my mother in the cathedral. And how I know so little about her and I have this pain right here and it rises in me, and I can't . . . Tess was bleeding again, the night's whiskey thinning her blood. She stood up from the chair, and sat down onto the mattress. Tadhg dropped a coffee in to her, and laid his own down, she lay back on the mattress and he lifted her foot and fixed the bandage winding it around again. Tess leaned forward and arched herself towards him, and let her face down onto his chest.

Thanks, she said softly into him. She felt his body stiffen. She heard the sounds an empty stomach makes. Suddenly, his heat was a comfort and she lifted her face and put her mouth on his, and kissed him. He didn't respond. And then she wrapped her legs around him, coaxed him down over her and down onto the mattress.

No, fuck, Tadhg said, moving back. Sorry, no, this is not good, not now, for either of us. You're upset. He rubbed her hair from her face. Get some rest, he said, and he went out to the galley as she tossed and turned.

20

Happy Christmas, Mam, Eoin said, opening the front door to Marie who was stood on his step with gifts and a baked ham.

Happy Christmas, love, she said as Eoin lifted the steaming plate from her.

Smells great, he said.

Happy Christmas to you, Marie, Jamie said formally. You are to come in here with me, Marie, Eoin is looking after the kitchen.

Grandmother and grandson sat side by side on the sofa together.

Get some drinks, Jamie, Eoin called out.

Jamie said: Oh yes. What can I get you to drink, Marie?

Without waiting Marie went rustling around Eoin in the kitchen, fussing with glasses and rinsing some crockery Eoin had used to prep.

Turn on the fan, she instructed. Marie found Christmas hard without Joe, she hated to sit still.

Go and sit down, it's an order, Eoin said.

She reached into her canvas bag: Here, some wine, think I'll have a glass of this. Were ye up early?

Around eight.

It was a habit of Marie's to ask the time everything occurred, and the cost. You're meant to be relaxing, Eoin said, gently pushing Marie to the living room. Her hands were shaking, and she had blistered fingertips that stung as she unscrewed the bottle top.

Shit, what happened? Eoin said, taking her hands into his.

I forgot my cleaning gloves last night. Mass was thronged, I thought all you young people had given up on it. But it was full.

Marie was in the cathedral just after midnight mass, cleaning brass plaques, washing down the pews and bleaching lavatories, then hoovering the huge space before Christmas Morning mass. Eoin leaned in and hugged her tight.

Jesus Christ, stop squeezing me, she said, you'll squeeze the life out of me.

Go in and sit with Jamie, he's finishing off the jigsaw.

Jamie regaled Marie about Terry and the boat, as he erected the Eiffel Tower. And he told her all about Arsenal, though just facts that Terry had given him.

How is Terry?

He's confused, Jamie said.

Confused?

Boy One has been calling us sissies, and we have been on a mission to figure it out. Terry is allergic to being a sissy.

Marie smiled and Jamie didn't understand her response.

Well, if you want my advice . . . she said.

No, Jamie said, quickly.

No? Marie said.

Yes, no. Father Faulks said that we are to try and foster relationships with other men, and not to take too much influence from our mothers and grandmothers, so I don't think I can ask your advice.

Oh my, Marie said, did he now? as she slotted together two tricky pieces. Jamie stared at her hands, all blistered. She finished the last of the tower's fourth leg. Jamie was impressed.

He's afraid of us becoming emasculated, he said, but he knew that not asking Marie's advice would be a hard habit to break.

He is? Marie said. I think that there is absolutely no fear of that happening to you. Or to Terry.

I don't know, Jamie said, and stopped talking. Marie was not the person to have this conversation with.

Have you looked it up in the dictionary? she asked.

Yes. I know what it means.

Well?

It means a boy that shows signs of being effeminate, Jamie said. And that we need to be careful not to— He stopped mid-sentence.

Womanly? Marie said slowly, as she fiddled with more pieces, and laid some over to the sides of the table in little mounds, ones she thought belonged together. It's good to be womanly.

I am a man-boy, Marie. A volcanic eruption, like you told me.

Yes, she said. I think what you boys need to figure out

is if you care what this Father Faulks thinks – being sensitive means you understand people. And that's the greatest power. To understand how a person might feel, see it as a compliment. That's how I'd see it. Sensitive people solve a lot of the world's problems, so they're problem solvers, ultimately.

Maybe, Jamie said, more confused now than ever, but that is a great leap, Marie.

21

Tadhg lit the stove as Tess texted Paul an insane Christmas greeting gif. Out of guilt. Out of fear. She had contem-
plated saying nothing, then saying something to patch it
all up, to get out of the situation she had backed herself
into, to make the chaos disappear. But in the end her text
sounded like a hybrid of an eccentric aunt and a lover he
might vaguely remember.

Have a good one, Paul responded. Make it about
yourself.

Agitated, Tess tried reading books that were strewn
about the place but she was too distracted. She lay silent
for long stretches of time, as Tadhg pottered about, tapping
and fixing things that garnered his attention.

In the distance they heard voices of children playing in
the forest, then crying, overwhelmed at new toys that did
not work on the mucky tracks.

By the afternoon, they grew unsure in each other's
company. But nevertheless Tess asked if she could stay a
little while longer, and Tadhg agreed.

They went out on the currach. Afterwards they drank

some more whiskey, and a bottle of wine that accompanied Tadhg's dinner of roast chicken and vegetables.

Tess got her appetite back and soon found she was ravenous.

I won't keep you fed, Tadhg said, as he sat opposite her on the school chairs, laughing.

But soon panic rose in Tadhg. It was a panic that he had not had since the dawn he left the island – that crippling familiar anxiety that came when something was added to his responsibilities.

What's wrong? Tess said, as she finished dinner.

It's just, we just . . . you . . . he left down his cutlery on the table, looking out of the window, you can't . . . you just can't hide out here, it is not sorting anything.

OK, Tess said. Her heart pounded. But I can't return today. Not like this. She wanted to say to calm down. Or add something that gave her back some control, but she had nothing to say, no real place to go, unless she returned home. Or went over to Ellie and Christmas Day was no day to arrive anywhere, uninvited.

I came here . . . you know, to Emory, Tadhg said but recognising her hurt, he stopped, and started again: I should explain, you know, he was repeating himself. I came here to sort myself out. Look, it's just, it's . . . he said, slowly, arching his hands, he brought them together in front of him. I have so much of my own stuff to figure out . . . I don't have the . . . I'm not the right person for this, Tess. For you.

He meant for another person in pain.

For what? Tess pressed, defensive.

Tadhg crossed his cutlery on the empty plate, to refuse a response.

Tess said: Right, I mean, it's none of my business. And you're right, I need to go, I need to get things straight in my head.

Tadhg replied: You do.

They were quiet and Tess was unsure. Arriving to him in the first place had been absurd, but she was so drawn to him.

I find it difficult . . . he said, standing up and pacing the small area now. I rarely left the island, you know, and as a kid . . . we didn't go far. I often tried, I really tried to . . . there was so much speculation, you know, it was fucking suffocating, all this talk about me, all the fucking whispers.

No, Tess said, I don't know.

. . . but I felt this shocking fucking guilt around leaving my mother, as if it was always my fault in the first place.

What's your fault? Tess said.

That I was born. That my mother was only twenty having me. That she was not equipped. That she was not ready. No choice. Tadhg looked at her. That's infantile, I know, but fuck it, I'm trying to be honest, and you know, Tess . . . there were so fucking many occasions when I'd pack a bag, just to try it out. I think I was goading myself, and I'd get up at some mad hour, and head down to the ferry at the pier all about myself, full of bravery. Pathetic really, he said, his voice unreliable. And then at dawn, when I'd sit down at the pier, I'd wait, and the longer I waited, the more I'd lose my bottle you know, my nerve. I was often following someone else, it's crazy just saying it, and finally I'd had enough, and I came here, to Emory, and I can't . . . I think why, I really don't know why I came here – maybe because it's close to the sea.

Leaving is the hardest, Tess said.

The kettle hissed in the galley. Tess picked at some cheese and went out and took the kettle off the hob. Her foot stung.

I was brought up to feel this responsibility to the island. As if leaving were a failure, letting everyone down. But it was so . . . stifling.

Oh, Tadhg. Look, I'm not asking you to look after me, I just needed a place . . . I needed to go.

Tadhg lifted his hand to his brow: I know you're not. I'm not great with . . . I guess what I'm saying is . . . Fuck sake, he said, throwing his head back. I would love for you to stay. And yes, he said, though she had not initiated a question, I'm lonely, but see, I've always been lonely, alone – or both. Maybe it's because like many children whose childhoods are lonely, I've grown accustomed to silence . . . it's dangerous to get close to people.

In case they hurt you? Tess said.

No, fuck no, he said, in case I hurt them. He sat a while, his head hanging down. I like being alone and I need it. I'm an outlier, I might be an outlier of outliers, he said and laughed nervously.

Everyone is an outlier, Tadhg.

Are they? Tadhg said.

Yeah, they are. People talk too much if you ask me,

221

she said, wishing he'd stop speaking. Knowing he'd talk himself out of whatever was happening. If anything was happening.

I can't start a relationship with you or with anyone – it feels like a trespass, or a gamble. And right, it feels right being with you. You know. But it's wrong.

I understand, she said. I'm not asking for a relationship. Christ, I just needed . . . a place to kip, she said.

Tadhg said suddenly: It'd be out of the frying pan, trust me, Tess.

Bit dramatic! Tess smiled.

I really need my space. Relationships, I can't commit, you need to know this, they're not for me. Friendships only . . . at a distance.

Tess reddened. His jumper was suddenly itchy on her skin and stuck to her chest, his jog pants smelled of burning wood and watching Granny Liz's coat dry over the stove, she wanted to be back in her own clothes.

I had nowhere to go, that's all, Tess said, lying. That's all.

Please, don't get me wrong, I'm glad you called. Called me. Maybe you could go and stay with Ellie, I think it's better if you go clear your head, and you need to talk to Paul.

Can we drop it? she said and got up and went out to the galley. Have you painkillers?

Small shelf, top right, he called out to her.

The box was by some unopened Christmas cards stuffed in behind the mugs. Tess opened the pillbox and pressed two white tablets from the foil. Her hands were shaking.

Sleep here tonight. And stay, stay a few days, stay until you feel up to sorting something out, Tadhg called out to her.

Tess slept on for most of the evening and when she woke she was filled with the panic of unfamiliar surroundings. She replayed moments of the last few days in her head. Back to the Square and Jennings; and then she spiralled back to the hospital, and right back to Granny Liz lying in her coffin, dead. Jennings in hospital. Jennings out of hospital. Jennings missing again. Letting Jennings go. And every time it was the same question: was it cruel cutting people from your life, like cutting off a piece of yourself? But she was used to it, to the see-sawing. And besides, it was too late to help Jennings. He was too hard to find. She'd have to wait for him.

She showered in a tiny space with whitewashed walls and a large mirror hanging from a bicycle chain. There was a stack of old engineering magazines and some books sat in a hazel basket: *Huckleberry Finn*, *Wide Sargasso Sea*, some Bolaño, an old *Hamlet*, two Orwells and *Pride and Prejudice* – which surprised her. There was a long crack through the middle of the mirror, so that Tess's reflection looked like a Picasso line drawing. A long shower arm with a large head came out from the wall and warm water poured generously down on her body. Wiping the steam from the cracked mirror, she didn't recognise herself, not her hips or her breasts, not the fringe that stuck upwards, wet now, with only Tadhg's comb to pull through it.

There's a toothbrush in the cabinet, Tadhg called out, and Austen, just . . . that's my mother's.

That's a very powerful shower for an eco-warrior, she called back. I love Austen, what's wrong with Austen? You didn't say your mother was a reader.

He ignored the comment. I harvest my own water, he said.

Of course you do, she muttered to herself, and it irked her.

It's bad luck to have a cracked mirror.

I know, he shouted.

Just another six and a half years so, she said.

It'll fly, he shouted back.

Tadhg's way of being in the world suddenly angered her. His talking, his not talking. All the upcycling. And with her own life toppled over, something about this realm, this mad place she was now washing her body in, to step back into the clothes of a man she barely knew, have them clutching her skin, was upsetting. Waves passed over her in the shower.

It was herself. She irked herself,

the corners she backed herself into

over and over

the way she ran from her life, running mad on Christmas Eve, running on from Jennings and Paul, rushing now to create new circles that too would ripple and crack in time. It was screaming to her, her life, her distorted Picasso face shouting at herself, asking questions, her body aching

but used to picking up the rhythms of pain that she fero-
ciously protected against, in denial, in the way she lifted
his towel to her face and dabbed it, and wanted to cry or
go into the kitchen,

and how really,

whatever the impulse, or her way of being in the world,

she so desperately wanted to fuck Tadhg Foley right
then,

hard

at whatever cost

fuck him on a futon he probably made from pieces of
wood that floated by him, and before he made the wicker
basket, all the stupidity of it, the juvenile way she was carrying on. But it wouldn't happen, he had rejected her, rejected
the chaos that came with her, she knew this, deep down,
he might say he was a relationship phobic, or whatever he
was getting at, but Tess knew she was unsteady. And this
was the most unattractive thing about her. It made loving
herself impossible.

Tadhg's voice sounded strange now, more cautious.
The laceration on her foot was opening again as warm
blood poured fast down the shower gulley. She sat on the
toilet and put pressure on it, slowed down her breathing,
traced the silvery scar on her hand from falling over on
the road.

And as Jamie would say: One mistake, Tess, is an accident, two is foolish.

You OK? Tadhg called in.

Yeah, yeah, I'm OK, out in a minute.

Slumped on the toilet seat, she couldn't exactly predict

her next moves. She suspected she couldn't do what she had always done: procrastinate, sit it out for some weeks with Tadhg – and make no decisions. Soon, this lack of clarity catches up on a person.

But Tess had walked out of the Clinic.

She had walked out of the hotel bar. She had taken the first steps.

Now, she just had to continue.

After she had dried and dressed herself, Tess sulked on a little for the afternoon, as was her habit when she had no defence, when she had messed up. It was a withdrawal from herself ultimately, a way to disconnect her body and her mind. She was exhausted. She took some more pain-killers and slept on and off, chatting a little,

but Tadhg was right,

and she knew he was, and as uncomfortable and lonely as she would feel to leave – she needed to sort herself out.

And the next day, she moved out of the Forge and into a tiny room in Brooke's Hotel, washed-out watercolours and a dark bedspread, a room with a small sink in the corner, and a tiny ensuite that she backed herself into.

Tess would spend some time there, and time would spend her, and eventually they would strike a rhythm where she would begin, slowly, to take responsibility, and face recovery, and that would begin with facing people, whether she wanted to or not.

Dead and alive. Starting with Paul.

22

So, you're sure that this is *really really* what you want to be doing on New Year's Eve, Jamie? Eoin said, driving along the motorway towards the university in Galway where Jamie was attending their Annual New Year's Eve Maths Lecture.

The radio kept losing station in the van. Jamie sensed his father's gentle challenge.

Yes, Eoin, Jamie said, he was definite. You keep asking me this same question and I keep telling you, there is nothing I would rather do.

Friday evenings should be strictly for kissing girls, Eoin smiled. Or boys.

Jamie didn't respond.

Any kissing and fun has to be better than listening to . . . what's his name?

Lucy Kovalevskaya. Them.

To them, Eoin said as he pushed up his sunglasses. The glare of the winter sun was strong. He drove fast now.

They both laughed.

Jamie said: They explain the fundamental flaws with

allowing too many people solve mathematical problems in a group scenario, and it's throwing a lot of questions at me.

Yawn, Eoin teased.

Jamie said: In *your* opinion. But I have been carefully considering the currach, now that my life systems have been thrown off-kilter.

Life systems? Eoin said, raising an eyebrow as he was changing up the gears.

Yes, we are making great progress with the currach. But I am not sure it fits its brief of being anything close to the machine that I really want to design, but since I always liked the idea of building the boat or machine alone –

Eoin nodded.

– I am accepting it for now. But my next machine will have nothing whatsoever to do with other people, what I am saying is, there's room for the communal approach, and the currach has a communal quality about the process, which to be frank, means the whole thing has a crudeness about it.

Right, Eoin said nodding. But just for what it's worth, I think that a boy should also like to hang out in CeX or get a pterodactyl maybe, or drink some beer on the weekend.

Jamie said: Why would I drink beer? I'm fourteen years old.

Not fourteen *yet*, Eoin said as he grabbed his son's thigh in jest, another month.

That weakens your argument, Eoin. I thought parents were not meant to encourage alcohol and drugs.

Eoin smiled as he drove through the city built on roundabouts, and pushed onwards to the Quincentenary

Bridge, backed up with heavy traffic. This route was the only way to go west, on to Connemara, and on again over the Atlantic to the islands.

Jamie, if you were to sum up 2019 in one word, what would it be? Eoin said, knocking off the engine as they stalled on the bridge. They watched a boat on the river covered in blue Christmas lights, a small Galway Hooker. The lights stayed on until the sixth of January, when they celebrated Oíche Nollaig na mBan, Women's Christmas. Eoin would have Marie round for some sweet cakes and a drink.

A let-down.

Really? Eoin said.

2019 has been . . . Jamie paused. A gigantic let-down, Eoin.

That's two words, Eoin said.

It is four, Jamie said, flatly. It was a let-down . . . it will be for ever known as the *year I was passed over for a prize.*

Jamie, you can't still be going on about that. What about the boat?

Yes, it has been an interesting experience, a highlight, maybe one or two moments in particular have been good but like I said, this currach – it's erratic.

Erratic?

Yes, drilling, talking to branches, it will be a miracle if it ever floats on water, and you know how we both feel about miracles.

I'd like to see it sometime, maybe I can come in to the College, or would that be embarrassing?

Embarrassing? Jamie asked.

Your dad in the school?

Why?

Eoin smiled and started to hum along to a song on the radio, and Jamie noted it was the only song he had ever heard mention a pencil case and school subjects. And then the news came on and Jamie turned it off completely. Eoin started up the van again as the lights changed to green. Eventually they crossed the bridge over the Corrib.

I think when people ask me did I go to film school, I tell them no, I went to films, Jamie said to himself.

Students were balancing a kayak down by the back of the Science Building.

Ambitious, Jamie said.

Why?

That's the fastest-flowing river in Europe, the Corrib, Jamie said.

Yeah, but they're skilled, Jamie. They love those currents.

Jamie considered this as he looked out on the water.

What are you going to call your boat? Eoin asked.

Does it need a name?

Yes, all boats need a name.

You sound like Mr Foley.

Eoin threw his arm around the back of Jamie's headrest as he reversed, parking at the back of the Marine building. Soon they walked along the Arts concourse, towards the O'Flaherty lecture theatre.

The university was filled with kids in hoodies and tracksuit pants, bags on their backs, bikes under them. Outside the

O'Flaherty Theatre, younger teenagers stood about, awkwardly, as guardians sipping out of coffee cups – mostly women in dark tight running gear – took out snacks and notebooks from large bags and handed phones and money.

Hi, said a student at the information desk. You here for Lucy Kovalevskaya?

Hi. Yes. I'm Jamie, Jamie O'Neill. Yes, yes, I am.

Great stuff, Jamie, you're welcome. I'm Ben.

Thank you, Jamie said. He wanted to sit in the theatre, take down whatever was on the board before Kovalevskaya would arrive. Jamie checked his notebook and pen from Nice, checked that it was working: OK. It had a little image of a beach along the side and a little swimming float that moved up and down.

Hmmm, we don't seem to have you on the list, sorry about this, just one sec, the student said, as he clicked his laptop.

That's OK, the man behind him said. He was in a white shirt buttoned down, with a lanyard that read STAFF NUIG. Find him by school, do a college search. They're registered by school now.

What school do you attend?

The line filled up behind Eoin and Jamie.

Christ's College Emory, Form 1A, Jamie said, clearing his throat.

I didn't know it was by school now, Eoin said. He's signed up for an annual pass. I registered him myself.

Oh, I am so sorry, Ben said, it's only by school now, but that's OK, I'm sure they have you on here. One minute.

But the student shook his head. I'm afraid, he said, I'm

terribly sorry, it seems . . . there's another boy registered from the College, only one can . . . now register, did your maths teacher not mention it?

Jamie thought of David saying his prayer at the beginning of every class, fiddling with the string of his glasses, pulling up his trousers. He thought of how far up his pen he held it. How much this said about his age. How kids hold it so very close to the nib and then adults move farther up along the stem of the pen as they get older. What? Jamie said, suddenly remembering the moment. It is a big hall, there are . . . there are exactly three hundred and fifty-six seats.

He's been coming since he was nine, Eoin said.

We understand, but there is such demand that only one student per school, a new national thing. A new programme. I'm so sorry but we can't bend the rules.

There's nothing we can do? Eoin said.

Let me sit on the steps of the theatre? Jamie said.

I'm afraid that contravenes Health and Safety.

Yes, Jamie said, his mind escaping to a visual of the theatre hall engulfed in flames.

You might need to chat to the school, the Principal even, it might be an administrative error. They could have requested more positions early on, when it opened first. Talk to your maths teacher?

Jamie shook his head.

Hang in there, and I'm sure we'll see you back, Ben said.

Right, Eoin said. Let's go, but Jamie's mood had changed now.

This is a travesty, Jamie said.

Eoin pulled him gently by the shirt, and they turned, Jamie's shoes clip-clopped loudly on the concourse tiles. That's appalling, Eoin said, I'm so sorry, Jamie, I had no idea.

They passed a coffee dock. Want a tea?

Jamie shook his head. His heart dancing now, feet fizzy. He wanted to throw up.

Smokey's tuck shop was open with pastries and chocolate squares out on the counter. Jamie turned away from them, and as he did, Piotr Pulaski came towards him with a girl who must be one of the many sisters, twirling about with a bottle of Coke in one hand and a glittery phone case in the other. Piotr's mother was paying for water. Jamie watched them, his head hurting, his hands itchy now like his feet. The girl arched backwards, then screwed the lid back on the Coke bottle, and lifting it in one hand, she flipped it up high into the air, and stood watching as it landed. But it crashed down along the corridor, hitting Jamie's foot, cracking open and spraying up over him. Jamie shouted in fright, then lifted his wet foot as though it was scalded, and in that moment he kicked the bottle back, hard. It flew low and fast and just as the sister looked up at it, it hit her hard on the chin. Her bejewelled phone dropped and hit the tiles of the concourse and smashed. The Coke sprayed for the longest time, up into the air as the girl screamed out.

Oh fuck, I'm terribly sorry, Eoin said, running towards the girl.

Piotr had his laptop under his arms, and he repositioned his glasses up on his face. He stared at Jamie.

What, what are you doing? Piotr's mother cried out at Jamie as she rushed to her young daughter.

Jamie started to sing.

And Eoin shouted at him to shut up: so he began to quote Tarantino loudly: Eoin telling him to shut up again. But then he walked back to Jamie, and left Mrs Pulaska to comfort her daughter. He put his hand on his son's shoulders, and softer now, said: Jamie, Jamie, look at me, be quiet, take a breath for a second, what happened?

You are comforting your child, what about my daughter? the woman shouted and wagging her finger in his face she said, so as far as I can see . . . your boy is an . . . animal.

We're sorry, Eoin apologised again.

But she threw a bottle at me, first, Jamie said. Eoin nodded.

She is eight years old – playing a game. Eight years old. He is a . . . he is a man, her mother said.

Jamie looked every inch a man with his broad shoulders. Eoin took him to one of the leather chairs by the coffee dock, sat him down and circled his finger around on his palm. Jamie, watching each student register down at the table and Ben flitter about smiling brightly, started singing.

Jamie ssshhh. Good lad. Ssshhh now, Eoin said.

Disgraceful, Mrs Pulaska called out, absolute disgrace as she clutched her daughter and lifted her satchel high up on her shoulder. What is wrong with him?

There's nothing wrong with him, Eoin shouted back, nothing at all.

23

Tess had arranged to meet Paul in Temple Café to talk. He was running late. Late enough for her to leave. Late enough that she was on her third coffee.

But she waited. And still it came as a shock when he arrived, pushing in the café's glass door with his shoulder and chatting loudly on his phone, crooked between his shoulder and his jaw, *byebyebyebye* he repeated as he banged off chairs and stuffed the phone into his pocket. He opened the top button of his pale blue shirt, elaborately stretching the collar out with his right hand as he sat down at the tiny marble table without looking at her.

Tess squeezed her cup to stop her hands shaking. Hi, she said.

Hi, Paul said, nodding at her as he looked over her shoulder to try and grab the attention of a server. He pushed up the sleeves of his navy sports jacket revealing red cufflinks.

Hi, Tess said again.

You cut a fringe? he said. Thought you hated fringes.

Yes, she said. And yes. She blew it up and out of her eyes.

Looks different.

She blew again.

Makes your face, I don't know, wider?

Tess said: Food? as she passed him over a large laminated menu.

Nope, he said.

OK. Tess propped the menu awkwardly against a small salt cellar. The salt cellar fell over and spilled.

What's this all about? Paul asked.

We need to talk. I think it's important that we . . . try clear the air, she said lifting the cellar back upright. Before we both, you know, move on.

You've moved on, all you, Tess. All you doing the moving. I haven't gone anywhere. See, Paul said, lifting his hands up and out and then pulling skin off his lower lip with his top teeth. He tasted the iron and dabbed it gently with a serviette. Same house. Same bed.

The miniature furniture in the Temple Café didn't help put them at ease. Their knees touched and the leg of the table proved to be in the way no matter how they approached it. Finally, Paul swung himself sideways and crossed his legs at the ankle, red socks matched the cufflinks.

I don't think we can . . . just *leave* things, Tess said.

You're up for talking, *now*? Here?! He turned his head to her. The woman wants to talk. Guess what? he said, flinging his hands into the air and slapping the palms on the table, bit late, no?

Tess's coffee spilled over.

Flat white, excuse me, hello, he said lifting himself

halfway up, where he waved at the wait staff and catching their attention, he sat back again. Flat white, double shot . . . double shot.

Sure, the woman said coolly, wiping down the salt spill. You want anything else, love? she said to Tess.

No, Paul said, brusquely. She's fine.

You OK, love? Would you like anything else today? she said again, eyes intent on Tess. And here, let me grab this, I'll just take that menu out of your way.

Thanks, I'm OK. Actually, Tess said, maybe just a glass of water. Thanks. Tap's fine.

The woman smiled and nodded.

You walked out, you left the marriage, and what – you want back in *now*? Paul hissed. After the way you've been behaving. He was wearing his wedding ring.

I didn't say that, Paul. I don't want *in*, Tess said.

No? What do you want? Your clothes, things. *Things*, is that why we're fucking here? Things?

There's no need to be like this, Tess said, quietly.

Isn't there? You fucked off, or did you forget?

Paul, please, please hear me out, Tess said.

Do I? Really, I need to listen to you? Fuck this. I am a mug, that's what I am. My mother was right.

Tess didn't react.

See, he threw his hands to the air. You're impossible. Should I have to sit here and take this? Whatever *this* is? He looked about the café.

No, Tess said, you don't need to listen, I guess, and you know what . . . you should have married your fucking mother maybe.

Mature, he said, clapping slowly. The server returned with water and some napkins.

It *is* the end, Paul. I know this. I was in the marriage too. Tess stopped for a moment, and then said: I called it.

Oh, did you? You *called* it. Fuck that, he said. And he wiped the corners of his mouth. His lip continued to bleed. Were you though? In it? Really?

You ended our marriage, Paul, a long time ago, Tess said, fixing the napkins on the table.

Don't fucking start, Paul said, jerking in the seat. Then suddenly: Have you lost weight?

No.

It's just you look thin, ghostly, that's all the exercise with the chippie, is it? Heard he doesn't even speak English.

Stop it. That's not what happened.

You *are* fucking him, right?

Paul, don't.

We came to talk but seems now you don't really want to talk. Please tell me one of us is getting laid.

Paul, stop. I want to say sorry, Tess said, finally.

No, you can't just, you can't just throw a fucking sorry at me, don't, don't do this, go on draw your line in the sand, Tess. You said that you wanted to talk about the baby. So come on, let's talk. How I didn't, what is it . . . understand enough about miscarriage, don't you think I felt it, too?

No, Paul, I'm sorry . . . this last time, Tess said, there was no baby. She was whispering now, her heart pounding as she played with her watch strap.

What? Paul said.

I didn't miscarry.

What? I don't understand.

There *was* no baby.

I know.

Tess coughed. No, no. There was no, no implant, no embr—

I don't understand. Oh Jesus, he said, suddenly. Oh my god, did you get rid of it?

PAUL! NO! Stop. I didn't go through with it. That day in the Clinic, I just – I bolted.

He stared at her, his green eyes wild and full of fear. Or anger.

I couldn't, she whispered.

What? Paul said. You couldn't what?

Flat white, the woman said, leaving a cup on the small table, and pulling the sugar close to Paul. You sure you're OK, love? she said directly to Tess. Tess nodded as she watched coffee soaking the paper napkin on the saucer.

She's fine, Paul said. Why is everyone so fucking worried about how she is, look at her – best form of her life.

I don't know what's your beef, man, but keep your voice down or I'll have to ask you to leave, she said.

The sisters who fuck together . . .

Paul! Tess said.

That's enough, sir – you have to leave.

A burly chef came from behind the counter, and watched over them until Paul got up to leave.

I'll get this in a takeout cup, he said.

Tess went to the counter, and tapped her bank card off the machine.

You just mind yourself, the woman said. Men like that, she said and wagged her finger. No good.

Paul ploughed up the street off the Square towards home.

Paul, Paul, Tess said, shouting after him, please, PAUL! Stop. Wait up, *please*.

He swerved right up an alleyway and was standing, leaning against a wall. He was breathing shallow. It was a Farmer's Market on Saturdays and the smell of raw fish lingered.

Tess caught him up.

What do you want me to say, Tess? He turned now to face her.

Nothing, she said. But please, Paul, I need to explain . . . it was remiss, it was actually terrible of me to just disappear like that. I am sorry. I just . . .

Remiss? What kind of a word is that, Tess? Speak English. Don't fucking *teacher* me. You left, Tess . . . and now you're telling me . . . you lied about the miscarriage? All of them, did you lie about all of them?

NO! she said.

A child ran by up the alley shouting and a woman followed and grabbed the child by its fur hood.

I need to explain why I didn't go ahead with it, Tess said. Please just let me explain. The baby. I mean the embryo, they didn't . . . I didn't go ahead with it. I ran out of the Clinic . . . I couldn't bring up a baby – she stopped a minute – on my own.

The flat white splashed on his leather shoes. Christ, you weren't on your *own*, I was with you.

But you weren't, Paul.

Fuck, not this again, how many times are we going to go back over this? If I could have had the kid, I would.

Would you?

He didn't answer for a second, then quickly said: I'm not taking this. I've listened to you for years, talking in fucking riddles. He left his cup on the windowsill of a barber's shop, where it rolled off to the ground. The wind whipped it up, and scratched it along the pavement. Don't dare make this about you, Tess, *I don't listen, I don't listen*, it's all I hear, how shit I am at listening. You'd have to talk to be heard. He threw his hands up again. I'm confused . . . it was *all* you ever wanted.

You don't get it, Tess said.

Correct, Paul said. Damn fucking right I don't. But I know this much, our marriage . . . fucking eggshells with you, Christ. He was waving his hand. Whatever we had, it was not like a marriage. Crying now, he wiped his nose off the cuff of the blue shirt.

Tess reached out to him.

Don't.

I just need to give you these. Here. She handed him two keys.

Tess said: But remember, you put yourself under all that pressure, that pressure comes from you, and from *your family* . . .

Here we fucking go . . . my family this, my family that.

That's not my pressure. I'm not taking that. I just need one or two of my mam's things. Tess was unprepared to go on.

Paul took the keys and rolled his eyes. You know what, Tess? he said as he kicked the wall, and through the window a man was having the back of his neck buzzed by a razor. He avoided looking at her. You know, you always had that desire . . .

She stared at him.

Yes, see, it was always in you, from the minute I met you . . . to come apart . . . to self-destruct. It's genetic, here in the mind . . . Paul said, as he tapped the side of her head, then he tapped her black hair with his index finger over and over, hard, maybe that's the real reason you couldn't . . . have a kid, you know, because Cathy – your mother – remember her, and what she did, well, I bet she couldn't bear the fucking sight of you, Paul Mahon said, that's why she did it, and he turned, walking through the archway, hands in his pockets.

24

Walking along the path in the opposite direction from her normal route to the College was disconcerting for Tess. She had dressed for the first day back in bad light in the sleepy hotel room on this January morning. It felt so strange: the low narrow window with the street light flickering like an old movie reel on the dark purple upholstery, washing her hair over the olive bath that drained so slowly. Still, there was comfort in it, an awareness and the alive feeling that doing something new evokes. She had missed that sensation. Over the holidays she had read some books and planned the new term properly for the first time in years. She came up with some lectures from MIT for Jamie too; and finally watched Maryam Mirzakhani late into the night. Though she understood very little of the lectures, she could see how Jamie was drawn to her. She was feeling OK, everything worked better when she prepared.

Frost made the paths glisten. Tess walked carefully, picking out her footing. 2020. An even year, it might be a good year, she thought. It was a morning you watched the white breath come from your mouth. The Turkish takeaway was cooking meats. Tess's stomach grumbled.

She couldn't face the hotel breakfast on any morning, the looming window looking out to the Square, the small talk in the stuffy breakfast room, the clash of steel teapots and ceramic cereal bowls. It was rash to stay there, very public. She should have booked into somewhere anonymous in the city, one of the big hotel chains with pleather couches and rubber plants, where the buffet breakfast was filled with little assortments of marmalades in individual tubs.

One or two shops on the Square still had the remnants of Christmas. A little mistletoe over a doorway. A forgotten bauble. Half-price foot cream. Tess felt her guts lurch as she pushed in the doors to the College, wondering if there was talk about her new place of residence. The doors to the workshop were closed.

It was a long month, January, and though it had only started, Tess was trying to focus on spring, new life, new light. At times she felt relief and then sudden and overwhelming waves of guilt, mostly in the night when she would startle awake, not knowing where she was, feeling intense moments of failure. Some nights she would sit for hours looking out the window, hoping that she might come across Jennings and his crew so she could sit with them a while. Other nights she'd do some yoga, though the room was frustratingly small, or cut her fringe, paint her nails, put a mask on her face. Slowly, over time, her appetite for books returned.

She saw Faulks waiting under the tall stained-glass window like an old crow.

Happy New Year, Mrs Mahon, he said, formally.

She wondered did he know about her, as marriage

separation was technically a sackable offence. A deviation from the expected ethos.

Many happy returns, she called back.

Faulks could go fuck himself.

In the staffroom, Tadhg Foley was stood with his back to the door in a green army jumper. He was watching out the staffroom window as two dogs skidded across a frozen flood.

Hey, Tess said to teachers sat around the table staring into their cups. She coughed gently. David looked up from his newspaper, turned about and wished her a Happy New Year.

Happy New Year, Ms Mahon, Tadhg said, turning about. She was happy to see him. She coughed gently again and muttered something about having a good year in return. She filled a cup with boiling water at the Burco, dipping in a herbal teabag as she steadied herself. She thought about kissing his mouth hard in the Forge. She had surprised herself, and yet, she so wanted to do so again.

But when Tess turned back around, just when she had devised a smart comment about the jumper, something to break the ice, Tadhg was gone.

Eoin O'Neill parked his van at the door of the College and walked Jamie into school. The boy was quiet. He counted the seagulls on a statue. It was still empty on the College grounds as they had timed it before many students arrived off buses.

Hello, Eoin called, pushing in the heavy door, and holding it open for his son. He saluted Faulks under the stained glasses.

Good morning, straight to assembly in the Oratory, Faulks said, no messing.

I was wondering if I could have a word, please, in your office?

Faulks said: Oh yes, my apologies, doing a double take and realising Eoin was not a student. Certainly, certainly. You are meant to make an app— But Faulks stopped. Eoin was assertive, anger did this to him, and it threw Faulks who took his keys from his pocket, and jangling them, soon had the office door opened.

Jamie followed Eoin inside.

Perhaps we can speak alone? Might be best? Faulks said.

It concerns Jamie, Eoin said. So he stays.

The College filled him with dread. He was unsure in what capacity he returned there. Student or parent. He hated the smell of cabbage and paint, the same boys in the same frames with the same cocky sepia heads on them, looking down from the same walls with the same silver cups that no one but themselves could name. Tin cups that gave them a sense of achievement at a very young age, one that they brought all through their lives; that was both a blessing and a curse, and would, in time, prove both.

What's this in relation to? Faulks asked, hardening. I would really rather all appointments go through Ann.

Yes, Eoin said. But no one answers the phones on holidays, so here we all are.

OK, Faulks said slowly, so what can I do for you?

Here's the thing, Eoin said, Jamie and I went to the university for the New Year's Eve Maths Lecture.

Pardon? Faulks said, confused: Here, take a seat.

We went up to the university for the maths lecture over the break. Jamie goes every year, you see, he never misses a guest lecture in maths up in the university, since he was, well, since for ever.

Not technically *for ever*, Jamie interjected.

. . . but we were told this year that it is the College, you effectively, it is you who chooses the boy and that you had chosen young Piotr Pulaski, Eoin said.

Yes, you're correct, we did chose Piotr, which is, quite frankly, none of your business.

But it is my business, because Jamie has never missed a session—

—and I understand an altercation occurred on the concourse of the Arts Building, Faulks said, ignoring Eoin. I had Mrs Pulaska on to me, immediately. That poor woman was so upset.

Great, so one parent can make contact on the holidays, Eoin said, wryly.

I don't think you're in a position to come in here in such a manner, given what happened.

It was an accident, Eoin said. And with all due respect, you weren't there. Tit for tat at very best.

A young girl struck on the face by a boy who must be, Faulks eyed Jamie, who must be, what . . . six foot tall? And she required medical attention, doesn't sound like an accident to me.

Eoin stood up: Look here, Jamie shouldn't be expected to play second fiddle to Piotr Pulaski. I'm blue in the face trying to explain this to David.

Jamie looked at Eoin. He had no idea Eoin had spoken with David.

Are you happy here, James? Faulks asked.

Jamie stared at an image of Jesus: Sometimes. But no. I am not happy, he said. I am discontented especially around the Maths Award. And Boys One and Two and Three. They are not good.

Faulks looked at him. Then waited for a moment.

Tess is good though.

Tess? Faulks said. Please address Mrs Mahon correctly. And if you're not happy, perhaps best for you if you moved on. This school doesn't seem to fit your . . . your needs. There are plenty of other schools would . . . manage you better. A better fit, perhaps?

Now hang on a minute, Eoin said. Move where? There's not a lot of options for schools in Emory, in case you haven't noticed. There's a boys' school and a girls' school.

I'm not talking about an education in Emory, Mr O'Neill, oh no, there are plenty of buses to the city, and the boy would be . . . might be . . . happier with a lower teacher–student ratio? Faulks said. And as for Piotr Pulaski, not that I'm at liberty to discuss him specifically, but he is exemplary. Look, here's the thing, Mr O'Neill – and young James, he added as an afterthought – we look for an all-round boy to put forward for events, a boy that can maintain decorum, live up to the name of this College, and for that reason, Pulaski is the right boy. I have no doubt you're full of . . . of a . . . certain genius. I've read your test results. But that temper of yours, and singing out along the corridors, and all the nonsense that I've witnessed . . . it's not . . . desirable. Nor safe.

He gets overwhelmed, Eoin said. That's all, but it's not hard to . . . manage. He was explaining, and losing.

Don't we all, Mr O'Neill, now don't we all? But we control our impulses.

Then you understand, Eoin said, and so if you understand, perhaps you can empathise. I can't figure out how it is so difficult to plan . . . adequately.

Jamie's eyes darted around the office.

Faulks was silent now. He never filled a silence for the comfort of another. Besides, he was right about one thing, Eoin thought, they should have had the meeting alone.

Eoin walked to the door, and opening it, said: Well, this was a mistake, coming here, and as he took leave, he beckoned Jamie to follow.

Perhaps, Faulks replied. And, he added, I'm sorry if you feel that way.

Out on the corridor Jamie was clearly upset as Eoin fumed, feeling fourteen again. He was stuffing his phone into his back pocket when Tadhg Foley, opening the door of his workshop for Monday morning, spotted the pair.

Jamie! Tadhg said.

Mr Foley, Jamie said, singing his name twice. This is Mr Foley, Eoin.

Eoin O'Neill, Eoin said, walking to Tadhg and he stretched out his hand.

Eoin, nice to meet you at last, Tadhg, Tadhg Foley, he

said, returning the handshake. Look, come in, come in, Tadhg said, beckoning quickly with his hand, let's get off this corridor.

You sure? Eoin said.

Yes, sure, sure. I'm free until break time.

Inside the workshop, Jamie was deadly quiet. Nothing fired in his head, no ideas, nothing. An unnerving, blank exhaustion came over him, he wanted to sleep, overcome with the buzzing in his head that made him want to curl up and shut off.

You OK? Eoin said to him.

Yes, Jamie said, yawning, I'm very tired all of a sudden. He sat on the café chair.

This is incredible, Eoin called out, looking all around the workshop. It was never like this in my day.

Tadhg said: Did you take woodwork?

No, Eoin said, sadly. Latin. They didn't offer it then actually, this place was a swimming pool.

So I hear, Tadhg said.

Wow. It's just . . . fuck, it's beautiful, Eoin said, as he walked about the large frame of the currach.

Jamie piqued interest.

Thanks, your son is the mastermind, Tadhg said.

He said so. But I never expected . . . I just never— He cut off mid-sentence.

No, Jamie said . . . it is not really me, mine.

What's left to finish it? Eoin asked.

We have to sew and stick the canvas, then tar it. Keeping an eye on the weather for the next few weeks, as with all the lads helping Jamie, I'd rather do it outside, and, then there's some work on the thole pins, and the last tacking.

Jamie stood up and the three of them walked around the boat's frame.

And oars? Eoin said.

They're done, I've two senior lads that join us, and they're great. Tadhg took Eoin over by the tall breeze blocks and showed him the long oars.

Yes, Jonesy and O'Toole, Jamie said, quietly.

You like boats? Tadhg said.

I don't honestly have much of a clue about them, Eoin said and then paused, but my . . . I mean, Jamie, Jamie's mum, Noelle, her father, Jack Doyle, he made them . . . currachs. He was a fisherman in Emory, Eoin said. She loved them . . . loved water.

Jamie stared at Eoin. His feet were fizzy. His head spun.

Jamie mentioned her. I'm terribly sorry, Tadhg said.

Eoin nodded.

We're working on the skin all weekend. It would be great if you could join us? Tadhg said. It's not weather dependent until we get to tarring her.

Sure, I'd love to, Eoin said, running his hands along the gunwales.

It, Jamie said. It's an it. Not a her. And besides, you're busy, Eoin, you're busy on Fridays and Saturdays.

It can wait, Eoin said.

I could do with another pair of stitching hands, Tadhg said. It's the part I'm least confident with.

Marie, Eoin said. Jamie's gran. My mother, she'd love to.

Great, Tadhg said.

See you Friday, Eoin said, if my temper dissolves.

Faulks? Tadhg said as he started sweeping sawdust into a little hillock.

Yes.

Want me to have a word?

Any point? Eoin said.

Not so sure to tell you the truth, Tadhg said. Doubtful.

Yeah, Eoin said. Seems like a man who's fairly fixed in his ideas.

A lizard brain in the body of a man, and little else, Jamie said. He's a prawn effectively, all body and no brain.

Tadhg and Jamie were alone in the workshop now, and Jamie was happiest, like the early days, but Tadhg started up with some difficult questions.

Tadhg pressed him: But what's this about you throwing a bottle at Piotr Pulaski's sister?

Jamie said nothing but his eyes widened and he put his head back as far as it could go, a habit from early childhood.

Everyone hears bad news, Jamie, Tadhg said, especially around here. Around here – they seem to wait for it. I can still see you, even with your head back!

It was an accident. I kicked her Coke bottle after she took a bottle flip, and it hit me, the liquid was spraying, and when I kicked it, it hit her face. It was just an accident.

Why did you kick the bottle in the first place?

Because she flipped it at me.

No, she didn't, she flipped it indiscriminately and hit you by accident. You going to have a fit every time someone crosses your path?

Semantics, Jamie said and shook his head. I was angry, angry with Piotr, he said finally. He took my place. I was mad and sad. I am overlooked.

No, Jamie, you're not overlooked. But he got his own place, and if Faulks wants to run this school on a manners-and-achievement basis, then he can. It doesn't make it right. But it is what it is.

It's not right. Her drink was fizzing all over me.

Look, them's the breaks, kiddo, Tadhg said, looking at Jamie from a workbench. You going to kick back at everything that hurts?

No.

No. You sure?

Jamie nodded.

Right, grab some sandpaper. I was thinking we should launch the boat, soon.

Soon? Jamie said.

Yeah, maybe your birthday.

My birthday?

Yes, what is it with you always reframing questions with a question?

Mr Foley?

Yeah, Tadhg said.

I have an idea.

You do?

Yes, for the boat. I have an idea for its originality piece, after it's tarred.

And?

We'll paint it.

Right, Tadhg said, a little deflated.

Jamie said: I'm working on inventing a colour, a shade of red. I visited Mr Bacon's studio at the Hugh Lane Gallery, and the paint cans struck me, just something about the crudeness of them, and then for many days I did a close inspection of all of his paintings.

You separating the artist from the art, Jamie?

Not really. But, maybe willing to . . . I don't know . . . You have heard of Yves Klein blue? Jamie said, changing course.

No, Tadhg said.

It's an invention of a blue by the French artist Yves Klein made from pure colour pigment, relies heavily on ultramarine to evoke the immateriality and boundlessness of his own vision of the world.

And what's your vision?

Vantablack. Like today, there can be no blacker.

Tadhg laughed.

But I'm not painting the boat a colour that takes so much energy from the sun, the sun is under enough pressure as it is, like you said, and after consideration – if I used Vantablack on the boat it would in fact reduce Global Warming, taking all that energy from the sun – but then I thought, we would probably need a million boats on the River Brú for that and the river is also under enough pressure as it is. So that's counter-productive, right?

Is that a joke?

Yes. Jamie stood with his hands hanging down by his hips. I love red. And . . . as you are a fan of Bacon, I'm wondering if you're familiar with the *Study of Red Pope*?

Yes.

The purple hue flooding the picture reminds me of veins. I have a thing about veins.

You have a thing about everything, Tadhg said.

. . . the systems of them, and the red is regal, and Dyer comes face to face with the Pope. I'm not mad about the nose on the Pope, it's a very ugly nose, but then again noses are ugly, and I think that's where the satire is built in. Analysing art is tough, as you know, but I am drawn to the colour.

That's wonderful, Tadhg said.

Jamie then said on one long out-breath: Problem is I am drawn to many colours, so I like the purple red, but I also like yellow. I liked the sycamore leaves turning yellow the day we went, when we collected the willows. I like the Japanese idea of sitting among trees, and just talking to them, and I like ladybirds, red ones, and I like the yellow gum boots with daisies left by the stile in the woods. They remind me of when I was small. Did you know that no one has retrieved them yet? And that makes me feel something.

Tadhg said: Sad?

No. Not sad. I don't know. Jamie shrugged, an unusual gesture for him. But something. I like the sun, and Marie always bakes me a yellow birthday cake. I have no idea of the why of that. But I also like the green wool of Maryam Mirzakhani's jumper. And here you are in class in a green jumper.

But why don't you just focus on your favourite red?

Yes. See, it is to do with the red of my mother's swimsuit. I think I can make a red, with a yellow and a green hue. And a purple? Well, that's what I'm working on. I

255

don't think I want it to be the exact same shade. But then I think that the fear surrounding that, is that I might fail?

I think you can do whatever you set that mind of yours to, Jamie. Do you think you'd be letting her down?

Jamie ignored the last comment. I use an app I have. *Pantone Create*. It'll be less messy that way.

Tadhg laughed. That maths lecture is up on YouTube, he said, the one you missed in the university, as he tapped the laptop. How about we both watch it?

Jamie said: Yes, let's, his mind filled with teeming reds pouring out in front of him.

They watched the mathematician curl and scribble and speak at an alarmingly fast rate and Tadhg was almost drifting off to sleep when Tess Mahon slipped into the back of the workshop and she too stood watching the screen for a moment and then she sat on a bench in the shadow of the boat, noting how beautiful it was, and how fragile.

Hi, Tadhg said when he saw Tess, and lifting himself up he walked over to her.

Hi – she said, whispering.

Look – they both said at the same time.

You go, Tadhg said –

No, no you first, she said.

I'm sorry, he whispered. I hope it's, you've been OK?

No, I'm fine. It's grand, she whispered.

Tadhg paused. He wanted to ask her whereabouts. It had irritated him how much he longed to know where she was, if she fucked off back to Paul, if she fucked Paul, all that she had been up to. Oh right, was all Tadhg said.

You were right, she said, I needed time, and I needed

to be on my own, and look – thanks again, I don't know what I would have done without you. But I feel very silly. Again. Third time.

I feel like I abandoned you, Tadhg said. Her absence made him slightly desperate.

No, not at all.

You're sure we're OK? Tadhg said, uneasy now.

I'm sure, she said.

She sat by Jamie as he watched the end of the lecture.

Tadhg was edgy now. So edgy he couldn't distract his thoughts, so he went to print off the Bacon Pope and framed it in silence as Tess and Jamie left.

He stayed in the workshop during break. He needed to avoid her. To avoid the staffroom. Tess was taking up all of his thoughts for days now. He found himself wondering what she'd think of his every movement throughout any given day. He was unsure that a woman who was so resilient could even allow herself to be loved. He thought about what colour the boy would concoct. About what happens when you allow people in. How you need to be vulnerable to allow another, just to be. But then he thought about how that can all go wrong. He watched the two male figures, the Pope and Dyer, how they were so controlled in Bacon's painting, though having an outburst, as though it is the condition of man, of the way Tadhg feels all the time. Is he Dyer or is he the Pope? Does it matter? It is most likely that he is neither, but he cannot settle himself to think this logically. Has everyone these parts inside them? In the painting, he thinks, Dyer always seems ready to turn off the light.

25

Tadhg spent Friday evening in the College, alone. He worked through to morning. He was tetchy about the canvas: it was the part of the boat that worried him. Being in the Forge now felt suddenly lonely without Tess, which was ridiculous, he knew that. But to that end, he had stayed in school and measured and remeasured the currach with Jamie on Friday afternoon. The wood laths, and gunwales and rods looked perfect, everything had settled, but he was always shy of the cutting. You couldn't patch it perfectly if you made a mistake. And this haunted him.

Some currach makers assemble the skin by using brown paper between two layers of canvas, some use animal hide, like Tadhg's grandfather, the most traditional approach – drying, then nailing hide over the skeleton. But growing up watching his grandfather, Tadhg was always overwhelmed by the feeling that there was not enough skin to cover the boat, and for some reason, the animals never felt dead to him. He did not like the feel of a currach that had its skin or canvas patched together, for in a storm, he knew this part of the construction was weak. Tadhg's grandfather would bring a half-pound of butter onto the boat, rub it into the skin when things got rough along the way.

Tadhg had loved going out to the ferry with his grand-father, watching all the currachs taking off from the har-bour, the boats filled with old men, dressed in skinny black trousers, worn boots, shirts tied up to the chin, caps on their heads backwards. Everyone spoke Gaeilge, the lan-guage Tadhg liked best. English felt like a traitor's tongue or a trespass into somewhere he didn't belong.

Tadhg lay down in the corner of the workshop on that Friday night, head on his jacket, but sleep didn't come for hours.

He worried he had offered Jamie too much.

He worried he had offered Tess too little.

At half past six on Saturday morning, a loud banging woke him.

I'm coming, he called out. One minute, he said, con-fused by his surroundings. The banging stopped. Then started up again.

Opening the doors of the workshop, he tossed his hair down with the palm of his hand.

Hello, Tadhg said.

O'Toole was stood there with his hood up.

You OK? Tadhg said.

O'Toole could not look at him.

Hi, he said, look, I'm sorry. Glad I caught you before the lads arrive.

Yeah, yeah sure, Tadhg said. That's OK. Come in.

Did you get the canvas sorted? O'Toole asked, moving inside the workshop.

Yes. Took a little time, I hope I'm right. Guess there's only one way to find out.

Shit, did you sleep here?

Tadhg nodded: I stayed, but not much sleep I'm afraid.

This place would creep me out, staying here, O'Toole said and ran his hand along the boat. Looks great, he said, quietly.

Tadhg asked: You OK?

Yeah, grand, he said rustling about.

Sure?

I'm good.

So can you stitch? Tadhg asked him.

Not a hope, O'Toole said pulling down the strings of his hood either side of his chin. He paced about. Thing is, Mr Foley, I can't stay, he said as he unravelled a dream-catcher caught up in its own string.

Right. That's OK, Tadhg said, we have loads of help, too many maybe, as I've only two sewing machines. But I'll need you later for painting.

No, he said, I can't. Thing is, Mr Foley, I can't help with the boat any more.

Is something wrong?

I'm also not allowed to continue woodwork. Dad hit the roof when Faulks told him how long I was spending here.

Right, Tadhg said. You don't like it?

No, I do.

He doesn't like it? Tadhg said. Your father?

Something like that.

O'Toole had taken woodwork as an extra subject. He eyed the cabinet he had made out of recycled woods he'd found down by the Brú. The boy was gifted.

Is it too much with your other subjects? Is it the HPAT?

No, it's not . . . O'Toole was struggling. I love the subject . . . you know. It's been. Fun.

Fun? Tadhg said. Here, make yourself useful, let's have a look at this canvas, and be sure we've it measured and tacked right.

O'Toole looked at the measurements. Faulks and my dad brought me in, O'Toole said finally as he worked.

Tadhg asked: In?

Over Christmas, they called us into the Palace.

The Bishop's Palace? Tadhg questioned.

I know. Mad, O'Toole said. Place gives me the creeps.

What for?

To tell me I was a disgrace.

What?

Going around with a motley crew . . .

Motley crew?

You and the boy, Jonesy and Terry I guess. The boat crew, they kept saying. They're not . . . He paused. They don't like you, they don't think you're the right influence.

Tadhg laughed. And what do you think?

He shrugged. They don't like me hanging around with Jonesy either and let's just say, they aren't impressed by Ms Mahon's father.

Ms Mahon can't help where she comes from, O'Toole.

O'Toole nodded, and pulled the drawstrings of his hoody.

I thought they loved Jonesy, Tadhg said, he's in the god-squad? Is he not the right sort of influence either?

O'Toole laughed. You could say – something like that. He's only in their *squad* because he's captain of the football team. They don't love him, Foley, they use him.

Right, and what have they against practical subjects? Tadhg already knew the answer.

Practical subjects are for the weak of mind, apparently, that they had a place, but not for gentlemen. I'm not meant . . . I'm not even meant to be here, they asked me not to talk to you again.

And what do you think? Tadhg said, threading a large leather needle, and leaving it tacked to the canvas on both sides.

I'm not meant to think. My father and Faulks will pay for my education.

Faulks. How so? Surely your family are in a position . . .

Yes, of course, but another . . . tradition . . . the College . . . They have digs and perks in a university.

The church? Tadhg said.

Yup.

And do you want to study medicine and live in their holy digs?

No.

Did you tell them?

O'Toole raised an eyebrow. No.

Tadhg nodded and leaned against the boat, folded his arms.

O'Toole said: All my family went into law, I'm the last son but I have no interest, I've listened to my father all my life going on about the courts. So medicine is my only other choice. Tell you the truth, I get weak at the sight of blood.

Does your father know how you feel?

No. But I have no choice.

So it's the easy route for you, that's what you're trying to tell me? It's no skin off my nose if you leave the group, O'Toole, but you're doing this voluntarily and from what I see, from September, you've been coming in here at all times of the day, giving up free time. That's dedication and if life's taught me anything, we go to what we love, eventually – we mightn't find it straight away, but we get there.

O'Toole stared at Foley.

Tadhg said: No such thing as a free lunch.

O'Toole didn't flinch.

Come on, the church paying for grinds and digs. I'm guessing your brothers have been through it?

We don't talk about it.

You'll do medicine and maybe you'll finish, who knows? But I know those places, paying for education, all fire and brimstone, that organisation, they feed into boards of hospitals and schools. You're bright – so I'll level with you, you're not getting nothing for nothing here, kiddo. And so to really escape, because you will eventually, because you have a mind of your own . . . you do know that, right? So hopefully you'll use it, some day. But you can only be in or out of your family, O'Toole, there's no middle ground.

O'Toole put his hands behind his head, leaned back. They're family, he said.

True. But that Head Boy nonsense, you not exhausted with the workload, telling back on teachers?

I don't do that.

Maybe, but it's part of the job right?

It's unwritten, O'Toole said.

But rewarded?

Sure, sure, especially for boys, boys like Jonesy, but you know he can get perks if he gives certain information.

Tadhg shot him a look. *Gives certain information?* And does he?

I don't know, O'Toole replied. We don't talk about it.

There are other scholarships. There's a great design college in Letterfrack, where I went, some of the best design and wood and eco projects coming out of there. We could look into it?

O'Toole shook his head.

Tadhg said: You're an adult.

I owe them.

You owe them?

I respect them, I have always worked hard to make them proud. He was growing defensive now, surly.

I came in to be polite, to say I couldn't continue with your boat.

Doesn't take much to ruffle you, O'Toole.

It's the fucking system, Foley. We play the system. It's not my fault, the system . . .

Ah. So as the Head Boy or Proc or whatever of this *great* College – well, you've got a bit of sway, right?

It's not like that. He shook his head.

You have a bit more than say, Terry or Jonesy? Right?

You have Faulks's ear. The board. And definitely more than Jamie, right?

I never looked at it like this.

Have you ever had this conversation with Faulks, about picking favourites? All the crazy shit he spouts about being top, being a man, all this shit that leaves so many out? Tadhg said.

We don't give opinions.

Just observations.

O'Toole nodded.

So basically you are a snitch? Think now though, if you think for yourself . . . you are capable of thinking for yourself?

Why the fuck are you giving me such a hard time? Plenty of other losers in this place.

Losers? Tadhg said.

You know what I mean, O'Toole said.

Hey, you're the one in my workshop at six a.m. on a Saturday. You came to me. Remember?

And then, suddenly, O'Toole started to cry. I have you all, coming at me, from all sides. I can't make the fucking boat. That's all. I just came . . .

That's OK.

I can't, you know they said it's not giving off the right impression? It's beneath the place.

Don't let me hold you if we're beneath you, Tadhg said, stung.

Look, I just came in . . . to try to explain.

You came in to be polite, to abandon your responsibilities. And you thought I'd understand, and feel sorry for your big position in the big world.

No, O'Toole said, suddenly. No, I came in to say thanks. It's been really great, it has. I am sorry.

Sorry? Tadhg said, looking up at him.

For letting you down.

You haven't let me down, Tadhg said, sharply. You've let the group down. But when someone puts pressure on you, you'll always bend and some day you will wonder who the fuck took your life, because you certainly won't have it.

Fuck you, O'Toole said, tears in his eyes now. Fuck you, he said again, finally, and he drew the hoody strings tight around his narrow face and walked out.

Path to hell paved with polite fucking nonsense, O'Toole, Tadhg said as O'Toole walked out.

26

Marie O'Neill felt out of place on Saturday morning in the workshop as she half-leaned against a bench. Jamie was going about humming, desperately unsure where to put her. She was unsure where to put her handbag. She had considered leaving it at home on the counter, but changed her mind at the last minute, and wondered how men go about with phones, tissues and whatever else they need to navigate the world, all stuffed in their pockets.

Jonesy was by the breeze blocks, polishing one of the larch oars with a soft cloth and linseed oil. The other oar was resting against the wall. He was waiting for O'Toole to arrive to polish it, undecided as to whether they were going with one thole pin or two, but O'Toole wasn't in yet. So Jonesy turned to Jamie who was chattering nervously and kept naming different types of wood for Marie. Relief flooded her when Terry's mum, Abba, arrived. She was immediately warm and open like her son.

Jamie, Jonesy said. Come here a sec. Jamie, he said again.

Yes, Jamie said, turning about.

These oars, Jamie, right, here's the thing, so we have

seen the double thole pins, and the single one of the more simple design, what do you think we should go for? Like, I'm favouring the Boyne currach and going for a single, but I wouldn't mind a second opinion.

Hmmm, Jamie said, anxious at the question, and though he understood and knew how he wished to reply, he took a moment. Tess had been telling him to take time, wait-and-breathe time, it helped to compose him.

Jamie went over and lifted the long oar.

What do you think, Jonesy? Jamie said.

I think what you think, Jamie, Jonesy said, smiling at him.

One pin as a lever makes most sense, because, if we look at it like a fulcrum and if we consider the angle from the pressure exerted, and versus the pressure of the water—

Suddenly he stopped himself.

One it is then, Jonesy said, it's your boat. And besides, you're the genius.

Jamie was excited now, and though it was weird (very weird) and strange to see both Eoin and Marie in the College, it relaxed him (also weird).

I'm not . . . a genius. There is no such thing. For instance I cannot play football. I cannot coordinate myself, Jamie said in a fast gush to Jonesy. In fact I have no spatial genius whatsoever and if I am not careful, I am prone to a quick topple down the stairs. Sometimes I think my head is too heavy for my body.

Everyone's head is too big for their body, Jonesy said.

Arsenal man, only team a sane man should support, Terry said to Eoin, laughing.

Get away, such nonsense, Eoin said, jesting. You any good?

Yes, I'm great, Terry said. I'm the best striker in my club, under-fifteens. And I'm only thirteen.

This was true. Terry was a talent, but Eoin hadn't expected him to be so assured. You play round here? Eoin said.

In the College? No, no, the Father, Father Faulks, he doesn't allow us play. It's an English game, a foreign game, Terry said.

Nothing's changed then? Eoin said.

I'm afraid not, Mr O'Neill. Terry shook his head. I play for United in the city.

Great team, Eoin said.

Abba and Marie threaded the industrial sewing machines, one Abba had borrowed from a curtain shop she cleaned for in Emory, and one Marie had borrowed from the Bishop's Palace. Without permission.

Right, Tadhg said.

Everyone turned to face him.

So today we need to stitch the canvas, and it's not something that I'm confident about.

What? Abba said. She wanted the day to start with confidence. You can sew? she said, taking control, and we can sew and we can see the boat, so we can see how to cover it, then you are fine, yes? Yes? We are all fine. This is not a hard job, you men – you overthink everything, she said, crossly.

Marie and Abba went back around the boat's skeleton, touching it as they talked about nipping and tucking as though it were about to undergo surgery.

269

It will be all-just-finefinefine. And Marie and me here, we will show you boys how to finish a job, you will have your boat, Jamie, and such a nice thing you're doing to remember your mother.

Silence fell heavy and fast in the workshop.

Jonesy looked at Jamie, and so did Terry.

Soon all eyes were on Jamie.

Jamie froze. Eoin looked at Marie.

True, Marie said. So terrible to lose a mother – to lose anyone really when you are young, life is hard enough, hard enough to be a boy without your mam, Marie said, or dad, she added, remembering Terry had never met his dad.

I think it's worse to lose your mam, Terry said.

And Jamie said: Why?

Eoin stood there, unsure whether to lean in or out, until Jamie said, defensively: Eoin knows *stuff*. A lot of stuff. He's very knowledgeable in areas. He considered Terry. Especially football, Terence. And the club you like, he knows everything about that, about all of the soccer clubs of the United Kingdom, even that one that sounds like a weapon –

Arsenal? Eoin said.

Yes, Jamie said, and Eoin knows about film and also how to plumb almost *any tricky situation* under a sink, and he knows how to cook moules-frites.

Terry said: To cook what?

Moules-frites, Terence, Abba said, like from that little place next to Liverpool Street Station where we used to go to?

Ah, yes, Terry said. Gross. Slimy fish, you like slimy fish, Jamie? So gross. I'm surprised.

Jamie knew it wasn't the correct time to proffer his dislike for cold fish in wet onions. Yes, I like it very much, he said.

I don't know about you, Marie O'Neill, but I could get very used to this, Abba said as Jonesy poured milk in her tea.

Maybe, Marie said, shyly, but it makes me feel uncomfortable too.

What? Abba said. Oh I see, I see, Marie, you like to be in charge, in charge of minding the boys. The boys should mind you, we are old now, no? Abba said, laughing, and Marie looked down at her fleece and her leggings.

Abba, you're not old, said Marie.

And Abba replied: No, I just feel old.

And Jamie saw how two women who had never met before took to talking at length, and even when they lifted the needles in the machines to begin to sew, they were still chattering.

Tess didn't turn up on Saturday morning, no matter how many times Tadhg watched the door, willing her to walk through.

He took to pulling and fanning the canvas in and out in places, it was beginning to shape like bleached whites on a green in Connemara. It was beginning to resemble a currach.

Joe would love this, Marie said.

Joe? Abba asked.

My husband. I lost him some years back, Marie said.

Oh, I am so sorry, Abba offered.

Thank you, Marie said, kindly. Are you married yourself?

No, no, I was. But I lost mine too. Not like you though. One minute he was there, the next, he disappeared, vanished, just after Terence was born. I am very clumsy with personal belongings.

And then they laughed so hard, Abba couldn't catch her breath.

Over by the prints, Jamie talked to Eoin about the Pope and Bacon and the colour red that he was mixing, and he showed him the final colour, in ten-part gradients, on Tadhg's laptop.

Mr Foley has ordered this paint in Galway, Jamie said. It is a specialised place.

It's really something, Eoin said.

By evening, they all lifted the canvas over the frame of the boat. Tadhg and Eoin stood at the bow, with Jamie and Terry at the back end. Jonesy, Marie, Ellie and Abba all stood along the sides, pulling it hard.

Just then, Jamie clapped and clapped and said: It fits on like a glove,

and right then,

a cliché was accurate.

Sunday promised a long dry spell, so they brought it to the pitch for painting.

It was the first time it was carried.

Jamie was standing under it at the bow, and the group lifted it up and over his head. Jamie chose Eoin to carry the back – despite it being so light he could have carried it on his own.

Outside on the pitches was muddy and damp, and they used the back of an old trailer to stabilise it. Jamie hated the smell of the paint, the speed that you needed to move with big gulping brushloads of it.

Terry and Eoin moved fast with their brushes. Terry didn't stop until the very last stroke was lashed on.

Later that evening as Tadhg was locking up the workshop, and everyone had gone home, he grabbed his wax jacket, and checked his phone. He'd had a text earlier from Tess in the morning.

> Sorry I won't make today.
> But wish Jamie all the best and I'll pop in on
> Monday, Tess

He was quick to respond without thought:

> All OK? T

There was an urgency to it. Tess replied:

> I'm fine. Just Brooke's rooms are so pokey,
> needed air. Sorry again. Did it go OK?

Tadhg didn't reply but he walked quickly out of the College. Outside the front door, he turned right, automatically, and allowing impulse to carry him for the first time in years, he turned left towards town and stayed walking until he found himself at the Square. His hands were covered in black paint that he peeled off as he walked. And though it was late, there was a stretch to the evening's light, purple crocuses budding and tentative green shoots of daffodil heads poking through the ebony soil in some window pots.

27

The small bar in Brooke's was much like the hotel bar on the island. Tadhg stooped under the low door and entered the cavern filled up with dark woods, polished tables, some brass, and purple and green flowers on heavy curtains that were never closed. A small bucket of ice sat on the bar counter and on TV a golf tournament was under way. The bar was empty.

What can I get you? the barman said, wiping the counter. He flicked a beer mat down.

Just a coffee thanks, Tadhg said.

Milk, sugar?

Neither, he said, tipping his head to the barman.

Great, I'll bring it over.

Tadhg sat under the front window looking at a golfer on the TV attempt a swing.

Tess was upstairs in her room, lying on the bloated bedspread. She had turned off the golf and was watching a programme about home improvements when Tadhg called her. A man on the telly was making a large expansive window at the back of a house, for a couple with three small children. She wondered how they would keep the glass free of small handprints. Then worried if it was reinforced glass.

It was unusual for Tess's phone to ring and it startled her. She answered immediately. On hanging up she shot up from the bed and glanced in the mirror by the cream kettle, itself plonked beside a line of books. Two beer bottles floated in a jug of ice that had turned to warm water, and the wet labels had slipped off. She quickly sponged some make-up across her face and licked a mascara wand down her oily lashes. She pulled on a clean sweater, pulled it off, pulled on another one. V-neck, red. And just as she was about to walk out the door, she turned, and sprayed a perfume, then walked through it.

Hey, Tadhg said, smiling as he looked up from his coffee when she approached.

Hi, she said. Nice surprise.

She sat opposite him, as the waiter came quick from behind the bar, wiped the table and laid a coaster down.

A beer, Tom, she said, please.

Any preference?

Tess said: Cold.

Tom nodded, lifting the hatch and slipping back inside the bar.

How have you been? Tadhg said.

Well, you know, OK.

What are the rooms like? He lifted his cup to finish the last of his coffee.

Small and dark. But weirdly liberating, she added then,

I think I need it, needed it, you know. It's comfortable, or comforting, I don't know.

Did you speak with Paul?

Yeah, she said, a couple of times.

How'd that go?

Messy.

You OK?

She shook her head. It was . . . bad, she said finally. It was awful, in fact.

I'm sorry to hear that, he said. He was sorry but he was relieved she hadn't returned to him. It had been driving him mad with jealousy, thinking of her returned to the house.

We just had to have it out, you know, and now I don't think it was the best thing. I am here since leaving you, she said, correcting herself . . . the Forge . . .

Look here, about that, Tadhg said, fiddling with his silver ring.

There's nothing to be said, she said. Please, don't.

Of course, Tadhg said, nodding. But, please, I wasn't rejecting you, and I don't know if that's how you took it.

It wasn't, Tess said. I was a mess.

You weren't, Tadhg said, quickly. Christmas drags up so much, then he leaned in and pinched the skin on her hand. OK, then you were a bit of a mess. And they laughed, all the blood gushing from you.

Hardly, she said, smirking.

He wanted to say he desired her. That he wanted to fuck her. Or that she did make him feel as though he wanted to lean in and kiss her, he wanted to say he was filled up with desire, that he regretted asking her to leave,

277

that seeing her in school was hard. But that was nonsense, he thought, stupid infatuation, childish shit. And he didn't like feeling out of control, but in the next moment, he desperately wanted to see what her room was like, what she might look like in the half-light.

Paul was nasty, she said, but quid pro quo, I guess.

I guess, Tadhg said, quietly.

Tom left down a bottle of beer. Glass? he asked.

She shook her head.

I mean, and from what you've told me, Tadhg said. And I know these things are complex, but sometimes . . . sometimes there's just an asshole, you know. An asshole is an asshole . . .

Is an asshole, Tess said, and smiled. But what of the asshole of the asshole?

That's a lot of assholes.

They laughed.

That's the thing though, Tess said. I don't trust myself.

He looked at her: How?

It's my story of a story, marriage, it's all a story you know – she was filling up with tears, her mouth, watering. She hadn't cried in weeks. I don't know what I'm at. I have no plan.

No plan is good, Tadhg said.

Is it? she said. And it's better if you're not nice to me. She was crying as she lifted the bottle to her mouth.

Do you want me to give out?

She smiled, no, fuck no, she said.

Tess, take a break, you've planned all your life. Breathe.

*

Tess had indeed been planning her whole life, even as a kid: how to get to school, how to make a lunch, where to buy a uniform, how to set alarms, to cook meals, to fill out forms, to have two keys at all times, to have some runaway money, to have emergency money, to water down the spirit bottles at home, to make excuses, all of the excuses why friends couldn't come over, in the end it is easier not to make friends, to be guarded, to self-protect at all costs. To keep going, to keep going. She started crying hard now.

Look, Tadhg said, it's a huge thing, marriage ending.

Is it? she said.

I don't actually know, Tadhg said. But it seems enormous.

That's right, she said, Mr I-Don't-Do-Relationships.

Yes, he said. I don't.

They were quiet as the telly replayed a golf shot over and over on some arid course in a Midwestern US town.

Lucky, Tess said.

Skill, Tadhg said. Jamie's going to launch the boat on his birthday and it'd mean a lot if you came. Just for the launch.

She nodded. I feel terrible for missing the weekend.

No, don't, he's doing great, Tadhg said. Even seems to be in Terry's company more and more now.

He's a great kid, Terry.

Tadhg nodded, then leaned across the table and clasped Tess's hands in his. Look, I'm not going to say it's not you it's me or anything, don't panic. And he smiled. I didn't come here for that. I just wanted to check in, you know.

She nodded.

And then Tadhg said, quickly, fearful he'd change his mind: It's not you it's us. It's a bad time is all . . . Tadhg didn't finish his sentence.

Tess shook her head. I don't think so, she said, I think you'll never know the right time. He gripped her hand tight.

The relationships, the phobia, it's not from nowhere, Tadhg offered. I have . . . He paused.

The habit of speaking in double negatives? Tess said.

Yes, it's a bit like that, Tadhg said. I didn't know my father, he said and pulled his hand away.

I thought he drowned, Tess said.

My stepfather drowned, Tadhg said. But I never knew my own father, my mother had me when she was very young, and no one ever spoke about it. I think that's . . . He coughed gently and watched the golf momentarily.

They never mentioned on the island how much taller and broader Tadhg Foley was than all of his fair and waif-like siblings that came after, everyone knew and no one knew anything real, no one offered anything tangible to tell him, explain.

Tadhg said: And I worry.

Worry? Tess said.

I worry that if I can't know, you know, if I don't know where I've come from . . . and I imagine it to be some awful act, or something ferocious.

Oh, Tadhg, Tess said. But it might not be. You can't think that of yourself.

True, Tadhg said. He sat up straight and folded his arms. She should have told me, you know, my mother, I've asked so many times.

So that's why you left?

Yes.

It fucking haunts me, and I can't, you know, he said as he drew in a sharp breath. I really wanted you, just to know, but that's selfish. I wanted to tell you. And then I really wanted you . . . but I can't encroach on you. Your . . .

Tess said: My marriage is over.

Just, he said. Just over.

It's over, Tess said. That's enough. It's all you need to know and Tadhg, you can't carry this around with you for ever, so many of us are from chaos. Jamie would say the whole world is chaos, and she leaned towards him. Wouldn't be here without the chaos.

Deep, Tadhg said, laughing, as he considered kissing her.

Another beer, Tess called to Tom, turning her head and gesturing her empty bottle in his direction.

And you? Tom said to Tadhg,

Same, Tadhg said as a golfer on the TV walked around the ball, eyed it, lifted his trousers up at the knee, then kneeled down in a squat and squinted, bobbed up and down, and up again.

28

Marie dressed quickly in the cold of her bedroom. Downstairs she lifted a cake box from the fridge, and gathered bags to go next door.

Eoin answered the door in his jocks.

Good morning, she said. Late night? She eyed his shorts.

Good morning, Mam, he said.

Jamie was dressed in his school uniform, and walked carefully downstairs as both of them cried out Happy Birthday.

Thank you, he said.

Fourteen is a great age, Marie said. Here, and she handed him a rectangular box, open it. She left a bright yellow cake down on the counter in the kitchen.

Jamie said: But I know what it is.

No, you don't, she said.

He opened his present of red Converse with bright yellow soles.

He smiled.

I had them made up. Abba said you can get these colourful runners online and we tried our best to match it to the Jamie-red of the boat.

Thank you, Jamie said.

How did we do? Marie asked.

Not bad, Eoin said. Not bad at all, he said again, holding the shoes and inspecting them.

It is a little off, I see some light hues of cerise pink, Jamie said. But that's OK, I like them, and he put the shoes on.

Across town, Terry and Abba walked to the College,
and Tadhg came in from the Forge,
and Jonesy was excited to see if the boat would float,
Tess was finishing up her first hotel breakfast,
and O'Toole was by the front door keeping watch for Faulks, on sentry duty for when they all started to arrive.

Hey, Jonesy said.

Faulks isn't happy, O'Toole said.

He's never happy, Jonesy said.

Look, thing is, O'Toole said, we know this launch is going ahead today, and Faulks is unhappy. He thinks it all looks very . . . common. So best just do it quick, with little fuss.

Jonesy laughed. And what do you think, O'Toole? He said, hopping a football on his foot to his hands.

O'Toole shrugged.

The fuck's a shrug mean? Jonesy asked.

If you go ahead with launching the boat, or taking part, O'Toole said, then Faulks said there's going to be repercussions.

There's repercussions to everything, Jonesy said, to every fucking move you make, O'Toole. And every move you don't. He left the football on the ground under his foot.

Is that a song, Jonesy?

I believe it is. Or it very likely might be, he said laughing as he pinched the back of the pin in his lapel and removed it, handing it to O'Toole.

You can give it back to him, O'Toole, he said.

Inside, the workshop was bustling.

The currach was waiting out on the pitches, tarred black, and the laths and inside were Jamie-red.

Terry brought over kids from Form 1A and Jamie was being wished Happy Birthday by students he could number but not name.

Right, kiddo, Tadhg said, sensing Jamie was overwhelmed. Come on with me. A wave of relief flooded Jamie as he left the workshop with Tadhg. They went outside and walked across the wet pitches.

I know, Happy Birthday, said Tadhg. How d'you feel? Feet out of the end of the bed?

Don't be absurd, Jamie said. It is a bittersweet day, he said. You know, good and bad. Fourteen is an even number. And you know. Noelle.

I know, Tadhg said.

They arrived at the currach, its black arch imposing on the green of the pitch. The strips of Jamie-red on the gunwales were electric.

She's beautiful, Tadhg said.

It, Mr Foley. It. *Every* time, Jamie said slowly.

I'm sorry, just a habit. *It's* beautiful. I have some things for you, Tadhg said, lifting off his rucksack, some bog cotton, Tadhg said, and here's a little jar filled up with soil.

Soil? Jamie said.

You put it in the currach for your safe return, Jamie.
You come back to the land you left.

Very reassuring, Jamie said.

Soon, everyone else came out with Tess, giddy on the pitch.

And then with six hands they lifted the currach over
their heads. Jonesy and Terry at the back and Jamie at the
front, and the three set off, walking in the direction of the
river, through the woods.

Jamie could only see the laths and smell the woods, as
Tadhg directed them over scrub and through the forest. It
was light enough for Jamie alone, but he was glad of things
in threes. Glad of Terry and Jonesy.

The willows they had replanted looked tender and
fragile. Sometimes it felt like this town could die but for
this river. They walked on, the group in their wake chattering and busy like sparrows, growing now with students
as the word got out.

David joined the walk, lost in his big anorak, and some
other teachers who had periods off came to watch, sipping
out of coffee cups. David remarked to Tess that he had had
no idea a boat was being constructed in the school, no idea
whatsoever he said a number of times, and shook his head.
But no one had any idea about anyone else in that school,
about their lives, or trauma, their business, or about the
weight they carried, Tess thought to herself.

The River Brú was high from snow that had fallen in
late January, and the water was quiet now. Snowdrops
were courageously sneaking through.

29

To some, the world is filled with threats. To others, opportunities. As people join behind the moving currach, anticipation grows, an energy that comes with seeing something out of place on an average Monday morning in an average town in the West of Ireland. Parents distract their young children, saying, *look!* An old couple, out walking a dog, pick the animal up into their arms and cradle it, fearful at first of all the young people interrupting their morning, giddy teenagers are chattering. But now the older couple are also stood by the river's edge.

Tadhg instructs the boys to slow their pace. They finally stop at the water, and lifting the currach over by flipping it, they place it gently on the grey surface, next to the *Joan of Arc*.

I can't, Jamie says, his eyes now on the people watching.

Tadhg is saying something, but Jamie's not listening. He hears only a buzzing.

Wade in first, Terry shouts. Go on, Jamie. Get used to it, go on,

and Jonesy says: Go on, good man, sure just get wet, we can change, but Jamie baulks at the cold water and Tadhg is crouching down to shove the currach along, and Jamie's red Converse are filling with water, he's up to his knees in the river and Tadhg says, hey wait up kiddo, you don't have to go so far in, Tadhg's laughing and it unnerves Jamie, and the water is making them all laugh, except Jamie, who is steering the currach with his hand on the bow, deep in the tar-slick black of the river now.

The currach floats and this is a mighty thing, it makes Jamie light-headed with relief.

Tess claps first, excited it floats, and then everyone cheers, and they wait a few minutes, the three around the boat, pushing it down and watching it bob back up, just to make sure it is capable of going farther.

Terry gives it one hard shove back and over now to test it, and smiles, Abba shouts at him to come in out of the water in the name of god, and not to get soaked wet with a full school day ahead,

and Jonesy clasps his hand again onto Jamie's back, and it settles him,

everything moves fast now

which gives Jamie no time to change his mind, distracted by the buzzing in his head, and a whooshing, the prickles on his skin, and Tadhg pulls the rope at the mooring bar and moves the boat back to the river edge a little,

and Jonesy and Eoin are in the water too, and they lift Jamie up and in and onboard he steadies it, and he sits and puts on his life jacket.

Tadhg leans in, checks the jacket, and Eoin checks it too, Eoin has taken off his shoes and there's something vulnerable and sad for Jamie watching his dad in jeans pulled over his knees, and the whiteness of his skin.

Eoin checks the jacket again, and is surprised when Tadhg slots the oars in the thole pins, how huge they are, how long and far out to the water they go, and the water is noisy now, alive, as some rain falls gently. Some on the bank open bright umbrellas.

Take it easy now, don't go far, Eoin whispers to Jamie.

Abba walks to the edge of the river with a bottle, and leans forward to bridge the gap and ushers someone to take it from her. It's a bottle of rum, she says, here take it please, she says to Tadhg, who walks to her, and she passes him the bottle, smash it off the boat, it's for Good Luck she says, to make the Shape be a good shape, and not to shift, never to shift, she says wagging her finger.

And Jamie is bobbing now

and looks bewildered

Marie says: Smile, Jamie, but he doesn't. He lifts the oars. His knuckles are white.

And Abba shouts out: Smash the bottle, come on, smash it, we're not asking the young boys to drink it. Eoin takes the bottle and smashes it off the bow, everyone cheers except Tess, who starts to cry.

Tadhg and Eoin and Jonesy shove the currach to the river,

and Jonesy says: Enjoy it, Jamie,

and Eoin says: Don't go too far,

and Tadhg says: Yes, Jamie, have fun, steady now, but remember, just to the buoys – no farther.

Epilogue

Jamie is gone far now,

the voices are paper thin then nothing, only rustling trees and his breathing, only the oars breaking the water surface, like the heart beating,

he rows along the river in a straight line.

Jamie knows a straight line by the way it makes his body feel,

curves make him dizzy, though sometimes he zigzags just to feel, or to confuse his brain, snapping it into other thoughts, as he crosses the street or stands alone on a pavement.

But now, he wants a straight line, to pick up energy, to flood himself with certainty.

Because lines drawn on a flat surface rarely meet again, in our average day we make thousands of lines – across our rooms, our schools, towns, cities.

Because we fire off, getting hurt, feeling love, unloved, all day long, we find meaning in the line we have walked, look hard to arbitrary things for symbols, and reassurance,

connecting many random sequences:

between a painting we once saw in a gallery and the face of a man on a train crying out loud,

between the white lines on a road whizzing by like all the seconds of our lives we have used up, between a moment in a park watching a person drink coffee and then a doctor in a hospital who made us cry out,

or a busker in bare feet singing on a grey street, giving off so much beauty that it derails our day.

And all these lines that cut off and curves that meet –

between a face we watched slowly arrive before us in an airport terminal, that would some day be the only person in the world who understood us enough to love us,

or

between a theory we once heard about motion and a child fallen down in a school yard with bloody knees that reminds us of a paint we might have once mixed,

or

a love heart on a card we once burned in a fire pit, and that fire pit reminds us of air, and trees, and how air can inflame, and a life bellows,

the river water is rowed by a boy making a straight line,

for now

but

a line, that will eventually circle back on itself,

in years to come.

As the currach moves now, all the wood and rods and paint, the drill holes, and the polished seat remember they have all been here before,

so, it's pulled to the ocean, where wild salmon shoals go out and swim until they finally, exhausted, return to spawn, where swallows fly to the sun in swarms on a feeling they once had in their wings, and these journeys we make

all this intersection, this criss-crossing

means we can also fall off the edge –

a line drawn off the edge of a square sheet of paper, a window washer returning to ground from a high-rise building, an ice skater on a rink, car over cliff.

Jamie rows his line on a curved surface – thinks about the coordinates of a car that once made a trip with a pregnant girl in the back seat from Emory to Galway hospital – these lines can close, even sometimes they close back on themselves, in completion like a spiral, infinity symbol or a tragedy that two people have felt for ever.

Brú means pressure,

and Jamie will always feel pressure. But today, the water cools him and he no longer feels a scalding on his ankles, his thighs are cold from where he waded deep and now the flicker of the winter sun comes like cat's eyes, whish-whish.

The oars feel lighter in his hand,

smooth

he soars

and as he rows he builds rhythm, feels his body move, it is always moving, but this is different. There is power in his hips, his flat foot on the currach belongs there, and there is a power in his back, in the curve of him, in his big hands. He likes being alone.

The faint light curves to a silver along the reeds,

he rows on to the estuary, where the drag is strong, and settles a while to catch his breath, right at where the horizon once was, or should be, but it keeps moving, and now he is no longer visible from the river bank,

and

like breathing it is as simple or complex as the day is on your lungs.

The river is splashing into the boat, coming coming coming,

he's into the salt water now

this is the edge:

a place that you should live your life sometimes, Jamie,

the world whitens as the wood green of Emory's forest fades and the bank with bog cotton evaporates after swallowing the heathers,

he can see his breath now

his wet school trousers make him feel alive.

The water is ever so black here,

currents rise to the larch of the oars, smacking them now, fast.

Soon, there is no guide, no bank, he shadow-boxes the air, moving the oars now,

repeat –

the freckles on his hands flicker in front of him, he would usually count them, but they move fast now as the bow pushes gently over the waves and the single hazel rods hold fast, bending to the water,

he thinks of splicing them from the branches – how they bend so compliant.

Maryam Mirzakhani never said, to the best of Jamie's knowledge, what curved surface was her favourite.

Perhaps she loved the mystery of them all. He feels strongly that Mirzakhani's was a planet, most likely earth.

Noelle Doyle was unable to tell anyone what exactly she thought about in those last seconds of her life. Jamie must now imagine it. He is sure that whatever she thought it was energetic and filled with the colour blue – he is surest, that she saw the depths of the pool.

That living and dying are like swimming for a swimmer.

Or beautiful patterns for a mathematician.

That they are the sea to a boat builder, sanding for a carpenter and tunes for a musician.

He thinks that you may be flooded with one or more considerations in your last moments, made up of the energy of your previous moments. Which is all you can ever have.

A corncrake calls out and it fills his ears, as waves and blood crash and gush.

Jamie, love – it's miles to the sea, settle here, good lad, you have gone far enough, feel the energy in your feet,

you need to change out of your clothes when you get back

you'll catch your death.

Jamie – chaos will scratch the scab of your mind, and the questions they will always be coming,

you will overheat

but remember everything starts with little warnings, listen to them.

A flock of mallards lifts to the sky. Remember flowers leak to the bees, because they are good,

everything good starts with a good impulse

his oars click now, listening.

To create you must feel and be uncomfortable, and sometimes you will feel isolation.

The currach is compressed between the sky and the river.

And you have been having difficulty in seeing the full picture but here's the thing, kiddo, there's no full picture, the picture is always filling, filling, let it, don't try to order it or organise it, listen to it, watch it fill.

Jamie remembers skipping through the woods asking Eoin to make him a bow and arrow top and suddenly his mind floods with colours, Jamie-red, and the Vantablack, and how easily he could breathe in the sky, the striking pain he feels when looking at Yves Klein blue,

and how maybe when you die

a beautiful colour

indescribable

should be the last thing you see.

The red of Noelle's swimming cap.

He lifts his hands from the oars, his heart is pounding now and he's crying. There is nothing but water around him.

What do I do now? he yells out. A seagull lands on the bow. Squalling.

Cross imaginary boundaries,

let go

throw paint,

sing

cut a tree and empty it out,

plant again

find something hard but delicate, watch spaces for tension, be near it, but not in it, think.

Design, redesign, build from what you have, you have so much already.

He turns the currach, and is rowing hard,
  going back now, fast,
  over his shoulder he sees faces on the bank, some are waving and some are clapping his return,
  and some are shouting in panic.

He was going back now,
  He would go back now.

And he would let Jonesy row out to the estuary to shout at it, maybe about O'Toole letting him down, and Terry should row out with Abba. And he would go out again very soon with Tadhg and Tess and they could talk about the importance of naming boats.

And he would row with Eoin and Marie, after some practice at keeping the currach steady, some day, when he was a little more accomplished, he would show them the open ocean, some September night filled with plankton,
  and among the sea stars,
  they'd go as far out as they could to feel the estuary's energy,
  shout out –
  await the echo.

Acknowledgements

Thank you to past students and teaching colleagues, most especially Jack McHugh (RIP) and Amanda Coakley (RIP). To Elaine Moynihan for her kindness and generosity in sharing her love of currachs and boat building with me – thank you.

In different ways, the following people mattered greatly on this journey: Sinéad Gleeson, Aoife Casby, Caroline Moran, Alan McMonagle, Jess Traynor, Conor O'Callaghan, Aoibheann McCann, Sarah-Anne Buckley, Lisa McInerney, Claire-Louise Bennett, Elaine Cosgrove, Dani Gill, Nicole Flattery, Helen Cullen, Douglas Stuart, Mike McCormack, Sarah Clancy and Rita Ann Higgins – thank you.

Thank you to the Arts Council of Ireland for a bursary to support my writing. Huge respect to book shops, libraries and book clubs for your support.

Mia Quibell-Smith, Hannah Shorten, Suzanne Dean, Leah Boulton, Morgan Dun-Campbell, Gray Eveleigh and Sorcha Judge – thank you for all your amazing work on this book, and to Hannah Telfer and all at Harvill Secker, Vintage and Penguin Ireland who were a part of this journey.

With love and thanks to family and friends, especially my mother, Catherine, who reads every draft closely; my sister, Andrea, for her early reading; and my brothers, Shane, Kenneth and Mark.

This novel would not exist without Kate Harvey and Peter Straus. To Kate, my editor and friend – I am indebted to you for your unending patience, trust, kindness and sharp intelligence at every step of building this book. To Peter – I am eternally grateful for your encouragement of my many mad ideas, for your friendship and great humour. Thank you also to all at Rogers, Coleridge and White for your support and work on this book.

As always, love and gratitude to Ray for understanding my artistic temper(ament). And to my sons, Jack and Finn, for helping me understand, again, the beauty and brutality of growing up.

Finally, Reader, thank you.